I Ran Away
to Find Myself

By Jillian Linares

Table of Contents:

Dedicated to my parents

Pamela & Cesar Linares

*for giving me **the world,***

enabling me to explore it,

and supporting my mission

to make it a better place.

Life is not defined by what happens;

it's defined by how you react to those happenings.

Prologue: Letter Home (Never Sent)

Dear Mom and Dad,

I'm on my way to Byron Bay. It's in the center of Australia's eastern cape. Way different than New York… and Connecticut. Byron is a surfer town. I've heard many people call it, Surfer's Paradise. I'm thinking of staying here for a little while. I want to take some time to figure out why I felt the need to run away across the world to escape my problems. If anything, that decision has made everything worse. I'm regretting coming to Australia in the first place.

I've never been on my own before, but I guess I should get use to it. I couldn't be any further away from everything I've ever known. I'm also regretting the decision to leave my phone behind, but it's too late now. Everything is too late now. Regrets are just piling up. I'm just going to focus on what's ahead and try not to look backwards. Does that make me selfish?

Maybe I'll try surfing. Or maybe I'll drown and die and not have to worry about any of it anymore. Just kidding… sort of.

Love,

~~Lucas~~

Lucky

Chapter 1: Ocean Kayaking

After a ten hour overnight bus ride from Sydney to Byron Bay, I couldn't wait to stretch my legs and breathe the fresh ocean air. It was refreshing to feel the warmth of sunshine after leaving Melbourne and Sydney, which were colder than I expected for June. I didn't realize that it was actually wintertime for countries on the other side of the equator, but I bet I learned it at some point in Social Studies...

Thankfully in Byron Bay, even the winter months were warm enough to go to the beach.

I didn't have to walk very far before I wandered into an upbeat hostel that resembled a college dorm lounge area. Not the ones in real life because those are usually made up of stiff polyester couches, a pool table that's missing the 8 ball, and a couple of HALO nerds.

This was like the college lounge you see in the movies with a big flat screen TV, leather couches, and bicycles hanging on the vibrantly colored walls. There was a row of five computers lined up off to the left with a sign on the wall that stated: *NO WATCHING PORN IN THE LOBBY*. It was a story waiting to be written.

I was greeted at the front desk a bubbly receptionist whose name tag said Cobalt, but said his name was Bradley. He informed me that they had an open bed in one of the dorm rooms, but it wasn't available yet because check-in wasn't for another couple of hours. He suggested hanging around the lobby or keep my stuff in a locker to enjoy the day until the bed was ready. After being stuck on a bus for so long, the beach was the obvious decision. Although the lockers were free, they didn't come with a lock, so I had to rent one.

"For just ten bucks more, you can buy a lock." Bradley said with a salesman's smile.

"That's alright, I'll only need it for a few hours."

"In the room there are lockers that we suggest using as well."

Places are always trying to get people to spend extra money any chance they get, "I'll take my chances."

Next to the lockers was a big fish tank with a plastic Neptune statue in the middle. I went up to the tank to admire the dozens of fish in an assortment of colors. That's when I saw Sushi, or Sushi's cousins at least. Sushi is my fish. He's a Cardinal Tetra with a most vibrant blue and red body. In nature, this type of fish only live about a year, but in aquariums, they usually live between two and five years. Sushi *defied* the life expectancy and is six! I attribute this to my mom.

My mom had him on a strict feeding schedule eating organic fish food (yeah, that exists!). She even went as far as to keep the same feeding time as the pet shop to make sure Sushi was comfortable with his transition from the pet shop to our kitchen counter. I told her I'm sure he'll be fine regardless, but mom would just smile and say, "I like taking care of him, he's part of the family."

We got Sushi because when I was a kid I was really into oceanography. I still am, but it's expanded into anything that has to do with science really. Sushi was technically supposed to be my responsibility, but that only lasted a couple of months before my mom took over because I kept forgetting to feed him. As I watched the Cardinal Tetras swimming around the Neptune statue in the aquarium, I couldn't help but smile thinking of my Sushi swimming around the plastic ornament of a fish holding a baseball bat. It was the first time in a while that I genuinely smiled from a memory of home. Lately the thought of home made me anxious. It was comforting to realize that not every memory I looked back on caused me anxiety. Maybe there was some hope for me after all. Maybe.

I grabbed my beach gear and secured the rest of my belongings in the locker. Neptune's was only a couple blocks from the soft white sand that I couldn't wait to feel between my toes. I walked aimlessly enjoying the warmth all around me and the sea breeze I hoped could cleanse my soul. I came across a little shop right on the sand called The Surf Shack. Just thinking about surfing got me both excited and nervous. I walked over to the shop to check it out. It was open, but there wasn't anyone there. On the counter was a sign that read: *SURFING, RING THE BELL (LOUDLY) TO BE HELPED.* I looked out towards the waves and there was a group of people surfing. I didn't want anyone to have to come in.

I took a moment to look around the shop. It had a lot going on in one organized mess. The surf boards were along the side of the shop and on the inside was a sign that read *Lessons/Rentals available.* Above that sign was a *Legend's Board* full of pictures of a dozen different surfers. I admired each of the pictures. I wondered what had to be done in order to get onto the *Legend's Board.* I turned and squinted past the sun to see surfers gliding along the waves like birds maneuvering through clouds. I wondered how many lessons I would need to glide like them… I continued walking on the sand, but I promised myself I would be back to find out more about The Surf Shack.

Further down the beach were about twenty people standing in a circle wearing wetsuits and helmets. I wondered what they were all up to. I must have looked curious because moments later an instructor with a wetsuit that read, *Ocean Kayaking* came up to me and asked if I wanted to join their group.

"We have an odd number, so another person would make the count... nine, fourteen, aaa... even! Have you been in a kayak before?"

He seemed to have made the decision for me, but part of me didn't mind. I needed a push to do something besides wander aimlessly, like I've done the past couple of weeks in foreign Australian cities.

"When I was a kid, I would go to Lake Michigan in the States during the summers. I'd rent a kayak pretty frequently."

"Great! Well, this is nothing like kayaking on a lake. Do you have a name?"

"Yeah... my name is Lucas."

Although my parents have always called me Lucky.

He started writing on his clipboard.

"What's your surname, Lucas?"

"Catano."

"Perfect, I'm Otto, come on I'll get you all geared up!" He exclaimed as he walked away quickly.

"What do you mean it's nothing like regular kayaking?" I asked as I hustled after him.

"This is the Indian Ocean, mate. It's a whole different animal out there!" He exclaimed while handing me a clipboard of paperwork.

"Is there anything I should know?" I asked, glancing over the contract that requires my signature at the bottom.

"Do you surf?" He asked me.

"Surf? No..?" I handed him back the signed paperwork.

"Well, when you're going out and coming back in, just pretend like you're surfing. Except instead of your arms doing all the work, you have a paddle."

"But I've never been surfing." I repeated.

"Woah, you've got to try it one day man!" He tossed me a wetsuit, life vest, and a helmet. "Put that on, mate."

I did as he said, but still had a lot of questions, only I didn't want to seem paranoid by asking anything more. Apparently I just missed the "training," but Otto said that they don't say anything that important anyway. I looked around and there were plenty of people who looked like beginners, so I figured it couldn't be so hard to figure out. Plus, Otto said I would ride with him in his kayak, so if anything went brutally wrong he'd be there to help... although that seemed very doubtful.

We pulled the kayak alongside the shoreline. The ocean was looking choppy and I began to realize that in order to get past the waves we needed to paddle at them, head on.

"Get in the front seat mate." He told me casually as if he didn't see the waves pouncing ahead of us.

"How are we supposed to get past the waves without them crashing on us?" I asked as I hesitantly climbed into the kayak.

"You paddle and I'll give us a boost! Let's go at it on an angle, and when the waves curl, lean in so that we don't barrel-roll in the boat. Alright?"

Suddenly he decided to give *really* specific directions when I was in a state of panic.

"And if we do barrel roll?" I yelled back.

"Yeah!"

"What?!" I exclaimed.

"Now!"

He began running and pushing the boat, then hopped in and began to paddle, pushing us much further, much faster. A wave was forming in the distance and we were heading right for it.

"How are we supposed to get past that?" I asked, trying to hide my anxiety.

"Keep paddling, mate."

"But it's going to crash right on us…" I pointed out.

"Right on!" Otto didn't seem to mind.

My heart rate increased, rushing faster than the wave that rose before me. I put my arms up over my face, disregarding any directions Otto may or may not have told me.

Suddenly I was under water spinning and flipping like a rag doll. I tried to swim up, but I couldn't tell which way that was. I could hear screaming, but knew it couldn't be me since I was underwater, unable to breathe.

Suddenly, my torso smashed into a hard surface and I came to a halt.

"Woah!" I heard a voice yell. And then I was under water again, swallowing sea water as the ocean tossed me around effortlessly. I flipped a few more times and then a hand reached out and grabbed my life vest, pulling me up to the surface of the water.

"Hold onto our boat!" Another voice yelled. I pulled my body up onto the stranger's kayak and held on. More waves came crashing around me, but I leaned into them this time, remembering what Otto said. I didn't want to get obliterated again. Another wave came and then another and another. I must have lost count, but it felt like I was under a crashing waterfall.

Finally, a calm developed around me.
Clutching the kayak, I heard the voice again.

"You alright?" A guy in the back of the boat asked

I rubbed my eyes, "Yeah, now I am." I answered.

"I think your partner is up ahead, hang on and we'll paddle you to him." Another guy in front said.

I hugged the center of their kayak with my torso and let my legs dangle as they dragged me along. I looked back at the waves pulverizing the other participants just as they did to me. The ocean didn't want any visitors today.

"Lucas man, that was a sick wipeout!" Otto raved, like he was proud of my painful fall.

I let go of the strangers' kayak and climbed back on with Otto, although I felt safer dangling off of the other boat.

"I thought you said you've been kayaking before." Otto continued.

I looked at him speechless and exhausted, then ignored what he said altogether.

"Thanks for the help," I said turning to my saviors.

"No worries." They replied.

"It gets a bit easier now that we're past the waves." One added.

I sighed in relief. My energy level from a mediocre night's sleep on an overnight coach bus was really catching up to me, but I tried to ignore that and continued paddling in sync with Otto's pace, while chatting with the other kayak. Their names were George and Kosta and they were from Greece. They were on vacation with their friends who were further back in the group. It was George's birthday the next day, so they were celebrating and invited me to join them that night. It turns out they were going to karaoke at the bar attached to Neptune's. I told them I would check it out, since they did save me after all.

We were kayaking for over three hours! After the mess of getting out there, I did just fine because it was just a lot of paddling, which I'm good at. About an hour in, Otto pointed out a whale in the distance that was swimming toward us! At one point it was only ten feet away, which both amazed and terrified me. I've only seen a whale in pictures and in an aquarium once when my dad took me to Sea World.

It was a father-son trip that my mom surprised us with as a combo birthday-father's day getaway when I was thirteen. My mom said I needed to spend more time with my dad since he worked so often and that she would stay back to keep Sushi company. My dad and I spent the whole day in Sea World, from the moment it opened to the moment it closed. I loved it at the time, but I won't ever go back.

I realized as I got older and more educated that it's pretty cruel to take a massive whale from the vast ocean and keep it captive in a tank. Orcas a.k.a. Killer Whales are at the top of the food chain in the ocean, meaning they don't have to worry about predators. Well, except humans. I use to have a dream of being a trainer at Seaworld, but now I have a dream of freeing all the animals in Sea World.

Otto said that mammals of the water can sense where we are and our energy. If we have good vibes, they'll come close, but not bother us, but with bad vibes we would have to watch out. Not that I felt like I should believe anything Otto said, but I was a little nervous because I felt like bad vibes were constantly following me. I tried to put that out of my mind and enjoy the natural sea world I was kayaking through.

Getting back to shore was as intense as paddling out except I wasn't getting crushed. We were going with the current and I was more prepared. At first I was tense as we approached the wave with Otto yelling, "Paddle! Paddle!" Then, there was this moment when we caught the wave just right and we were soaring without even having to paddle at all. Every worry just seemed to evaporate. Not just the worry of barrel rolling, or falling out of the kayak again, but all the worries I hoarded inside myself seemed to dissipate for those few moments.

I looked back at the wave as it curled and for that moment it was a feeling of euphoria, something I've only felt once or twice in my life and could never fully explain. I wish I could take that moment and capture it, save it somehow, because if I could, I think I'd have the answer to all my worries.

Chapter 2: Byron's Beginning

When I got back to Neptune's, my bed was ready. The room was on the first floor close to the bar where karaoke was taking place that night. The room had four beds, one in each corner. There was stuff on all of the beds but one, which was neatly made until I laid down on it, messing it up with my damp and sandy swimsuit. I was exhausted, dirty, and hungry, but couldn't decide which of those problems to address first. I wanted to sleep, but I was too gross to get any more comfortable in bed. I wanted to shower, but was too hungry to wait. I wanted to eat, but I was too tired to get up. I told myself five minutes, but five minutes turned to ten and soon enough I was fast asleep in a very sandy and sweaty bed.

I must have been asleep for a few hours before I was woken up by whispering in the room. It's pretty awkward to wake up with barely any clothes on to three girls I've never seen before. But it's my fault for putting myself in that situation.

I grabbed the towel folded at the side of the bed and sat up. They turned to look at me.

"Sorry! Did we wake you up? We'll be gone in a second." One said very considerately with an accent I've never heard before.

"No, no, don't worry. I didn't want to fall asleep in the first place." I told her as stood up.

"Where are you from?" Another asked.

"New York City."

They smiled at each other, "I like your accent." She giggled.

They had the accent. I didn't realize I had an accent...

"Thanks. Where are you from?"

"We're from the Netherlands. I'm Nancy. This is Bella and that's June."

"Nice to meet you. Do any of you need the bathroom? I was going to shower."

The three giggled again.

"No, it's all yours." Bella answered bubbly.

I took a long hot shower, got dressed, then headed out to the town to find something to eat. I landed in a Turkish spot after seeing a picture of an irresistible kebab that I just needed to have. As I was waiting for a table I saw a group of old ladies congregated near the window talking about the waiter. They each had a big sun hat and colorful outfits on like they were headed to a cabana... or Sunnyside Retirement Beach Condos.

"When I'm on vacation with The Girls, I can flirt with whatever cutie I want. Waiter, taxi driver, goodness- even the pilot from the plane, my husband cannot ask any questions!" One woman said as they all giggled in delight. I was happy that a table opened up for me because I didn't want to be that old woman's next target to flirt with.

I was seated next to a family of four who already finished eating. There was a 5-year-old sitting on his mom's lap as she read him a picture book. She had a different voice for each character that spoke and told the story with animated gestures that made him smile and laugh with each new voice. She would pause between pages, leaving just enough time for the boy to marvel at the pictures with his oo's and ah's. It made me really, *really* want to be 5-years-old again, giggling in my mommy's arms.

The waiter came over to take my order, then I continued to people-watch. It's hard to not watch others when I sit alone. The family had an older son who had his face buried in his iPhone and his music so loud I could hear it from where I was. His dad had a "Discover Australia" book in his hand and every once in a while he would nudge his son and point to something on the page. The kid would barely glance over and nod as if he already could predict how few shits he gave. I wanted to throw something at him, shake him, wake him up.

Everything around me reminded me of how much I missed my parents. I was that kid. How many times have I blocked my parents voices out because my text conversation was so fucking important? How many times did I run to play video games rather than ask my parents how their day went? So many things blinded me and now I can't have them back. All I had were the layers of heavy regret that pressed into my chest so deeply every time I realized how many memories I overshadowed because of my inability to appreciate the ones who gave me *everything* in this world.

I was happy my food came out because I was drowning in my own thoughts again. I've been doing that a lot ever since The Night My Life Fell Apart. The family got up after they paid their check and I tried to focus on my kebab to avoid resurrecting any other unwanted emotions. The meal was delicious, but my mind couldn't escape   somersaulting down a well of remorse.

After I left the restaurant, I went down to the beach. I began thinking about the last two years of my life. I was forced to move away from NYC to live in the middle-of-nowhere: Storrs, Connecticut. My parents didn't even *ask me* if I wanted to go. They just started talking about a new school I would be going to that had an awesome baseball team and then BAM!

We're moving and there's nothing you can do about it!

Well, they didn't say it like that, but that's what it felt like. The whole situation caused me to become really bitter. I think because of that move and my stubbornness to accept it, the past two years were wasted. I wasn't fully there because I was angry and I wanted to shut everyone out. My dad would tell my mom it was because I was a teenager, but that's not a good enough excuse. I wish I could jump back into those wasted moments and shake myself out of my self-created sense of misery. I wish there was some way to change the past. I would change so, so much.

I was going to watch the sunset, but I ended up watching the surfers instead. I thought about Otto's advice to get on a board and try it myself as well as the euphoric feeling of riding the wave in the kayak that morning. If surfing was like that, then I couldn't wait to catch a wave.

There were seven surfers in the water, squeezing in every second of sunlight they could. One of the girls in the group really showed-up the guys. Effortlessly cutting in and out as the waves curled behind her. I could have watched her forever.

"She's really good, huh?" I heard a woman say from about ten feet away. She stood alone as well, watching the surfers.

"Yeah, she's something." I turned to answer. I wanted to see who was talking to me, but it was dark.

"The sea shows you about yourself. It's truly an amazing thing." She spoke.

"You should really get out there one day and try it for yourself." She must have seen my look of admiration for the group out on the water. And as a local, she probably never saw me around and could gather that I was most likely a tourist. I nodded.

"I'm Elsie." She said.

"Lucas." I responded, admiring her welcoming sky blue eyes.

"How are you liking Byron, Lucas?"

"It's beautiful, I just got here this morning."

"It's a great place to slow it all down. Life can be too much sometimes."

I nodded and I stayed quiet. There was no way I could tell her why my life felt like too much.

"I came here to restart… a long time ago. And now I feel as free as the birds in the sky." She smiled and talked like she knew me. "It will get better."

I fake smiled. *How could it get better? How could she make it sound so simple?*

"It can't always get better... some problems have no solutions." I said as I watched the surfers in the distance ride the waves as I navigated the storm in my own mind.

"You can't expect the water to always be calm. Why would you want it to be? You just gotta learn how to surf the waves and enjoy the ride. The bigger the wave, the more discipline you have to have. And if you fall, you gotta know how to swim."

Even though I knew we weren't really talking about the ocean, I realized I needed to learn how to surf, and soon.

Chapter 3: Karaoke

Karaoke started at eight. I showed up on time because I really didn't have anything better to do. I really wasn't even sure if George was serious when he invited me out for his birthday or if he just did to be polite when I asked him what he was doing. For some reason I was being so paranoid about showing up, especially on time. It was mainly because I was the only one at the bar for a while and I had a lot of time to think about how awkward I must have looked sitting there, all alone.

I learned a lot about being alone over the past few years. I guess it started after the move to Connecticut when I sat with no one in the cafeteria for at least three weeks before anyone noticed I existed. It wasn't that the students were mean, I just didn't really make an effort to talk to people. I really didn't want to be there.

Traveling alone is different though. It's a good way to meet a lot of new people and have time alone to think, but I go back and forth between loving the space and detesting the isolation. I could go from having a good conversation to being completely annoyed for no reason. It's like I don't know what I want. I don't know what happiness looks like anymore.

Initially, I really wanted to go to karaoke to be in a room surrounded by happy people celebrating nothing and everything. It was supposed to keep me distracted, but when I got there and had all that time to sit at an empty bar thinking, my mind brought me to all the wrong places, again. I walked outside, thinking I'd go for a walk down to the beach again, but I heard George calling my name from down the block. I ignored it at first because I suddenly got that feeling where I wanted to be with no one, even though being with no one was what was getting me so down in the first place.

"Hey, you made it!" George smiled as he began a slight jog in my direction.

"Yeah." I replied pausing. "Happy birthday!" I finally exclaimed patting him on the shoulder.

"Not until midnight!" He corrected, as Kosta and their two friends caught up.

"Lucas, this is Jon and Nick." George introduced. I shook both of their hands.

"How is it in there?" Kosta asked.

"Pretty slow right now." Although there was about a dozen more people who had arrived.

"Well, let's liven up the party!" Jon exclaimed eagerly, leading the way inside.

Karaoke started off mellow, but as people gained more liquid confidence, the performances became more and more dynamic. I made sure to stay away from the sign up list at all costs.

"George and Nick think they're getting some." Jon laughed pointing at his friends getting close to two girls across the bar. The three of us were standing in the back, staying under the radar.

"Well, I don't see you with any girls Jon." Kosta commented. "I have a girlfriend, what's your excuse?"

"I could talk to any girl in this place, I'm just waiting to find the prettiest one." Jon boasted.

"Oh yeah, what about you Lucas? Why aren't you out there?" Kosta questioned.

The truth was, girls haven't really been on my mind since The Night My Life Fell Apart. Any time I found myself in a conversation with one, I'd make an excuse to leave. Of course, I didn't say that to them, instead I said, "Same as Jon, no girl has caught my eye yet."

They both laughed.

"Alright Kosta, point out the most attractive girl you see at the bar, and I'll get her number at least. Someone with a pretty friend, so my man Lucas can play too."

Kosta laughed and agreed. How did I become a part of this scheme?

Kosta pointed to two gorgeous brunettes in tight dresses and heels chatting near the patio area just outside the doors, not too far from where we were standing.

"Okay Lucas, here's the plan." He began to explain. "It's called the Joe Swisher
pick up, I learned it from my cousin in L.A. Now, listen carefully. We're going to walk over there, Kosta can come if he wants to see magic in motion, and we're not going to just walk right up to them. We'll stand a small distance away and we'll talk for a little while, whatever. What you need to do is act really excited and worked up about that big guy near the DJ booth. The one over there who's acting like he owns shit. I'm going to bet you 100 bucks that that's Joe Swisher."

"Who's Joe Swisher?" I asked.

"Exactly. I need you to be so sure that that's not Joe Swisher that our argument
gets their attention. Don't be too loud, but just enough for them to hear you say that you bet me 100 bucks. Got it?"

"Uhm yeah, then what?"

"Then after a bit of us arguing, I'll politely interrupt their conversation and ask
them if they think that is Joe Swisher."

"But who's Joe Swisher?" I asked again.

"Exactly. They won't know who Joe Swisher is, but by our excitement they'll be damn interested in finding out. I'll explain who he is, and how I bet you a bill that guy is him. I'll hype it up, you just have to play along. But after we've chatted with them for a bit, I'm going to go over to that guy to ask him if he's Joe Swisher. That's when you're in the spotlight. You gotta keep them interested, keep talking to them while I'm gone and when I come back that's when we move on from Joe Swisher and start talking about them."

"And then?" I said with skepticism.

"And that's it. Our charm and good looks will captivate them. We'll get some drinks at the bar, tell blasphemous stories about our travels, and four or five rounds later they won't want to leave our sides."

He made it sound so simple. I had no epic travel stories.

"Game time." He declared. Although a big part of me didn't want to be involved in Jon's "game," I was kind of curious to see how his plan worked, so I went along.

We did just as he said. We walked over there and talked about baseball for a while. He explained to me who Joe Swisher actually was, which was some ex ball-player that I never heard of, and I know baseball! I guess no one can ever know who he is in order for Jon's plan to work.

Then he started pointing and saying, "I know it is. It has to be! How much do you want to bet?!" And just as he predicted, the girls turned to look at us, then turned toward to DJ booth find who Jon was pointing to. That was my cue, "I bet you 100 bucks that isn't Joe Swisher!"

That's when Jon turned toward the girls. "Excuse me ladies, I don't mean to interrupt, but could you help settle a dispute I'm having with my friend here." The girls glared but nodded. Kosta and I joined them.

"My friend Lucas here doesn't think that guy over there is Joe Swisher. And I know it's dark, but can either of you back me up by telling him that it is." One girl turned to look and the other one said, "Who's Joe

Swisher?" Jon acted surprised. "Who's Joe Swisher? He's a famous baseball player. An autograph from Joe Swisher would be like gold!"

Their faces lit up. "He's really famous?" They asked.

"Yeah! He was one of my favorite athletes growing up," Jon replied.

"I bet Jon 100 bucks that it wasn't him." I played along. Kosta just stood there, smiling.

"Alright. The suspense is killing me, I think I'm just going to go over there and ask him. Pardon me, ladies." Jon walked away.

I realized it was my turn to be in the spotlight.

"He always has these ridiculous claims, I swear, right Kosta?"

Kosta just laughed and nodded.

"I'm sorry, I didn't get either of your names."

"I'm Makayla."

"Scarlet."

They both smiled.

"Nice to meet you girls. I'm Lucas, this is Kosta, and the Joe Swisher fan over there is Jon. How are you liking Byron Bay?"

"It's lovely. We love it here. We hate that it's our last night. The week flew by." Makayla sighed.

"Where you off to?" I asked.

"More north. To Cairns. Then we'll leave Australia and head to Fiji for a week before ending in New Zealand."

"Wow! That's amazing." I said, genuinely impressed. My first thought was, *I wish I could take a trip like that*, until I realized how ridiculous that statement was. I was *on* a trip like that, I was just too depressed to realize it. I was glorifying their travels and sulking in my own.

"What about you Lucas, where are you off to next?" Scarlet asked.

"Next? Well, I don't really know. I just got here today, so I'll just take it day by day I guess."

"Going with the flow. I like that." Makayla nodded with a smile.

I saw Jon walking back towards us with a smirk on his face. He walked over to the group and the girls turned toward him, anticipating what he had to say about Joe Swisher.

"What happened?" Scarlet asked.

Jon let the suspense linger.

"I'm right aren't I?" I smiled.

"You're right Lucas, but he said he gets it all the time, so at least I'm not crazy!" Jon exclaimed. "But do you know what that means?"

"What?"

Jon pulled out a hundred dollar bill and slapped it in my hand. "Drinks are on you now!" The girls smiled wide and with a $100 in my hand I led the group to the bar.

I got to give it to him, Jon was a smooth talker. We got a table next to the bar and while I tripped over my words, Jon took the lead and ordered a round of tequila shots followed by some mixed drinks. Jon was drawn toward Scarlet and her to him, as he told stories about his epic travels in Asia through Singapore, Malaysia, and Thailand.

Everyone I meet on this trip seems to be a world venturer and I, kind of wandered here by accident. These people have experiences that I only see in movies or read in books. I've been telling people that I'm taking a gap year to travel, which is kind of true. Telling people I ran away from home could lead to a lot of unwanted questions.

In the middle of one of Jon's stories, Kosta said, "Hey, isn't that George on stage?"

Our whole table turned to look.

"Yeah! It is." Jon laughed and whistled loudly using his fingers. "Alright Georgie!" He yelled. "That's our friend George, it's his birthday!" Jon shared with the girls. They cheered along.

I turned to watch the stage as Makayla reached up and touched my disheveled hair that hadn't been cut in over a month.

"I like your hair."

I wasn't sure if she was mocking me because I did absolutely nothing to my hair that night and all the days before.

"Thanks." I said, unsure how to respond. My hair was getting longer and my kinky curls were getting a bit wild, but Makayla ran her fingers through it like she was my hairdresser. One time I touched a girl's hair because it looked really soft, and she pushed me into a fence. That was in the fourth grade. I learned to never touch a girl's hair after that. Obviously Makayla didn't have a phobia of touching hair like me. I certainly wasn't going to push her into any fences.

George was on stage with the girl he was dancing with from before. They were singing, *Walking on Sunshine* complete with harmonies and stage props including a black feather boa. The bar filled up by this point and the strobe light turned on; that's when you know it's serious. I wondered if it was short circuiting or something because I began to smell burning. Everyone else was having so much fun, they didn't seem to notice at all.

Our group got up from the table and moved to the dance floor to support George. Makayla grazed my hand as we were walking over, but she was far too intelligent, beautiful, and intriguing to be interested in me... I figured it was by accident. I was paying more attention to how happy everyone looked. It seemed like the whole bar wore smiles, besides me. I wondered if they were actually happy or just happy on the outside. I wondered what problems they had bottled up behind their brews and smiling faces. I wondered if anyone else felt so alone in a room of people. I wondered what the point of all this was... running away... life.

They all wanted to get another round, but I didn't want to take a sip of anything besides water. I told everyone I was going to the bathroom and instead left the bar through the back door in the direction of my room. I felt kind of bad not saying goodbye, but I was getting that feeling again where I just wanted to be away from everyone and everything.

It was nice only having to go to another part of the hostel to get to my room, but what wasn't nice was realizing the door was cracked open, not locked at all. I went inside cautiously, but couldn't see a thing without any of the lights on. I could hear people sleeping and didn't want to wake them. All I was hoping as I made my way in the dark was that there wasn't anyone inside who would jump out and attack me.

I rushed to the bathroom for a light source to ease my caution. I flicked the switch and used the light illuminating from the bathroom to scan the room. Nobody was up and as I looked at each bed I noticed that every single bed had someone sleeping in it. I wondered if I had walked into the wrong room. I walked over to a bunk. My duffel was on the floor, sticking out from under the bed. It was most definitely my room. I recognized my towel hanging on the bedpost. I walked closer to the bunk only to find a girl fast asleep in my bed.

Chapter 4: Excuse me, you can't sleep here...

I've never had a situation quite like that before, so I just stood there for a moment looking around the room contemplating my next move. *Should I just tap her awake? What if she wakes up in a screaming panic and wakes up the whole room?* That's a pretty incriminating situation for me. I went outside to think.

I could see the light on at the reception desk. So, I went in to inquire about what they do about displaced beds by sleeping strangers past midnight...

"Hi." I said not knowing what I was going to say next.

"Hello, what can I do for you?" A receptionist, different from before, asked as he lowered a magazine with a naked girl on the cover. Awkward.

I guess he didn't care about the *NO WATCHING PORN IN THE LOBBY* sign.

"Well, I went to my room just before and there's a girl in my bed and I was wondering what to do about that."

"There's a girl in your bed?"

I nodded.

"Do you know her?"

I shook my head

"Did you bring her there?"

I shook my head.

"So, she was just there when you got back?"

I nodded.

"I'm trying to figure out what your problem is here." He smiled creepily. I knew by his mustache that he was either a butler or a douche. It didn't take me long to figure out which he was.

"I'm not going to just jump in bed with her." I said as I began getting frustrated.

"I know, I know, I'm just having some fun with you. Have you asked her to leave? Is she refusing to leave because then mate, you need to tell me what you're doing right or what this girl is doing sooo wrong."

I narrowed my eyes at him. "She's sleeping in the bed I paid for, so I want her to leave. I just want to go to sleep."

I think he began to see that I was pretty annoyed, because he got up from his desk and followed me to the bed.

We both stood looking at the sleeping girl, just as I did before. He took out his flashlight and shined it in her face. She squirmed, rolled over, then pulled the covers over her head.

"Well, at least we know it's definitely a sleeping girl and not a dead girl." He joked. I didn't laugh.

"You gotta get up, this isn't your bed." He said, poking her with the flashlight.

She mumbled something indistinguishable and pulled the pillow over her head.

"No, no, you need to wake up. You need to go."

"Why?" She said perplexed.

"This isn't your bed." He reiterated pulling back the covers. She was wearing a tiny blue dress that was pulled up above her waist exposing her thong. He began eyeing her. Looking her up and down. I put the covers back a little, covering her again.

He just looked at me with a sour face. "I thought you wanted her out."

He continued shining the light at her eyes. "Up, up, up." I was beginning to regret asking for his help to begin with. He was making a lot of noise and being really aggressive, pulling at her wrist and trying to grab her waist.

When she finally stood up, he began leading her outside. "Goodnight. Sorry for the disturbance." He disingenuously apologized.

"Where are you going to bring her?" I asked.

"Aaa... she can crash on the couch out front. I'll watch her." He replied without turning back, holding the stumbling girl by the waist to hold her up. Her dress was barely covering her.

Even though I didn't know the girl and just wanted to go to sleep, I didn't have the stomach to leave her inebriated and alone with the creepy reception guy in the middle of the night. I couldn't have that added to the heavy regrets lingering on my conscience, so I followed them out.

"Maybe we can find out where she's staying." I suggested.

"She doesn't have any ID on her, I don't think that's possible." He denied.

"Maybe we can ask her."

"She's drunk. She can't tell us nothing."

He plopped her on the couch in reception, her dress hanging off, body limp.

"Hey, what's your name?" I asked her.

"Just leave her, kid."

I ignored him. "Do you know where you're staying?"

"Hereeee." She groaned.

"See, she wants to stay here, just leave her."

His persistence only made me more skeptical of his intentions.

"Are you staying at Neptune's hostel?" I asked her.

She nodded. "Twenty-two." She mumbled.

"Twenty-two? Are you staying in room twenty-two?" She nodded.

"Can you get the key to room twenty-two?" I turned to ask Creep.

"How am I supposed to know she's not just giving us a random number? I'm just going to let her into a random room, so that another person can come down complaining to me to kick her out?" Creep argued.

"Well, look up who's staying in that room." I demanded. He rolled his eyes.

"Hey, what's your name?" I asked her again.

"Annnah." She slurred.

"Do you want some water Ana?" I asked. She nodded.

I walked over to the water dispenser on the other side of the reception desk and began filling a cup. "Who's staying in that room?" I asked Creep.

"A Thomas and an Anastasia, that's it, that room's a double."

I looked at Creep pridefully then walked over to Ana. "Ana, do you know who Thomas is?" as I handed her the water.

Her face lit up. "Tooommmmy! My boyfriend. Where's Tommmmyy?"

"We're not sure. He might be in your room. Do you want to go check?"

She nodded her head as she gulped her water to the last drop.

"Come, I'll take you there." I told her as I helped her up.

Room twenty-two was on the second floor, so she had to take the steps very slowly. I tried to encourage her up the steps while thinking about what I was going to say if a huge man opened the door fuming, asking what I was doing with his disheveled girlfriend in the middle of the night. We made it to room twenty-two and stopped outside.
"Are you sure this is where your room is?" I asked for reassurance. She nodded.

I thought about knocking and then running away, but it seemed too cowardly. I took a deep breath and gave three loud knocks.

We waited. I knocked again.

Each time I knocked I secretly wished no one would answer, so I wouldn't face the possibility of getting punched in the nose.

I went to knock again, but stopped after I heard the doorknob rattle. I froze, prepared to defend myself. When the door opened there was a shirtless guy about my size standing there with messy hair, tired eyes, and a look of bewilderment. Ana jumped in his arms.

"I found her passed out on the floor near the bench. She told me she was staying here." I mildly lied to avoid the long unnecessary story.

He rubbed his eyes. "Ahuhhh," he groaned and shut the door.

While I was thrilled to not get punched in the face, I was surprised at how nonchalant Ana's boyfriend acted after I delivered her drunk at his doorstep. Did he even realize she was gone?

Thinking about the last hour infuriated me. I put it out of my head and went back to my room, to my empty bed. Byron was off to a wild beginning.

Chapter 5: Beach Escape

For once, the dream I remembered was pleasant, for the most part. My parents, uncles, aunts, and cousins were with me in the dugout of a huge baseball stadium. I could tell it was Yankee Stadium by the signs in the outfield. The lights were bright, the crowd was cheering, and it all gave me a good feeling. Baseball was always huge in my family, on both my parents' sides, but especially from my mom's Puerto Rican roots.

My mom was born in New York after my grandparents moved from Guayama, Puerto Rico. My family claims we are related to Roberto Clemente who was the first Latin American and Caribbean player to make it into the National Baseball Hall of Fame. It's a really big deal, especially for a baseball crazed family, but when I asked my abuelita *how* I was related to Clemente, she said he was my great-great-grandfather's second-cousin, which seems pretty distant. When I asked my mom if she really thought we were related to the famous Hall-of-Famer she told me, "all Puerto Ricans are related if you go back far enough. It's a small island."

So does that make Marc Anthony my uncle?

In the dream I was up to bat and the whole crowd was chanting the nickname my dad gave me.

"Lucky! Lucky! Lucky!"

From the dugout I could see my family on their feet rooting for me.

I lifted the bat, dug my feet into the dirt, and focused my attention on the pitcher. That's when the dream shifted.

The pitcher had a deceitful face I recognized, with a douchey looking mustache. Suddenly, the crowd's cheers turned to gossipy whispers. People's faces of excitement turned to judgment and shock. I lowered the bat and looked around at the stadium that had now turned dark as storm clouds moved in quickly. My family had moved outside the dugout, faces full of sorrow, and were standing over two graves. When I tried to walk over to them, my feet were stuck, and they just drifted away until they were no longer in sight. That's when the baseball hit me right in the head and I was awoken.

I rolled over in bed and realized that I was slightly sunburned and there were floating whispers about me. June was telling Nancy and Bella that I had a girl over last night and security had to come kick her out.

"They woke you up?" One asked.

"Mhmm."

"Ew. Did you hear...? Were they...?"

"I think so."

"Ughh, that's disgusting. With a room full of people?"

"I thought he was a nice guy."

I pretended I was still asleep, hoping they would leave soon, but they just kept gossiping. I felt really awkward and I really needed to use the bathroom. I turned to my side with my back facing the girls and tried to put my full bladder out of my head. I concentrated on what they were talking about, but it was making me so angry that the tension was building everywhere; I could practically hear a stream of water that didn't exist.

I waited long enough. I threw back the covers and stood up yawning to try and indicate that I wasn't awake long. None of the girls said a word when I got up, but continued whispering once I shut the bathroom door.

"Oh my gosh, do you think he heard us?" One whisper-yelled.

Didn't they realize how loudly they actually whisper? I didn't have to explain myself to these girls, but hated the false impression they had of me.

As I went to the bathroom I looked into the mirror. I hadn't gotten a haircut since I was back in Connecticut, before I ran away. I usually get it buzzed once a week, or at the very least a shape up, but lately I've been thinking about growing it out again, like when I was in elementary school. I patted the top of my head wondering how much longer it would need to be in order to get it braided. My hair is dark, curly, and thick. I've never been able to braid it all myself. My mom would be the one to do it for me and she would make the coolest braid designs. One week would be cornrows and the next I would have criss-cross. She learned from her friends growing up. My friends at school would even notice when the design changed, but more importantly: so would Kendra Walker. Kendra loved my braids, and well, I loved Kendra.

I mean, if love exists in the fifth grade.

In the lunchroom my friends and I sat near the vending machine. This was a strategic move because we would sometimes strike up a conversation to score some other kids' snacks. But I was more interested in seeing who went to *get* the snacks. And if that person was Kendra Walker I was ready because she wasn't in my class, so lunch was the only period we had together. Well, *ready* didn't mean much except being able to stare at her from a little closer. Until one day we finally spoke.

It was a Tuesday right after P.E. so I was still sweaty, which made me extra self conscious. Kendra walked over to the vending machine in her baby blue Jordan's, put in a dollar, got a strawberry pop tart, and walked over to our table.

"Hi. I'm Kendra."

Oh, I know.

"And well... I was wondering..."

The whole room got blurry around her.

"...where do you go..."

I just sat there transfixed.

"...to get your braids done?"

Is she talking to me?

I was so entranced that Kendra was only two feet away from me, I forgot how to speak.

"His mom does them. They're sweet, right?" My friend Mateo answered for me, saving me from the awkward silence.

"Oh really! Do you know how to braid too?" She asked excitedly.

"Aaa… no." I stuttered.

Another silence.

"Oh. Well, never mind then. See ya." And she turned and walked away.

My friends shoved me.

"What are you doing!?"

"This is your chance!"

"Lie or something!"

I stood up from the lunch table and did the bravest thing of my entire childhood.

"Wait, Kendra!" I called. She turned around. "If you want your hair braided, you can come over after school today."

Kendra smiled. "I'll have to ask my mom."

"Yeah, me too."

So my braids got me my first date.

If dating exists in fifth grade.

Kendra came over that night and many other nights where we would watch a movie while my mom braided both of our hair. The movies were perfect because I didn't know what to possibly talk about with her since I was always so nervous when she came around. She came over almost every other week, and each time I wanted to ask her to be my girlfriend, but each time I decided that I would ask her *next time. Next time. Next time.* Until next time turned into summer and I didn't see her because she went to visit her grandparents in Haiti and then I started sleepaway baseball camp. It was a long summer of missing Kendra.

There was no first day of school that I looked forward to more than the first day of sixth grade. I was so excited to see Kendra. I even had a list of movies picked out for us to watch. She seemed just as excited to see me as she walked over. I noticed she got her cartilage pierced over the summer. Sexy. If there's such a thing as sexy in sixth grade.

"Lucas! Can I come over after school today?" She squeaked after giving me a *hug.* She smelled like bubblegum and peach body mist.

Of course. "Yeah, I should be free."

"We have to catch up! How was baseball camp?"

"Good." *But not great because I didn't get to see you.*

The bell rang.

"Well, see ya after school." She giggled and skipped away toward her classroom.

I found out during last period that Kendra not only got her cartilage pierced over the summer, but she also got a boyfriend. A seventh grader. My day went from amazing to terrible. It was the first time I sat next to Kendra and couldn't wait for her to leave. I wanted to speed up the movie, even if her braids weren't done. I wanted to shout *LEAVE!* But of course as usual, I just sat quiet.

As she left she said, "Next week, I pick the movie. I want a love story."

I wanted to vomit.

The next day I shaved my head. No more hair meant no more braids, which meant the perfect excuse to not invite her over again. Kendra took away my hair and my heart. And since then I've had a buzz cut.

In the smudged mirror, I examined the fro that was beginning to form. I wasn't trying to look good for anyone, so I didn't care if my hair was a huge mess. Plus Makayla even said she liked it the other night, maybe it wasn't as bad as I thought.

I washed my hands, splashed some water on my face, and walked back out into the room where Dutch girls had their backs to me as they rummaged through their suitcases.

"Someone left the door open last night and that girl wandered into our room." I said as I walked over to my bed and grabbed my towel.

They looked at me without a word, pretending to be clueless of the conversation they just had about me, right in front of me.

"She drunkenly wandered into my bed." I repeated as I began walking back toward the bathroom. "I was helping her find her way back to her room, so the creepy front desk guy didn't have his way with her." I explained, then shut the door without giving them a chance to respond.

My shower was longer than usual. I wanted to ensure that the girls had plenty of time to get their stuff together and leave before I got back out of the shower to avoid further awkwardness. I also had nothing planned for the day and was thinking of ideas for things to do. I considered going to the front desk for ideas, but didn't want to run into Creep. I was exhausted from kayaking and a long night, so I put my desire to surf on pause for a little longer. I decided that I would spend a day relaxing on the beach.

My plan went well. The girls were gone, so I didn't have to hear their awkward apologies. I got dressed and grabbed my writing notebook, hoping to clear my head. Since I left New York, I've been carrying a notebook to write down my thoughts, experiences, and letters to my parents. The notebook has been my travel companion.

I headed down to the hostel's bar turned breakfast buffet. I stopped by to grab a chocolate chip banana muffin and some Crunchy Nut cereal, which was like an upgrade from Frosted Flakes. When I went up to get some OJ, I ran into who else but Annah and Tooommmmy, fully clothed and polished to the point where I almost didn't even recognize them. I made eye contact with Ana to see if she recognized me. She smiled, so I smiled back. I wondered if it was because she remembered last night or because she was just being polite. I looked over to Thomas, who was glaring back at me. I looked back down at my cereal. *Who knows?*

I stopped on my way down to the beach at a convenience store to pick up a bottle of water, some snacks, and sunblock. Then I walked along the shoreline toward a cluster of rocks in the distance on the other side of the beach. There was a dark grey cave in the mountain surrounded by green trees blanketing the beach's backdrop, but for some reason the darkness stood out over the vibrant canopy. I walked toward them in a daze thinking about how relaxing the sand felt between my toes, and how tense the rest of my body was. There was a guilt tangled inside of me that was difficult to escape. Even when pockets of happiness made their appearance, my guilt gradually slithered around any sense of positivity, suffocating every trace.

I sat in the sand near the rocks in a deserted area of the beach. It was a day where I felt like I just wanted to be alone. The previous day out on the ocean I got a little sunburnt on my face. It wasn't too terrible, but it reminded me of all the times my parents told me to put sunblock on so I wouldn't burn. I was always convinced that since I had tanned skin I didn't need sunscreen, but that wasn't always the case. My mom who was darker than me even got sunburnt sometimes. But I was often too stubborn to listen. I took out my notebook and wrote to clear my head before letting my madness build up inside of me.

Dear Mom and Dad,

It's been two years since I've been on a beach, since Mexico. When I think back to that trip it gives me a heavy feeling in my stomach. It was an incredible resort, with delicious food, white beaches, and the most perfect weather I could have asked for, yet I still managed to mess it up. I always mess it all up. I started off bitter because I felt like you were trying to buy my happiness to compensate for forcing me to move away from NYC. I just couldn't let it go. I just made it worse for myself, and for both of you. I ruined the trip for all of us.

I'm learning pretty quickly that you both always knew what was best for me. Even as simple as telling me to apply sunscreen before going to the beach. Of course, I didn't listen and of course, I got sun poisoning that trip. The crazy part though is that even after my moping and sulking and inability to smile for the entirety of the trip, you didn't call me a lobster or even say, I told you so. Mom gave me Advil for my heat fever and Dad, you ran to the store to get me aloe to ease the pain. And even after ordering my dinner to the room because I was too embarrassed to go out and show my face, I still didn't have the decency to say thank you. For anything. I'm sorry. For what it's worth... thank you... for everything.

I know that it's too late to say a lot of things I wish I said in the past, but I think it's at least a start for you to know that I do remember these times and instead of disregarding them out of frustration, I'm learning from them. Or I'm at least trying to. I know it's small and silly, but I bought sunblock this morning and I just wanted to say thank you. Thank you for being my parents and putting everything you had into raising me and pushing me to do the right thing even if I didn't appreciate it at the time.

Love,

Lucky

I closed the notebook and looked up to find Elsie walking slowly along the beach. She looked sad. Her head was down as she dragged her feet along the sand.

"Hey Elsie!" I called, waving.

She waved back and returned a half smile. I motioned for her to come over. Reluctantly, she did.

"How are you?" I asked her.

"Could be better. Feeling a bit down today." She sighed.

"I'm sorry… if it means anything, I was pretty upset when we met on the beach and talking to you helped."

She smiled. "Feeling better now?"

"Well, no… I'm trying, through writing actually." I told her, showing her my notebook.

"Oh yeah? What are you writing?"

"About my trip. Letters to my parents." I told her hesitantly.

She smiled. "Do you miss them?"

"More than I could ever explain." I took a deep breath, and held back the tears that I felt building.

"That's normal, you know. Emotions can hurt deeper than physical pain."

I wanted to change the topic.

"I know I'm a complete stranger, but if you want to just vent, you can talk to me." She said.

"Thanks..." I wasn't sure how to respond.

"Anyway… I should get going. It was lovely talking to you." She began dragging her feet in the sand again.

"Yeah, same. I'll see you around."

After Elsie walked away something caught my attention. Out in the distance in the ocean was that surfer crew again. That girl was with them. I sat up and closed the notebook putting it safely back into my bag without taking my eye off the surfers. Well, one surfer mainly. They were taking turns catching waves, alternating between being serious while they surfed and goofing off in between. It looked so liberating and they made it look so easy. I decided that tomorrow I was going to sign up for surf lessons.

I wanted to glide on the waves and get that feeling of euphoria again. Part of me hoped that somehow surfing would connect me with that girl, even if it was as simple as a quick hello on the beach. *Anything* to cross paths. Just to see if her grace on the water matched her personality.

Chapter 6: First Wave

I went to bed before anyone got back to the room and woke up before anyone was awake. I didn't want to see those girls again, too awkward. I'm pretty good at avoiding people. I'm not sure if that's a talent or a weakness. At breakfast I ran into the front desk guy Bradley. He asked what I was doing that day and when I told him I was going to check out surfing, his face lit up.

"Alright! Today is sunny and mellow, perfect for learning. You're going to have an awesome day."

Bradley said the instructors were these local brothers whose logo was: *Guaranteed to stand during your first lesson or the second one's on us.* That was pretty assuring. I had an open ended trip in Byron, so even if I completely spazzed during my first try, I could keep trying. Although, I hoped it wouldn't have to come to that.

I remembered the way to the Surf Shack. There were three guys when I walked up. The one with the sandy blonde dreads looked up to greet me.

"Sup mate, looking to surf today?" He asked with a smile.

"Yeah, definitely." I nodded enthusiastically. "I want to rent a board and have a lesson."

He looked at his left wrist as if there was a watch there. There wasn't.

"You can be in the eight o'clock surf session. My name is Spiggle, but you can call me Spigs." He introduced himself, shaking my hand.

"We're going to get started soon." One of the other guys said.

Spigs assisted me by setting me up with a wetsuit and a board. I asked him if they owned the shop and he proudly smiled and introduced his two younger brothers Budd and Coco. Coco had dark hair, green eyes, and was taller than his brothers by a few inches. Budd, the youngest, looked exactly like Spigs: athletic, tan, and dark brown eyes. Only Budd had a baby face and had a buzz cut, instead of sandy blonde dreads.

"We started pooling money to fund this dream since I was sixteen. Budd was only nine and he still gave in half of his allowance money." They all laughed. "Ten years later here we all are."

I zipped up my wetsuit. "Living the dream," I added, not just because they spend every day on the beach doing what they love- I'm sure that helped though. It was because of how close they all seemed. Starting a business with your two brothers... I always wondered what it would be like to have siblings.

We set up on the beach with the seven other people participating in the lesson. It was a group of friends and a couple. We played a corny icebreaker to introduce ourselves where we had to say our spirit animal, which had to be alliterative with our first name. I was Lucas the Lion.

Before running straight for the waves, like I wanted to do, we learned the basics on land. Spigs taught us some lingo and safety. We practiced popping up while Budd and Coco gave us tips on how to improve. After about a thirty minute sand sesh, we all grabbed our boards, enthused to try out the real thing.

The waves seemed small, which seemed perfect for surfers just starting out. Spigs broke us up in smaller groups to work with Budd and Coco out on the water. I was with Gabe the Gorilla and Hazel the Hyena. Initially Hazel said her spirit animal was a hippo, but as soon as Spigs started calling us by our spirit animal names, she opted to switch. I don't think anyone wants to be called a hippo on the beach.

I was first in line for my group after we paddled out to where Coco was stationed on the water. He dragged my board over *to get closer to the break* and explained the type of wave we were looking for. I watched the waves building behind us as Coco pointed out and told me, "that's the one."

My heart was racing, but that good kind of race like when you're next in line for a rollercoaster you've been waiting two hours for. "Start paddling!" I cupped my hands and put all my energy into propelling through the water.

"Angle! Angle! Turn a little left!" I heard Coco call from behind. I tried to shift my body, dipping my right shoulder. I glanced back and the wave was curling behind me. I popped up just as we practiced on the beach and *CRASH* I tumbled down flopping on the wave, my board barrel rolling behind me. The wave kept me under, whipping me around like a mere strip of seaweed. When I finally breached the surface I took a huge breath, wiped my eyes, then squinted out to Coco who was asking if I was okay from what felt like a hundred feet away. I gave him a thumbs up then hopped back on my board and began paddling back out there again.

Coco was helping Hazel the Hyena with her first attempt. Gabe the Gorilla already bailed and washed up around the same spot I did, making me feel not *as* bad. I looked up and Hazel's board was moving like it had a motor. "Up! Up!" Coco yelled. Hazel popped up and balanced on the board, as the bubbly sea-foam curled behind her. Shock and thrill overtook Hazel's face as she let out a big "WHOOOOHOOOO" before slipping off her board shortly after. Everyone cheered, excited for Hazel's successful first attempt. Now I really *had* to prove myself.

I continued the cycle. Paddling out to Coco, looking for the right wave, trying to catch speed, attempting to stand, then finishing it off with some form of a brutal bailout. After the seventh or eighth attempt I couldn't decide what part of me was hurting more: my arms or my ego. Paddling back out each time was exhausting; my arms were beginning to turn into noodles and my ego was accumulating on shore beside the children building sandcastles. Hazel continued to rip it up, a surfing natural, along with Lincoln the Leopard and Giana the Giraffe in the other group. Coco was working with Gabe one-on-one when Spigs came out to help me out.

"You're not angling yourself right. You're trying to ride the wave straight on, but you need to hit it on an angle." Spigs explained as he treaded water, holding onto the front of my board. "You want to ride the wave while facing your board toward the lighthouse." He pointed in the distance. "You're going to keep nose diving if you try to take it head on." He swam my board over to a *better spot.* "Let's give it another go, but remember, angle the tip of your board toward the lighthouse." I nodded my head, absorbing all he just told me and organizing it with everything I learned in the past hour.

By then I could pretty much read when the *right wave* was forming behind me. I began paddling. I felt Spigs give me a huge boost from behind, sending me off with solid momentum. I paddled vigorously ensuring the board was facing the lighthouse.

I glanced back to find the right pop-up timing.

The wave was curling.

I felt the board begin to connect with the water, as if they finally agreed to work with each other.

I popped up and found my balance.

I was riding the wave!

The water carried me as the misty wind danced around my wetsuit.

I heard a loud cheer from behind.

Smiling, I picked my head up to soak in the view of the breathtaking beach while euphoria tingled throughout my body. As if I thought my heart was already racing at its peak, it spiked when I saw that surfer girl standing looking at me from the beach.

It's like she was able to look into my eyes and right *into me* so far away. I think she even smiled.

Of course, in that moment I bailed. I completely washed up, but as soon as I found which way was up, I hopped right back on my board and paddled back out, hoping she wasn't laughing behind me. I didn't even notice my noodle arms boiling in fatigue.

"That was sweeeeettt Lion!" Spigs exclaimed awarding me a high-five.

"That felt incredible!"

"You had it there! Just gotta keep your balance there at the end. You kind of just stood up, you gotta keep your knees bent."

I turned to look over my shoulder at the beach, for that girl. I didn't see her anymore.

"Let's do it again!" I've never felt so free.

Chapter 7: The Bondfire

The rest of the day was incredible. After the lesson ended, Spigs, Coco, and Budd invited me to their place for a party that night. Actually they insisted that it wasn't a party, they called it a Bondfire.

"No mate, not a bonfire, a Bondfire," Spigs told me. "It was Coco's play on words to encourage more *bonding* time."

They said they have a grill to cook up whatever anyone donates to the food fund. I wrote down Coco's directions on the back of my hand because I didn't have a phone and I always lose pieces of paper.

Nancy, Bella, and June must have checked out of the room because their beds were stripped and their luggage was gone. I kind of felt bad about ending on a bad note and for avoiding the problem instead of fixing it. After all, it was all just a big misunderstanding.

I sat down on the bed and took *The Perks of Being a Wallflower* by Stephen Chbosky out of my bag. It was a book I bought back at the airport in New York to help get my mind off reality. It was the reason I started writing letters to my parents, since the book is comprised of letters from Charlie, the main character.

He would write because he had no one to talk to about the problems in his life. He just wrote down what he was thinking in a letter to someone he hoped would listen and understand. It made me wonder about all the individuals in the world with innumerable untold stories bundled inside of them. It made me wonder how many stories are never heard because nobody bothered to listen. Like Charlie, I had so many thoughts racing through my mind and it was so difficult to filter out the poisonous ones that threatened to pull me down beneath the surface of negativity. Writing gives me someone to talk to, even when I'm alone and nobody is there to listen.

I stopped reading *Perks* for a couple of days because I was getting to the end and didn't want to find out what was going to happen. What if everything gets worse and then there are no more pages left to turn and change what happened? I thought leaving it a mystery was somehow a better solution. Over those last couple days though, I thought about Charlie and what was going to happen to him. I decided I needed to finish the book to find out. Sometimes when I'm reading I wonder how the characters would be if I knew them in real life. Would I be friends with Charlie? As I began analyzing his character, my thoughts shifted to thinking about if Charlie would want to be friends with me. *I didn't even want to be friends with me.*

I thought about my last two years in high school and why I usually sat alone in the cafeteria. Why was I being a person that I didn't even want to be friends with? I gave that a lot of thought since I started reading *Perks.* While part of me continues to sink, another part of me wants to pull myself up, to persevere, and become a better person. I'm trying to appreciate each day because today only happens once and I can't change yesterday, but I do have control of how I live my tomorrows. Or at least that's what I keep telling myself...

I got lost in the pages and didn't realize how much time had passed. When I finished, the sun was already going down. I was right about everything getting worse in the end... sort of. It's like Charlie hit rock bottom, but still believed that things were good, or at least would be, *soon enough.* I couldn't figure out how a guy can have so much optimism with so much heaviness in his life. It's admirable.

Charlie reminded me that everyone seems to have something going on, something that tries to throw them down, even if the outside world doesn't see a thing. I realized that adversities are opportunities to overcome and become stronger. However, realizing this alone won't necessarily solve my problems because realizing something and living with it in my consciousness is different. I knew I needed to be more proactive in piecing my life back together because running away at that point was a *disaster*.

I got ready for the Bondfire then stopped at the front desk where Bradley printed me out walking directions to the house which was on the other side of town right along the beach. I stopped at a store on the way to pick up some offering; I couldn't just show up empty handed. In the store I saw Italian sausages, which immediately drew my attention. My dad is Italian and his specialty was grilling sausage and peppers on the BBQ. My dad was born in Italy, grew up in London, and moved to the U.S. when he was in his twenties. He had a very distinctive British accent that has sustained, even after living in the States for so long.

In Connecticut, it was entertaining when someone would hear my dad speak for the first time. His British accent caused mixed faces of amusement and bemusement. He often seemed like a fish out of water, compared to back in the city. In New York City differences were so common, they often go overlooked or unacknowledged, but in Storrs, Connecticut Dad's differences were very apparent. Some would ask his story, but others would sit with questions dancing around in their heads until they left without getting answers. I've always loved my dad's accent, so being in Australia brought back some good memories.

Don't get me wrong: I'm not saying a British accent and an Australian accent are the same, but they often use the same words like rubbish for garbage, sunnies for sunglasses, swimmers for bathing suit… many of which I've adapted just because they make more sense. You're not *bathing* and it's not a suit, so swimmers makes much more sense. Anyway, I'm going off on a tangent. Moral of the story: The English language is confusing as fuck.

Even when I was a few minutes away from the Bondfire, I was still battling the voice inside my head that wanted to go back to my room to sleep or do nothing. Going to parties was not something I usually do, but I wasn't really too happy with who I was, so it only seemed right to do the opposite of what I would normally do.

Social situations sometimes intimidate me. I get my timidness from my dad because my mom is the complete opposite. Mom made it a point to talk to everyone because: *you never know what kind of story you're going to hear.* Mom always heard the best stories and unlike many gifted storytellers, my mom was also an excellent listener. Friends and even strangers would exhaust the burdens of their lives for my mom to absorb, and although she couldn't always solve the problem, she had the words of reason that everybody could trust.

For some reason, I never went to mom with my problems. I always kept things to myself. Sometimes I wonder if things would have turned out any better if I asked my mom for advice. I guess I'll never know because I never asked.

I could hear music from down the road, that led me directly to their house. I could hear people in the back, but didn't want to just walk in. I wasn't sure how to approach the situation. I went to the front door and knocked, waited, but nobody answered, so I knocked again. I was about to knock a third time when the door flew open and some guy was in my face.

"Delivery is here!" He yelled behind him where I could see people congregated in the kitchen. "Hellloo!" He looked at me with a growing smile. "You're my hero right now mate, 'cause I'm starvvving. How much do I owe you?" He asked looking at my bag. I recognized him from somewhere. "Did you bring us beer too, mate? Best delivery guy ever!" He cheered as he reached into his pocket for his wallet.

"No, no, I'm not the delivery guy. I'm here for... Spigs, Coco, and Budd invited me to come by tonight. But yeah, I brought beer... and sausages." I clarified as I lifted the bag for him to see.

"Well, I love beer and *sausages*." He said then looked down at his wallet. "So I don't have to pay you?"

I shook my head no. I realized that he was one of the guys hanging around in that surf group.

"Do you want a beer?" I asked to break the awkward silence.

"Sure!" He glowed. "I'm Zane."

I handed him a can.

"Lucas." I introduced myself. "Nice to meet you."

"Come on in. Spigs is out in the back, Coco is making out with his girlfriend upstairs, and Buddy is on the half pipe, per-usual." Zane said leading me inside. "So, you from America or Canada, mate?"

"America. New York." I told him.

"That's sweet. I've been to America once. Cedar Rapids, Iowa."

"Yeah? That's random, what's there?"

"Grandma. She moved there last year. I had to go visit Grams." He shared as we opened the door to the backyard and the volume turned up immediately.

Walking outside I saw the fire in the center of the yard, with people gathered around eating, drinking, and playing the guitar. To the left was a half-pipe that Budd and one of his friends were skateboarding on, casually. Beyond the half-pipe was a row of bushes that acted as a barrier from the beach to their yard. There was a hole right in the center of it, a pathway, for people to get to the beach, easy access.

"Lion man, welcome to my humble abode. I'm glad you made it!" Spigs said.

"Thanks for inviting me. Your place is sweet!" I complimented, gesturing at his set-up.

"Thank you, thank you, we try."

"I brought some food and beer."

"Oh thanks, mate. I have more brews in the cooler over there, of course you can help yourself to that too." He grabbed his can from the table next to the grill. "Cheers! Welcome to Byron!"

Spigs continued grilling and I went over to grab a seat at the Bondfire next to Zane. He introduced me to everyone sitting around the fire. That's when I noticed her. That girl. She was leaning against the half-pipe with some of the guys, drinking a beer. She was barefoot in short-shorts, a bikini top, and a zip-up hoodie, unzipped. My heart began to speed up. Her skin was tan with light freckles underneath her eyes and on her nose. Her smile paralyzed me. Like Kendra Walker, times a million. She was the first girl who stood out to me since I ran away from home. I needed to get near her, and *somehow* talk to her.

She was right by the cooler that Spigs was referring to before, so I concocted a plan. I needed to finish my beer and go over there to get another one. I could buy myself more time by putting my beer cans in the cooler too, while taking off the pressure of having to drink them all. I chugged my beer and stood up.

"I'm getting another beer and putting the rest of mine on ice, anyone want anything?" I asked Zane and everyone else around the fire.

"I'll take a Carlton." One guy said. I looked what he was holding already because I had no idea what that beer was.

I walked toward the cooler, looking at her, without making it obvious I was looking at her. I heard her laughing, which made me crack a smile. Even her laugh was beautiful.

I got to the cooler, which one of the guys was using as a seat.

I politely tapped him on the shoulder. "Excuse me, could I get into that cooler?" I asked.

He looked up. "Sure…" He said as he stood up. Budd was next to him and beside him was Skye.

I made eye contact with her. Her deep blue eyes consumed me like the swell of a wave. I smiled and she immediately looked away, as if she didn't see me. Or worse, saw me and chose to look away. I kneeled down and tried to stall at the cooler to think of something brilliant to say to her… *I saw you on the beach and you're an incredible surfer…* too forward. *I just wanted to tell you that you're insanely beautiful…* way too forward. *I want to talk to you, but I can't get past looking at your eyes…* my ideas were no help.

I grabbed the beers and went back to the fire, defeated without so much as an exchange of words. I talked with Zane for a while then got up to use the bathroom. I noticed Budd grilling me from the half-pipe when I stood up. I looked away then glanced back to confirm and yes, he was definitely glaring at me and he definitely didn't look pleased. I wondered if he could tell I was into the girl who was standing next to him before. I wondered if Budd was her boyfriend. I walked inside to avoid any more tension from the direction of the half-pipe.

Spigs was in the kitchen with Coco cleaning some things up.

"Thanks again guys. This is a really sweet party." I told them.

"Not a party. It's a Bondfire! We can't have our neighbors thinking we throw parties every week." Coco laughed.

"Coco and his word-play." Said a girl with long healthy beautiful braids, who reminded me of my childhood crush, Kendra. I ran my hands through my hair in admiration. Her hair gave me nostalgia. *Should I grow my hair and get braids again?* I thought to myself.

"Where's your bathroom?" I asked.

"Right behind you, someone is in there though." Spigs responded.

I walked over to the counter. "Do you need any help?" I offered.

"No worries, mate. Take a seat." Spigs said, motioning at a stool next to the counter. I sat down.

"This is my girlfriend Jade. Jade, this is Lucas." Coco introduced.

"Nice to meet you. How long you in town for, Lucas?" Jade asked with her soft light eyes and smooth dark skin. I couldn't stop staring at her braids. I recalled the flashback of touching a girl's hair in fourth grade and getting pushed and shook myself out of the trance.

"I'm not sure, just playing it by ear right now." I wanted to ask if she did her braids herself, but felt too shy.

They all looked at each other and smiled.

"Stay long enough and you won't ever leave."

I laughed along with them. "I can see why, this place is beautiful."

Just then the bathroom door opened and *She* stepped out. I froze and looked down at the creme colored counter hoping it would spell out the perfect words.

"Hey Skye, come over here. Meet my mate Lucas the Lion." Spigs said.

My spirit animal!? Now Spigs, really? My face must have turned brick red. Better than Hazel the Hippo, I guess. I smiled at her, then turned to get up. I tripped over the bottom of the stool, making an absolute fool of myself. Everyone laughed, *especially Skye.*

"Nice to meet you, Trip." She said as she continued laughing. *Trip?!*

"You all are big on nicknames, huh?" I said to take the attention off of my klutziness.

Her face changed and her head tilted to the side.

"Where you from, Trip?" She asked, ignoring my comment.

"New York City." I told her.

She looked at me for a second, squinted her eyes, then looked over to the guys. "Spigs, why you inviting tourists to our Bondfires? It's for Aussies to unwind! He's on holiday, what does he have to unwind from?" Skye snapped.

She was standing right in front of me, but acted like I wasn't there, demanding answers from Spigs.

"Aww Skye, c'mon, be nice. You were new once too." Spigs said, but Skye wasn't having it.

"Whatever." She pursed her lips and in the next moment, she was gone.

"Daddy problems." Coco said. Spigs and Jade punched him in from both sides.

"Sorry about that, Lucas. Everyone's pretty friendly. Just avoid Skye... she's not very kind to... some people."

I nodded. But I didn't want to avoid her. Even if she was sour and thought I was a klutz. It just made me want to talk to her more.

Chapter 8: HideAway

I devoted the next few days to surfing. I rented a board from Spigs and only took breaks to eat, write, and occasionally nap on the beach when I was over exhausted. I was committed. Surfing was draining, especially on my arms. While learning to surf was my main priority, I had ulterior motives for being down on the beach all day. I wanted to see Skye. I wanted to talk to her again, redeem myself, even though Spigs told me to avoid her.

I was surprised when I didn't see Skye at all the first two days after the Bondfire. Maybe she goes to different locations to surf. Maybe she came down to the beach conveniently when I left to get lunch. Maybe she saw me and left immediately. Maybe I was overthinking the whole situation...

Not having Skye watching me as I learned definitely took the pressure off. I had quality surf time with no beautiful distractions to avert my attention. I was getting up on the board consistently and began to practice controlling my direction. It was hard because it defied my equilibrium and I usually fell right off. It was like day one all over again.

It wasn't until mid-morning on Monday that I saw her. She was alone and didn't even have her board with her. I watched her from the ocean as she walked right past me toward the rocks at the end of the beach, her head buried in a book, entranced. Her light brown hair was pulled back and she was wearing ripped jean shorts and an oversized T-shirt. I wondered if the shirt was hers or if it was her boyfriend's... was Budd her boyfriend? I laid on the surfboard out on the water, staring at her, wondering. She took a seat right near where I went to write in my notebook a few days ago. I wondered what book she was reading.

After realizing how creepy I was being, I turned the board around and paddled out. I wanted to get her to notice me. I caught a wave and rode it in, proud at how natural it began to feel. I glanced over my shoulder, to look at Skye, hoping she could see my improvement. She remained sitting there, head down, consumed in her alternate world. *How do I get in her world?* I caught a couple more waves, then rode in because I was hungry. I decided I was going to ask Skye if she wanted to grab lunch, even though I knew she would probably turn me down, but she just disappeared. One moment she was there, delighting my peripheral, then the next she was gone, like a mirage.

I was pretty bummed that I missed a chance to talk to her when she was sitting right in front of me. Not that I would even know what to say. I beat myself up over what-ifs and tore myself down with the events of my past. It was like nothing I did was ever the right choice. Maybe I should always just follow my opposite intuition.

I went into a cafe I stumbled upon right off of the beach. The *HideAway Cafe* was nestled in the trees on a back road along an overt sand pathway. It had a wraparound porch with worn wooden benches out front and green windows with glass missing from its panels. The door was painted green, yellow, orange, and brown, emulating a bohemian tapestry. Nonetheless, its shabby look was inviting.

I walked in past the beaded entryway and took a seat at a corner table alongside the empty-paneled windows.

The barista behind the counter looked over, "G'Day! How you going?" He asked as he fiddled with a knob on the espresso machine with one hand, and poured a container of milk with the other.

"I'm doing alright. How about you?"

"Happy the sun is shining the coffee is brewing!" He smiled. "Your waitress will be over in a moment."

"Thanks."

I opened the menu, which was already on the table and began to peruse my options.

They had a huge breakfast menu and an extensive list of paninis, wraps, and homemade pie. My eyes grew wide in excitement because of the nostalgia I felt from picturing fresh baked pie.

My mom was not just a fire cook, she was also the sweetest baker. Everyone raved about her pies, but my favorite was when she made quesitos: a soft flaky pastry with cream cheese filling that makes my taste buds reconsider everything else it has ever been fed. My mom's abuela in Puerto Rico taught her how to make them when she would visit their hometown of Guayama in the summertime as a kid. Besides quesitos, the only other dessert that makes me salivate on the spot is her pies. Apple pie, blueberry pie, pecan pie, mixed berry pie… all of them were out of this universe!

"What. Are you following me, Trip?"

I looked up from the menu.

Skye. Her bright blue eyes scowled down at me.

"Uh, no." *Uh, no?* That's all I could come up with?! Days of envisioning what I wanted to say to this girl. Trying to figure out how to sculpt my words to make her smile.

She rolled her eyes. "Well, what do you want then?" She said with an attitude.

"What do you have against me? What did I do?" I asked her.

"Did you come here to bother me? Or are you going to order something?"

"No… I mean yes. Yes, I came here for lunch. I didn't know you worked here."

She stared at me, the fire in her eyes giving me a warm feeling inside. She was cute when she was angry, even the way her jaw tensed up.

"Well...?"

I realized she was waiting for my order. "I'll have the roasted red pepper chicken panini with mozzarella." It was the first one on this list.

"Anything on it?"

"Hot sauce."

"Okay."

"And what pie do you recommend?"

"All of them."

"But what's your favorite?"

"All of them."

"Okay... I'll take a slice of blueberry."

"Drink?"

"Whatever you usually get." I said smiling.

She rolled her eyes, turned on her heels and walked away.

"Number one with hot sauce!" She called to the back. "And a large quad shot soy upside-down caramel macchiato iced with two straws."

The barista looked at her puzzled. "Skye, your shift just started, you can't have two in a row."

"It's for him." She said with attitude.

I gave the barista a half wave, unsure about what in the world I just ordered. He chuckled to himself.

Skye was a terrible waitress. She plopped my drink and food in front of me and didn't return. It was definitely a step back from the Bondfire, which was barely a step at all. I didn't want to be too pushy, so I didn't bother her. I finished my panini, which was delicious, and even drank the entire macchiato, which caused my hands to start shaking from so much caffeine. I ripped out a paper from my notebook and left it behind with the check:

Skye,

What's your story?

-Lucas

*P.S. Straws are really bad for the environment. Do you really need **two** each time?*

Chapter 9: The Night My Life Fell Apart

After breakfast the next morning I noticed that there was a bookshelf in the lobby with a sign that read: TAKE A BOOK, LEAVE A BOOK, 'CAUSE EVERYBODY NEEDS A BOOK.

I've always loved reading. My dad would come read stories to me when I was little and preparing for bed. He would act out the characters to match their personality. He has all types of accents mastered, but somehow I would giggle the most when he would talk with an American accent. His natural British accent was barely detectable when he did impersonations. When dad would read to me, I would be in ultimate delight with the turn of every page.

Soon I started practicing my reading to him, as if he hadn't heard the story a million times already. I don't exactly remember when dad stopped coming into my room for reading time before bed. Like baseball catches every Sunday and jumping into his arms when he got home from work, it kind of just gradually decreased until it eventually stopped altogether. During my teenage years, I put up an invisible wall in front of my parents. I didn't even remember building that wall, one day it just felt like it was there.

I stood staring at the selections on the bookshelf, unable to make a choice.

"Looking for something to read?" Bradley asked.

"Yeah, I just finished my book. I'm going to add it to the shelf, but I don't know what to read next.

"What do you suggest?" I asked him.

He walked around the front desk and came over to where I was standing next to the bookshelf.

"A lot of them are great, it's really about what you prefer, but this one's my favorite." He said picking up *For One More Day*. "It's written by my favorite author, Mitch Albom. I literally get goosebumps as I read. He makes me think and appreciate everything in my life, you know? It's short, but don't let that fool you. It's really heavy, in words not in pages, but worth the effort of taking on. I've read it a bunch of times."

His passion for this book made it hard to turn down, although it's heaviness made me somewhat reluctant.

"You can always come back and re-trade whenever you'd like, but give it a shot."

Getting a new book is like holding a mystery in your hand. All the answers are on the pages just waiting to be figured out and when someone hypes it up, it only makes those answers more mysterious, more enticing. I took *For One More Day* down to the beach and sat against the rocks away from families and foot traffic. Skye was out on the water with her crew surfing, shredding the waves aggressively to mimic her attitude. I continued to wonder why she was so hostile.

I dove right into the book. I knew by the first couple of chapters it was going to tear me inside out. The protagonist, Chick, is an older guy looking back on his life and regretting all the things he did and didn't do with his mom. He never fully appreciated all that she did until it was too late, and she was gone. She died after Chick lied and left her on her birthday. He drank his life away in depression doused in nostalgia and decided to take his own life, until he was given another chance to be with his mom again, for one more day.

I almost couldn't continue, but it was like he was saying everything I was feeling, everything I wish I could avow to my parents in the letters, but could never get all out. Chick was pulling it all out of me and it was agonizing. My stomach was twisting, my eyes burned, my throat would barely let me swallow. It was like experiencing the emotions from The Night My Life Fell Apart all over again. The night both my parents died.

Halfway through I wondered why I was torturing myself. I ran away to escape my wretched thoughts, but somehow this time was different. I felt ready to feel these emotions and more prepared to face what I could not erase. I couldn't let my life spiral out of control like Chick's. My parents raised me to make them proud and I felt obligated to do so. That's why I needed to get away. I wasn't trying to run away from the past, I was trying to diverge from a dreary future. I couldn't let the routine of crying and helplessness morph into my life's fate. I needed to design a different path. In life, you always need to feel in control of your own future, even if you're running blindly, you need to depend on the strength of your other senses to keep you in control. You gotta keep that strength.

I was always bitter... even on The Night My Life Fell Apart, before the bad event happened... It was the day of my high school graduation. My parents planned a dinner to celebrate, but I wanted to go to a party someone from school was throwing, which is so not like me. I never went to parties. To be honest, I didn't even know the name of the person throwing the party, but I knew it would be my last opportunity to go to a high school party. I figured we could get to dinner and get back early enough for my friends to pick me up. They were guys from my P.E. class, who I got along with because I was pretty good at sports and I was on their team. I didn't ever tryout for anything at my new school because I lost my motivation after my parents forced me to move to Connecticut, but my competitiveness came out during P.E. games, awarding me an invite to the party of the year. I would normally pretend that I didn't care about going to parties, but that was when I wasn't invited. This was different.

My dad came to my graduation in the morning and then worked the second half of the day. I was watching for his car by the window because I wanted to go to the restaurant as soon as possible to ensure we were back in time for me to go to the party. I was waiting by the door when he walked in. Just like when I was a little kid. I was usually busy doing homework or watching TV when he gets home, so I didn't run to the door super-excited like when I was seven. I guess that's why he looked surprised that I was waiting for him. His face lit up. For me.

I don't even think I was smiling.

"Lucky! I'm so excited for tonight! We haven't really spent a good night as just the family in a while, you know?" My dad has called me Lucky since before I can remember.

"Your mother and I, we're just so proud of you. It's nights like these we're really going to miss when you head down to college." I was accepted to NYU and couldn't wait to move back to the city.

He kind of looked down at the floor, still smiling, but he lost that glow.

He looked back up, burying whatever thought just ran through his head.

"You ready for tonight?" He asked me.

"Yeah, I wanted to talk to you about that. There's a big party tonight that everyone in school is going to."

"A party? That's great. Do you want us to drop you off later tonight?" I could hear the tone of surprise in his voice because my dad knows, I usually don't go to parties.

"No... My friend Asher is going to drive. He said he'd pick me up at like ten."

I can't have my *parents* drop me off at a party.

"Ten? We won't have time to go get ice cream after dinner, Lucky."

"I mean, yeah I know, but I don't need ice cream. I know you're proud of me and all."

My parents are firm believers in celebrating and honoring accomplishments, particularly with ice cream. They know how much I love ice cream. It started when I was a little kid. My first home run in little league won me a big ice cream sundae. I couldn't even finish it. I got ice cream after I passed my drivers test too. Even though I failed twice. I couldn't parallel park.

My dad just half smiled and nodded at the change of plans.

"Okay," he said flatly. "How's your mom? Is she ready?"

"She should be. She's upstairs." I said as I walked away toward the den.

I heard my cell phone ringing, so I *didn't even listen* to the end of what my dad was saying. I just walked away from him, on the very last day I had with him. My ringing phone took priority.

We were seated right away at the restaurant. The truth is, I wanted to eat and leave as soon as possible so I barely talked, I just kept my head down and ate my food with haste.

"Slow down, Lucas. And don't forget to save room for dessert." My mom said.

I made eye contact with my dad, finished chewing my raviolis, and wiped my mouth to tell mom we didn't have time for ice cream.

"Ma, I told dad that I have a party tonight and since my friend is picking me up back at our place at ten, I think we should skip the sundae this time."

She paused, "Oh... but you love sundaes."

"Yeah" I said, "but dinner is enough really, this was awesome."

"We could do both! We can drop you off at the party after we go for ice cream. That's no trouble." Mom smiled.

"No, I already told my friends I'd go with them."

"You could text them to say that you'll meet them there."

Mom didn't get it.

Dad stayed quiet.

"We could take the ice cream to go and eat it in the car on the way over to your party."

"I don't want to do that." I said.

"Why not? You would probably get there about the same time as your friends, or even before! If they're not there we could wait with you outside till they pull up."

"I don't want to pull up to a party and have my parents dropping me off! I'm going to college, mom. I don't need to get ice cream, I'm not a child anymore." I snapped.

The words nearly shattered the whole evening.

Mom stayed quiet for the rest of the meal. *Our last meal. I ruined it. I ruined it all.*

The busboy began to clear the table as we finished up. "I'm going to use the restroom before we head back home. Don't worry Lucas, I won't keep us long." Mom said as she got up and headed to the back of the restaurant.

I didn't mean to hurt her feelings, but my pride swallowed my sense of decency and I didn't speak another word nor apologize. I just let her walk away.

I looked down at my phone for the time.

9:27PM

"Why don't you pull up the car and drive us home tonight, graduate?"

I couldn't help but sit there in shock. "You sure?"

My dad had a brand new Audi TT convertible. All black. He's never let me drive it.

"Yeah Lucky, now go outside before I change my mind."

He gave me the keys and I walked out of the restaurant with a smile ear to ear. Probably my first real smile all night. A materialistic smile coated in the guilt that would soon swallow me whole.

It was drizzling a little so I hid under the awning of the restaurant and handed the valet the ticket.

9:33PM

I'm gonna be late, I stressed.

I got into the car and adjusted the leather seat and played with the mirrors a little. I felt like I was about to fly a plane for the first time. The seat hugged me like I was a ball turret gunner. I gripped the steering wheel, foreign to my fingertips and ran my hands down the smooth, black leather.

9:37PM

When are they going to come out? I need to leave.

I got a text from Asher: *heading to ur house now*

He only lived about 15 minutes away and our drive home would be just over 30.

I didn't want to make everyone wait for me.

My parents came out to the car. My dad opened the door and helped mom climb into the back.

"How does it feel?" Dad asked.

"Incredible," I told him as I grazed my hands over the steering wheel.

I didn't know if my heart was beating fast because I was driving this car or because I was nervous about the party. Either way I was feeling very anxious.

I pulled out, blinker first, and accelerated down the street toward the highway. From the back seat I heard my mom say, "There's my coffee mug! I've been looking for it for weeks now."

"Oh yes hunny," my dad remembered, "I borrowed it one morning and totally forgot it was back there.

She unclipped her seat belt to reach over for it on the floor.

9:46PM

I knew I wouldn't make it home in time, but with this whip I knew I could get there pretty quick. I wanted the guys to see me pull up driving the TT. Nothing would make me look cooler.

I merged over to the left turning lane and saw the light was changing to yellow.

Gotta make the light. Gotta make the light.

I accelerated and the engine roared.

"Lucky be careful, slow down!" Dad yelled gripping the doorframe.

9:48PM

My heart was racing.

The light turned red.

I made the turn anyway.

The next thing I heard was my mom

s c r e a m i n g.

I wasn't going that fast…

I was.

I thought she had her seatbelt on…

She didn't.

I thought I could make the light…

I couldn't.

    I didn't.

        I can still hear her

        s c r e a m i n g.

Chapter 10: The Day After My Life Fell Apart

It was the first day since my surf lesson that I didn't touch a board at all. I read *For One More Day* in one sitting and was so mentally drained afterwards that I knew there was no way I could find the energy to paddle myself out. I went down to the beach and wrote pages and pages in my notebook, which really helped me process everything running through my mind.

Bradley wasn't kidding, that book was heavy.

"Writing again?" I heard a voice say.

I looked over to see Elsie, smiling. A smile so contagious that I couldn't help but do the same.

"Hey, yeah. Another letter to my parents."

"That's great that you can do that, just sit down and write. I was never much of a writer."

"Why? Because you don't? Or because you don't think you can?"

"Both I guess."

"Can't hurt to try." I shrugged. "No one even has to see it. That's what makes it so cathartic. It's yours. You decide if it says what you want it to say. You decide if you keep it or toss it. You decide if you share it or hide it. It puts me back in control, when I feel out of control."

"I never thought of it that way. That makes a lot of sense." Elsie nodded. "Do you mail your letters home to your parents?" She asked. I dropped my head into my hands. It's implausible how quickly I could go from hopeful to hurt. The claws that dig out the guilt I've managed to bury, stung to the root of every nerve inside of me.

"I can't." I painfully managed. My hands were stiffening up, blood rushing out of them.

"Why?" She asked.

"I can't."

She looked at me, waiting for me to continue, explain myself. I didn't feel pressure from Elsie, but I did feel the pressure of my secret pushing out from inside of me. "It's the reason I ran away. It's the reason why I'm in Byron in the first place."

I was tired of staying quiet about The Night My Life Fell Apart. For so long I've felt like I needed to vent. *To someone.* Sometimes a stranger can seem like the best confidant. I told Elsie about the crash and how I didn't wake up until the next morning in the hospital.

White. Pure white. That's all I saw.

I thought I was dead.

I tried to focus my eyes. I saw a man. He had his back to me. He was wearing all white.

There was a clock on the wall in front of me.

7:15AM

"What happened?" I somehow managed to say.

The man turned around. I realized he must have been a nurse. "Hello Lucas, you're at the hospital. How are you feeling?"

"I feel lightheaded, what's going on?"

"You were in a car crash. A truck ran into you going pretty fast. You lost a lot of blood, Lucas. You had a blood transfusion last night so you're probably still feeling a little groggy. So just sit tight and I'll go get the doctor." He said.

"Wait, where are my parents? Are they in a room nearby?"

"The doctor will be right in." He left.

The eggshell walls were closing in, *suffocating me* as I waited weightless and confused.

The doctor walked in and the walls bounced back to normal. "How are you feeling? A little disoriented?"

"Yeah, I kind of remember... I don't remember a truck though."

"You were in and out when the ambulance got there. You stayed with us the whole time. We're proud of you." She paused, as if to say something else, but stopped.

"Where are my parents? Are they okay? Can I go see them? Please."

"Lucas, I'm really sorry to be the one to tell you this-"

no

    no no

no no no

    no no noooo

"-your parents were not as fortunate as you-"

Dontsaytherestdontsaytherestdontsaytherest

      "-they're no longer with us."

The world drifted away from me.

I can hear myself s c r e a m i n g silently.

    It's my fault.

      It's all my fault.

        I killed them.

          I killed my parents.

Elsie sat there listening. I spoke faster with each word pouring out faster and heavier than the last. I needed to relieve my thoughts, but I needed to explain the full story, so that she didn't think I was crazy. I didn't know what to think after I finished. I looked up at Elsie. I worried about the judgment she might have, but there was none. She nodded and somehow, I felt like she understood.

When I was able to leave the hospital after The Night My Life Fell Apart, I didn't want to see anyone or do anything. I just wanted to be alone. I laid in my parents' bed and cried until my eyes burned like meteors, intense and alone.

I wrapped myself in their comforter and inhaled deeply, so that I could smell their scent and try to picture them laying next to me. Like when I was little and would crawl into their bed in the middle of the night when I was scared. I would nuzzle between them and feel the warmth from the covers and their love.

Until I was seven, my parents and I lived in a tiny one bedroom apartment in Brooklyn. It was the same apartment they had since they first moved in together when they were dating. It took a while for them to upgrade. I shared a room with my parents.

Thinking back, those were the best years of my life. On Friday nights, they would let me stay up late to watch cartoons with them. It was our thing. I always got to pick what we watched too. We were in close quarters; the dressers were in the living room, my mom kept her heels on top of the cupboard in the kitchen, and my dad's clothes overflowed into the coat closet near the front door. It wasn't much, but in many ways that's what made it so great.

Mom was caring, understanding, and kind. She spoke with remarkable elegance which reflected the shelves and shelves of books that filled our living room. Her collection grew every time we moved to a new place as more and more books seemed to appear. She read each and every book and marked the books she decided that I must read as well.

My mom was a butterfly, and the type of butterfly who could touch hearts and entice minds with a single flutter of her wings. My mom was beautiful, inside and out. She always made the world feel like a warmer place even when I was too stubborn to really listen to her words, too proud to seek out her embrace, and too embarrassed to accept her kisses, even when I really needed them.

Of course I love my mother and of course I always will. But there's something about being a teenager that made me want to reject all the care mom tried to spoon feed me. As if an eagerness to grow up replaced the yearn for Mommy's softness. It takes maturity to find a balance. Mature enough to handle responsibilities, yet mature enough to realize that there is no love like a mother's love and no age too old to receive advice from the person who created you... who'd do anything for you.

My dad was hardworking, loving, fun, and admirable. I always looked up to him... More than just how he had a solution for everything or how he dug his foot before a massive hit in baseball. Baseball was only a small reason as to why I wanted to be just like him when I grew up. He helped me realize how important it is to be persistent with something you really wanted. *If you're not persistent how are you supposed to show people, or even yourself, that you really really want something?*

It seemed like my dad never got tired either. I use to think his coffee gave him his superpowers, but I started drinking coffee too and I still don't know how my dad accomplishes so much with so little sleep. He did so much because he was persistent. He was persistent in giving me all the opportunities I could dream of and work to ensure nothing would hold me back.

It wrenches my stomach to think of the many nights when dad would come through the front door exhausted- still with a smile on his face- and I'd lack the energy, no the *decency,* to greet him at the door with the love and appreciation he truly deserved.

If only I reflected upon all of this beforehand...

If only swallowed me just as much as the *What if...* that drowned me.

Dear Mom and Dad,

It's been six weeks since the crash. It's weird how time seemingly goes by so slowly, but then before you know it, so much time has already passed. That probably doesn't make any sense, but you know what I mean. Mom always told me to be smart with my time.

Spend time more carefully than you spend money.

I never really understood what she meant. When I was younger, I always had the mindset that time was free and I had to earn my allowance money. I figured whatever I didn't get done today I could just do tomorrow. Money was always more relevant than time. Dad worked extra hours to make more money so that we could move and go on vacations and live more "comfortably." What I didn't realize until now is that the more money that was made, the less time we had, together.

If I could go back to any time in my life it would be when we lived in the small Brooklyn apartment and ate dinner together every night and watched cartoons and mom kept her heels in the kitchen. I wish we spent more time so and that we had less money so that we never moved and never got a nice car for me to crash. All that stuff just distracted us from what is most important, time. Quality time with the people I love the most. I'd do anything for more time with you. I'd do anything to have you both here. Anything...

Love always,

Lucky

Chapter 11: Sunrise Surf

I went to sleep early so I could wake up before the sun. Normally I would never *wake up* when it was still dark out, but I remembered that Spigs and the surf crew often went out for their morning surf before they opened the shop. I haven't gone out with them yet, but they told me to join when I felt comfortable out on the board.

By the time I got down to the beach, the guys were already putting on their wetsuits. There was another guy I didn't recognize sitting on the sand with his back to me. Coco saw me walking toward them first.

"Hey, how you going?" He called.

I waved and picked up my pace to jog over.

"Hey, hope I'm not too late to rent a board and catch some morning surf with you guys."

"No, just on time." Coco smiled.

"You've been practicing a lot I see. Feeling good out there?" Spigs asked.

"Yeah, I'm getting up consistently now." I shared proudly.

"That's deserving of a Tim Tam," the guy I didn't recognize said, as he extended a blue box of cookies. "I'm Kenny, nice to meet you. Grab one."

I took one out of the box. "Thanks, I'm Lucas"

"Welcome to sunrise surf. Have you ever had a Tim Tam?" He asked.

I shook my head no.

"Well, I feel honored to be the first to introduce you. You have to have it properly then, a Tim Tam Slam." He said as Budd brought over a cup of tea.

"Now bite each end of your Tim Tam, just enough to make an opening." He directed.

I took two bites and let the chocolatey goodness wake up my taste buds. "That's delicious!"

"That's only the half of it," he raved. "Now use the rest of the Tim Tam as a straw to drink your tea.

I did as directed, letting the hot tea flow through the chocolate and into my mouth. I sipped tea through the Tim Tam straw until the cookie began to crumble from the temperature and it quickly started melting in my mouth and fingers. I chomped the rest of it in one bite. It tasted like a warm chocolate lava cake.

"Wow! Who had that idea? That was out of this world!"

"It's an Australian thing. My grandma would even do it as a kid. Take another," Kenny offered.

Without hesitation I did, enjoying the gooey slam just as much as the first time.

"Let's head out to the water boys." Budd said as he brought out the surfboard and wetsuit I've been using since my lesson.

"Alright, my niece is just going to have to meet us then. She told me she'd be right behind me when I left the house, but she takes forever in the morning, so who knows." Kenny said as he got up and picked up his board. That's when I noticed his leg. His right leg was a prosthetic. I figured it was rude to ask him any questions, so I just pretended like I didn't see it.

"Jade is coming soon too." Coco grinned. I remembered seeing Jade's beautiful braids at the Bondfire. I suddenly became conscious of my hair.

"We got a sweet surf crew this morning!" Spigs exclaimed.

I cracked a smile. He said I was part of their surf crew.

We were out on the water for about fifteen minutes before two girls came walking down the beach with boards. As they got closer I realized, walking next to Jade was Skye. *Is Skye Kenny's niece? She could be his sister.* The girls paddled out.

"Hey, how'd the waves wake up?" Jade called as she paddled closer to Coco and gave him a kiss.

"On the right side of the bed. They're real nice." Coco answered. They kissed again.

"Alright you two." Skye rolled her eyes, landing on mine.

"Hey." I attempted.

She paddled away.

As Spigs was saying all morning, the Surf Gods were in a good mood. The sun was shining, the waves were perfect, everyone was having a great time, even Skye. She was actually talking to me. Although sometimes she would catch herself being nice and immediately halt our conversation, as if she suddenly remembered that she had to be an asshole to me. I didn't get it. Kenny was always giving me feedback on my technique and suggesting ways for me to get better. He was an impressive instructor. I wondered why Spigs didn't have him working at the Surf Shack. He helped me to get a hold of the board. I felt like I was really starting to get good, until I would look up and notice the skills of everyone around me. *They* were good. I was still just a beginner.

"How long have you been surfing?" I asked Skye as she paddled up behind me after catching a wave.

"Since I was two."

"Two?! How did you even carry a board? Or paddle out?" I asked intrigued. Two!

"Well, I would ride with my mum on her board until I was five. That's when Kenny carved me a board of my own."

"Wow, your mom must be really good."

"Was. She was pro when she died."

My heart dropped.

"Oh, I'm sorry Skye, I didn't know."

Everything went silent. Even the waves stopped swooshing. I thought about my mom and my dad and how hard it was to talk about their death with other people. I wondered if Skye's mom passed recently. Is that why she was so tightly wound?

Skye paddled away to catch a wave alongside Kenny. Skye brought her board so close to his that she could have reached out and grabbed his arm. They both had so much control. Even Kenny with a prosthetic leg owned the ocean. I wondered what his story was.

It seemed like everyone in Byron had a story inside of them. It seemed like a good place to hide mine.

Chapter 12: What's Your Story, Skye?

The guys invited me to the Bondfire again and I was psyched. It was the first thing I've been actually excited for in a very long time. I could already smell the burning of the fire all the way from Neptune's.

I brought over an offering again- some chicken for Spigs to throw on the grill and some beer to toss in the cooler. Although, I still haven't grown too fond of the taste of beer, I'd still probably drink it all night. There seemed to be more people at the Bondfire than last week, but it felt good to walk in and know a few people. "Hey, Lucas the not-delivery guy!" Zane put his arm around me when I walked in. It felt nice to be remembered.

I made my way to the yard and found Spigs near the grill, Budd on the halfpipe, and Coco with his arm around Jade. I turned to look near the cooler to see if Skye was where she was standing last week, but she wasn't. I didn't see her anywhere. I tried not to be obvious as I looked for her. I took a seat alongside the fire and chatted with some locals. Some of them I've seen talking to Skye. Did they know where she was? There was no way I could ask them. I'd look like a creep.

We talked about surfing mostly, well, they did. I didn't have much to contribute besides my one week of experience, but these guys were like surf encyclopedias- from the lingo to the best regions and even down to the science of the waves. I listened mostly and scanned the yard as the amount of people increased and the amount of personal space decreased.

Then suddenly I saw Skye. She weaved through a group of people near the grill and slid out from the yard through the bushes, making her way to the beach. I told the guys I was going to get another drink, which I did, then headed through the bush onto the sand. I looked around then saw Skye sitting on a log down the beach with a drink in her hand, alone. I walked toward her. In my head I fumbled words attempting to come up with a clever reason why I was also out on the beach, alone. As I got closer, she saw me.

"Hey." I said. Simple. Expected. Normal. Good.

"What do you want, Trip?" She said with an air of aggression.

"Just wanted some quiet for a bit. There are a lot of people there tonight, huh?"

"Yeah, too many. It's cause Spigs invites everyone, even *tourists*." She said, emphasizing tourists.

I needed to change the subject.

"What were you reading the other day?" I asked her.

"The day you stalked me and followed me to work?"

"I swear I didn't know you worked there. I saw you reading when I was surfing. I was on the beach first." I said innocently.

"You were on the beach first? So, it's your beach, now?" She snapped.

What was her issue with me?

"No, I'm just saying I didn't follow you there. Or to work. Chill out Skye, it's not always all about you." I chided.

She went silent, stared me dead in the eye, and started laughing.

"Wow, growing a set, are you?"

I was taken back by her bluntness, but still, it made me laugh too.

"You don't hold back, do you Skye?"

"Hold back? Why should I?"

"You shouldn't." I told her. "You're honest." I smiled. Honest was one way to twist words in describing Skye's interactions with me.

"What were *you* reading the other day on the beach?" She asked.

I smiled. She noticed me on the beach.

"It looked like you were crying." She continued.

My smiled disintegrated.

"It was a really good book I traded for. And I wasn't crying, I was concentrated."

"I don't care if you were crying Trip, that's your own issue. I just wanna know what kind of book made you cry. It must have been good."

"I wasn't crying."

"Alright Trip, so what was that book that made you *look* like you were crying?"

I exhaled to compose myself. Her attitude was annoying, but oddly I was attracted to it.

"It's called *For One More Day*. It's about a guy who loses his mom. It made me miss mine."

"Homesick Trip?" She poked at me. I was surprised she could be so rash, especially after learning about her mom's death.

"Something like that... Do you want to trade? I just finished it. How about you give me what were you reading on the beach?"

She looked up at me and attempted to bury her smile. "Yeah. I guess we could trade."

"I'm warning you, the book is pretty heavy." I added.

"You think I can't handle it? Because it made you cry?"

"No... I'm just saying..."

Right then she she took out a lighter and lit a cigarette.

"Why do you smoke those things?" I asked. I hated cigarettes. My grandma died of cancer from them.

She exhaled, filling our clean air with smoke.

"Do you want a hit?"

"No. They're not good for you. You can get cancer."

Skye laughed at me.

"That's not funny." I said seriously.

"This isn't a cigarette, Trip. Calm down. If anything, it could help someone with cancer."

I never smoked anything before.

She inhaled deeply. "Why do you follow me?" Exhale.

"I don't follow you."

"You followed me out here."

"No, I just left the party for some air."

"Then why are you sitting here? Right now. With me." I looked at her beside me.

"Because you're interesting." I replied.

"Do I interest you?" She looked at me, tilting her head, and squinting her eyes as if to analyze my reaction. I remained quiet.

"Nothing clever to say now?" Inhale. "You can't even look at me. Do I make you uncomfortable?" Exhale.

"No, you don't." I said, fidgeting my fingers.

"You can't look at me in the eye, Trip." She dared, flicking the ash toward my feet.

"I'm looking at you right now." I said, with confidence as I turned and looked at her ocean blue eyes that reflected the moonlight.

"And what do you see?" She asked, moving her face a bit closer to mine.

Her proximity made my heart race.

"I see a beautiful girl who hides behind weed and tough talk to come across as a badass." I smiled and moved my face closer. Inches.

"Wow, that was bold." Skye kept her eyes locked on mine and put the J to her lips. "Very bold, Trip." She exhaled and puffed the cloudy smoke in my face, making me pull away, coughing. She laughed.

"You're smart, you know that? You really have me figured out." She stated sarcastically.

I stopped coughing and composed myself. She took one last hit and stood up.

"Stalk me some more tomorrow. I'll bring that book to work. We'll trade." She said without turning back, leaving me sitting on the log, alone. I got up to go back to the party, until I realized that it would look like I was following her, which I was, but I didn't want her to know that.

Skye was about twenty feet away when I called out to her. "Hey Skye!" She turned around. "What's your story?"

She laughed. "You wouldn't be able to handle it."

Chapter 13: The Book Trade

I still felt selfish pushing away the painful regret when I thought of my parents, but I knew it was the only way for me to avoid getting sucked into a well of guilt again. There are too many mistakes that cannot be repaired. Is running away from reality an acceptable escape?

I went down to the HideAway Cafe with Skye's words from the previous night still replaying in my head. I hoped Skye would be there like she mentioned. My hopes were fulfilled when I saw her behind the counter organizing a shelf of mugs. I tried to think of what I could say to someone who always seems angry with me. Her back was to me, so she didn't see me go sit down at the same table as last time. I thought about getting up to grab a menu, but I just sat there and watched her stack mugs until she realized a customer had walked in. Her pace quickened to finish what she was doing until she realized it was me. She looked up, slipped a half smile, and her face softened. For once Skye didn't look at me like she hated me.

"Same drink as last time? No better way to start the day." She smirked. Only a crazy person would willingly drink that over-caffeinated heart attack and I already had it once. The caffeine spark it gave me shot me through the roof. No wonder Skye was an unpredictable ball of sporadic emotions.

"I think I'll tone it down and stick with a regular coffee."

"Would you like sunshine and rainbows in that coffee?" She asked with a smile, confusing me.

"Huh?"

"Sugar and milk…" As if that was obvious.

"No black, please." The way my parents both would drink it.

Skye brought me my coffee, a slice of pie, and *Looking for Alaska* by John Green. I could tell the book had taken a beating because the cover was worn and the pages looked soft, like it had been devoured time and time again. Carter was written down the side in black marker and even that was fading away. I pictured Skye reading while surfing, because if anyone could do it, it was her.

I gave her *For One More Day* along with another warning. After finding out that Skye lost her mom, I was nervous that this book could hit her in the wrong way if she wasn't ready.

"What's this book about?" I asked her.

"A kid trying to figure out his problems." She vaguely described.

"Well isn't that every book? Someone trying to figure out a problem."

"The protagonist reminds me a bit of you." I perked up in my seat. Someone reminded her of me! "He's new, and a loser, and looking for answers that don't exist in places he's unfamiliar with." New, I get. Loser? Ouch. Looking for answers?

"What answers am I looking for?"

"Well, why don't you tell me that, Trip?"

What was I looking for here? A distraction? An escape? A reminder of why I am alive.

I didn't tell Skye any of that. That would have gotten too deep too fast. I was already treading water to stay on the surface. I stuck with my pre-college backpacking story.

"If that was the case you wouldn't have stayed in Byron for more than a week. Why are you here so long?" She pried.

I never thought of a response to that kind of question. Why so long?

"There's a lot of beauty in Byron." I flirted, looking up toward her.

Skye broke our eye contact and looked past me, seemingly through the window, but it was clear by the depth in her eyes that she was looking far beyond the HideAway porch. Her eyebrow curved like the tail of a question mark.

"Are you scared of heights?" She deflected my subtle compliment.

"No." Our eyes reconnected.

"My shift gets off at 4. Meet me at the end of the beach, near the rocks. Your crying spot." She insisted.

"Where are we going?"

"To the most beautiful place no one has ever seen."

Chapter 14: I Need Your Help

I was down by the rocks before 4:00. I was eager to see what adventure boiled inside Skye's labyrinth of a mind. I saw Elsie walking around the bend of the rocks. I called out to her, but she didn't respond. She kept her head down and kept walking. I didn't chase after her. I sat and read the book Skye traded me, *Looking for Alaska,* until I saw Skye in my peripheral walking toward me with a tangled cargo net slung over her shoulder. I got up and tried to take the net from her, since it looked like it was swallowing her upper body, but she refused to hand it over.

"Don't treat me like I can't handle carrying this. I brought it all the way here didn't I?" I quickly noted Skye's irritable mood. Maybe she gets bitchier as the day goes on as her dose of caffeine dwindled, I thought.

"You can hold these I guess." She handed me two headlamps.

"What are these for?"

She ignored my question and continued walking past me, climbing up the rocks toward the trees overhead, holding the net on her shoulders with one arm, and stabilizing her balance with the other.

"Where are we going?" I followed behind her.

"Be patient, will ya? Bloody hell." I gathered that Skye didn't particularly like questions.

We got to the top of the rock scramble and began walking up a steep path that was barely cleared. I tripped on some roots with my sandals while Skye effortlessly navigated through the densely wooded pathway barefoot. We didn't exchange many words besides when the net would hook onto branches with thorns that would whip back into my face and arms breaking through my skin, to which I'd respond with some variation of a curse and she'd mutter an apology she didn't mean, trekking on. This went on for almost an hour until we finally got to the top.

I peeled off my blood stained shirt covered in sweat and threw it over a tree while Skye propped the net in front of a rock and laid against it, breathing heavy. Her face was flush as she gazed out to the sun that was just beginning to set. Her rosy cheeks reflected the shades of pink in the horizon.

I walked closer to the ledge and admired the numerous facets of the earth's natural beauty…

The sunset with strokes of every shade.

The soft white sand that stretched to disappear around the curve.

The treetops that waved from the same gentle breeze that cooled my face.

The rocks that chiseled to form the very mountain enabling such a view.

I peered over the cliff to the aqua water down below. The cliff extended beyond the mountain's base.

I was hovering over the water.

"It's breathtaking." My back still to her, I continued to look out painting a permanent picture in my head.

"It's only half." She replied.

I turned around. "Where's the other half?" I looked around for a hidden trail nestled in some more thorns, but we were at the highest peak, there couldn't have been a better view.

"It's below us."

I turned to look over the cliff again.

"The water?" I asked puzzled.

"Stop asking so many questions, be patient." She stood up. "Follow me. We have about another hour before it gets too dark to see." She walked off to the opposite side of the mountain's peak and began descending. We hiked for another fifteen minutes until she stopped at a landing.

"Loop the headlights around your arm so they don't get lost when we jump into the water."

"When we jump!?" I looked down at the water over 50 feet below.

"Yes, Trip. You told me you weren't afraid. You can't back out now."

"I'm not backing out, I'm just... clarifying." She threw the cargo net down into the water.

"Good. Point your toes to break the water and reduce the harshness of the impact. Jump as far as you can to the right of the net. And don't bitch out."

Without another word or window for any questions she jumped, breaking the water with her toes, just as she instructed. She disappeared below the surface and I waited for her to come up for air, but she didn't. I waited a few seconds more, which morphed into a minute, which felt like a million, triggering my panic.

"Skye!" I screamed from overhead. My heart began to race. Where did she go? Why didn't she come back up?

I heard a familiar scream from below.

"Skye!" I yelled even louder, my voice echoing.

I hesitated for a moment as I approached the ledge. I couldn't waste any more time. I took two huge steps to propel myself far from the rocks like Skye said and plunged myself into the water, my legs smacking painfully upon impact. I didn't come up for air. I stayed below the surface looking all around, expecting to find Skye's limp body drifting. The water was clear, but I couldn't see her anywhere. I thought of the worst. A shark?! Did she get caught on washed up scrap metal at the bottom? Did she hit the rocks without me noticing? I swam furiously with no clear direction in mind, using the last of my oxygen to scream her name under water.

I came up for air then looked around. I caught my breath and screamed her name again. It had been minutes since she jumped. The cargo net was beginning to sink. My stomach knotted up. Should I go for help? Should I continue diving to find her? Bodies don't just disappear, they float. The thought of Skye's floating body became a scarier thought then it never appearing.

"Skye!" I cried coughing on my own racing panic. My throat burned from saltwater screaming.

"Yeah!" I heard her call behind me, right where she landed, next to the cargo net. I hastily swam over to her.

"What the- how?! Where?!

"What did I say about so many questions, Trip?"

"No. No, Skye! You will answer my questions this time! You scared the shit out of me." I began raising my voice. "What just happened? How are you alive after being underwater that long? Are you like some pro diver where you can just hold your breath for minutes at a time? Why would you do that to me?!"

Skye began to laugh. I splashed her in anger because there was no other way to express my frustration. "Is this some kind of joke?" I was beginning to get tired of treading water.

"No. Calm down. I'll show you."

"No, no! You're going to tell me before you show me because the last time you tried to show me you disappeared under water for I don't even know how long! Where did you go?"

"I went inside the mountain." She told me.

"Inside? Like a cave?"

"Exactly. Part of the mountain is hollow and I found a way inside."

I envisioned a frigid, dark den filled with bats.

"How do you get inside?" I asked, already knowing the answer to my question.

"You got to swim down. The entrance is underneath. I went inside first to get this rope I keep in there." She revealed a rope in her hand from underneath the water. "I want to bring that cargo net inside the cave, but need help pulling it down. It's heavy and under water it only gets heavier. I've tried to pull it once before but the resistance is too much for the depth. I can't do it alone."

"Are you saying you need my help?" I smirked.

She scowled at me. "Yeah, Trip. I need your help. If you're not too scared."

"Scared? Why do you think I'm scared of everything?"

"Because of how you panic when I present adventure."

"I don't panic!"

"I heard you screaming like a madman." Skye laughed. "Not to mention the look on your face before I jumped. I knew you wouldn't have even followed if I just came right back up. You needed a reason to come after me."

"So you just disappeared? Anyone would have screamed for you!" I defended.

"I'm not here to argue with you, Trip. Are you in or not?"

I was already exhausted from trying to find Skye and treading for the entirety of our conversation. How much more did I have to swim? It didn't matter. I couldn't wimp out. Skye *actually* needed me.

"What do I need to do?" I asked, implying my consent.

"Okay, so I compacted the cargo net as much as possible to reduce resistance in the water. Here," she pointed to the net, "I looped the rope through and made two loops, one for each of us to pull. I'll take the lead with the loop in front and you'll follow me under the water to the entrance of the cave. Once we get through the entrance, just swim up. You can't really get lost in there."

She explained her plan so simply. I had so many questions. How did she find it? How deep down was the entrance? What was inside the cave? All these questions floated in my mind, because I knew with Skye, I dare not ask a single one.

Chapter 15: Underwater Cave

Skye gave me goggles that she had secured to a tree branch that extended into the water. She said I would need them more than she would. I didn't argue with that. I grabbed my part of the rope and took a deep breath while Skye made sure the cargo net was tight and secure. I was only getting more and more tired with each minute that passed treading water. I wasn't an avid swimmer like Skye. I was nervous that my energy would fall short when pulling the net through the water. I didn't tell Skye my worry because she probably would have just snarled and told me to leave. This was my chance to help her. To impress her.

"The entrance is about ten to fifteen feet under water. It's not too deep, but you may feel pressure in your ears. Just hold your nose and breathe out to release the pressure. It's called equalizing." Skye explained. Then she made me practice, warning that if I did it wrong my eardrums could rupture. That was comforting. She was very knowledgeable. I absorbed her advice hoping it would ease my nervousness.

We both put on the headlamps adjusting them to fit snugly.

"Ready?"

No.

"Yes." I lied, securing the goggles.

And we dove down.

We swam effortlessly until the rope slack ran out, then it felt like we were dragging another person behind us. We headed toward the rocks that supported the base of the mountain.

Down.

Past the swimming fish.

Down.

Toward the darkness of the water.

Down.

My ears began to tighten.

Down.

I equalized.

Down.

Until an entryway appeared in the rocks and Skye led the way inside. The only source of light came from the lamps on our head, everything was dark at that depth, like swimming in black water. I couldn't even see the rope trailing behind me.

Skye began swimming up and I followed, until suddenly I couldn't pull the rope anymore. It was stuck. I gave it a stronger tug, but it wouldn't budge. My oxygen was rapidly escaping my lungs from panic. I turned to look back, but only saw pure blackness and pulled again. Nothing. Fear twisted in my stomach. I turned to see Skye was gone. Again?! Was this girl serious? I dropped the rope. I barely knew which way was up, but swam with the little energy I had left. Kicking and reaching my hands for the surface, my head throbbing from the pressure. In that moment I felt trapped, captive in the inky water.

This is it, I remember thinking. Giving up felt easier than pushing on, but it wasn't what I wanted. A month ago yes, I would have gladly let the ocean wash me away, cleansing my problems, erasing my existence, but that day, in that moment, I felt compelled to push on, eager to embrace tomorrow.

Letting the ocean win felt cowardly. I fought my body's urge to shut down and kept swimming until I broke to the surface gasping. I swam over to a rock to rest, panting, until I realized where I was. I looked around. There was a light on the side revealing the capacious cave, illuminating the stalactites hanging all around like icicles. It was astounding.

Suddenly Skye broke the surface with the cargo net beside her. Who was this girl? The Little Mermaid crossed with Wonder Woman. She paddled over to the opposite side to a ledge and tossed the net down, collapsing on top of it like she did at the top of the mountain.

"You alright, Trip?" She called across the cave.

No.

"Yes. Are you? What happened down there?" I asked. How did she manage to bring the net up on her own, after I panicked and bailed?

"The net got caught on the entrance when we changed directions and began swimming up. I had to swim back to untangle it." Skye had unbelievable composure.

I swam over to her ledge and sat down next to the net-turned-recliner, looking around at the entirety of the cave. I almost began to spew out all the questions erupting in my mind, but organized them into one statement, remembering Skye's previous reactions to my questions.

"I have so many questions right now." I stated simply.

"Like what?"

"You hate when I ask questions, so I'll just stow them in my thoughts."

She turned her head, her eyes narrowed at me, brows morphing to resemble question marks. "No, Trip. I hate when you ask questions that spoil the adventure. And, the adventure has been had." She sat up, an idea in her eye. "And now the work begins." She rose to her feet.

"Begins? You're telling me dragging a colossal cargo net into the depths of darkness didn't constitute as work?" I stood up beside her with my hands crossed over my chest.

Skye began unfolding the net. "That? No, that was the fun part. Now, I don't even know if this net will accomplish what I want, so we need to get to work to figure that out."

What? That sounded promising. Skye turned to survey the cave.

"And what do you wish to accomplish, Skye?"

I stared at her, waiting for a response. I could almost hear her ideas shifting. She reached out to hand me a part of the net.

"Grab this end, and climb up there."

I glared at her like she stated a really offensive joke. I looked up at the part of the cave she was pointing to. I made it that far.

I grabbed the net and helped.

It took us almost an hour and four false successes, but we did it. I found out Skye previously measured and cut the net to fit that corner of the cave. Like some engineer-mermaid-goddess. Secured in eight different corners, we fastened the cargo net to hang from the rocks overhead, like a canopy hovering over the water. The industrial waterproof battery powered flood light continuing to illuminate the cave, forming shadows that resembled teeth on the cave's ceiling. We laid there in fatigue staring up at them.

"Did you know that stalagmites only grow about ten centimeters every thousand years." Skye said, pointing up toward the cave's ceiling. "That means everything around us is tens of thousands of years old."

I was impressed and kind of turned on by her scientific knowledge.

"Actually the ones on the ceiling are called stalactites. Stalagmites are the speleothems that are on the ground." I added.

"Speleothems?" She asked with surprise.

"Those are cave formations. All of them form from water simply dripping. It's amazing."

"That's why I love coming in here. Everything about caves are amazing." She let go of a deep breath.

You're amazing.

"How did you find this?" I asked her. I let my questions flow freely now that the adventure was complete.

"The mountain used to be a popular cliff jumping spot. Mostly on the front half where we walked up when the path was clear. People stopped coming about ten years ago, but I still come up for the view and to think. I liked discovering new spots to jump from and began jumping off of the back of the mountain. I always would dive down pretty deep and when I did at that spot we jumped from, I realized a part of the mountain that was darker. I got some goggles to check it out and realized it was a hole. I didn't want to go in since it was almost impossible to see, even in the daylight, so I bought a headlight and discovered it was an entryway. I swam in without knowing where it would lead or if there would be air or an animal on the other side. I just needed to discover more. And look what I found."

I shifted my eyes from the cave's stalactite teeth to Skye's smile.

"Beautiful" I whispered.

Never in my life had I experienced a moment like that moment in the cave. Laying with the most interesting and alluring girl I've ever met, floating in a space that few or none have ever witnessed, and feeling weightless, hovering in a world so vast and undiscovered. Skye allowed this moment to occur in my life.

"You weren't very fond of me for a while, what changed?" I asked her.

The cave's cold air creeped over my skin.

"I like you Lucas, but everything I stand for hates you."

I let her words float in the stagnant air. "Good thing we're not standing." I toyed.

She didn't find my joke very funny. "I refuse to succumb to your fabricated American charm."

"Why do you act like you hate me?"

"Because you're American."

"Seriously?" I griped.

"An American knocked up my mom. And I don't hate that an American is my dad, but I hate that a spoiled tourist on his daddy's penny abandoned my mom at eighteen and never sent a word nor a dollar. You tourists skip through here in your own fantasy world, stepping on real people's lives with any regard for anyone but yourself. It's not just my father, I've seen your type, it's especially Americans. You're so... ethnocentric and self-centered, it's disgusting." She fired.

"So then why bring me to your cave?"

"Because I knew I couldn't set up the cargo net alone, but never wanted to reveal my secret to anyone."

"What makes me different?"

"You're a mirage. Temporary. You'll go away soon, my secret will be kept, and my cargo cradle constructed."

In an instant I went from elated to deflated. She just wanted to use me. She did use me. AND she almost killed me in the process.

I gripped the cargo net tightly in a fist. I felt so used. "Do you think if people saw inside of you, they would still think you're beautiful?"

I immediately regretted the words as soon as they left my lips.

She turned to face me. "Fuck you, Trip. You know nothing about what's inside of me. And what kind of backhanded compliment is that?"

I didn't know how to respond to a remark I knew I shouldn't have said.

"You come out here to party, call mommy and daddy every time you run out of money, and think you can just make judgments about people. You fit the formula, Trip. Point proven." Judgments?! Skye was the one making extreme judgments.

101

I gripped the net tighter, infuriated. "DO NOT MAKE ASSUMPTIONS ABOUT MY LIFE!" I yelled at her, my voice echoing through the cave. She didn't say a word. The silence calmed me. "For someone so against judgments, you're pretty quick to judge."
For once Syke didn't have a smart remark.

We just laid there, examining our flaws and imperfections in silence.

Chapter 16: Burgeroo

It was a dark walk back from the cave, but Skye instinctively knew her way and I was able to manage not falling on my face thanks to the headlamp. There was barely even a path, yet Skye brought us back to the end of the beach without deviation.

"You have a good sense of direction. Have you always lived in Byron?" I asked.

"No, but for most of my life. Since I was six." Skye began. "You know, I remember the day I moved here. My mum and I walked down to the beach and I turned to her and told her I wanted this to be home. She asked me why and I told her, *because it makes you smile and I haven't seen you smile in a while mummy.* Then she started crying and I was six so I didn't understand why. I told her I was sorry and wanted her to stay happy.

She picked me up and said, *I'm happy now because this is home.*

I never want to leave Byron because this was the only place that made my mum happy. Every other place we lived was like a nightmare."

I was surprised how much Skye revealed after a long hike in silence. Through the darkness, she was helping me see inside of her. Skye told me stories of when she and her mum were homeless, moving from town to town until her mom caught a break with a surf sponsorship landing them in Byron.

"She died when I was ten. I was in foster care for three years until they let Kenny have full custody of me. He had to get his shit together before they'd let me live with him. He was more of a big brother than an uncle. We're only ten years apart."

I was beginning to understand why Skye was who she was.

We walked along the beach, past the block of my hostel, Skye talking and me listening for a while.

"So what made you want to tell me your story?" I asked. Her demeanor had completely changed. She seemed more comfortable with me.

"Same reason I showed you my cave, I'll never see you again after all this."

There's some kind of safety when confiding in strangers. I thought.

"I don't usually talk to anyone about personal stuff. I didn't really expect to tell *you* all this, but somehow it just felt good after I started spilling."

"We have more in common than you think." I told her as I rubbed my already throbbing temples. My heart was beating through my chest. My secrets were knocking to get out again. Skye stayed quiet, waiting for me to say more. My face felt hot. I was sweating. I opened my mouth to speak, but the words wouldn't come. The words were only ever put together in my writing and my thoughts.

Skye stopped walking.

"Listen, I don't want you to think I'm saying sorry or anything, but I shouldn't have passed such harsh judgments before. I know how it feels to be on the judged end."

I was sweating, probably visibly, thinking about my parents and then Skye completely shocked me with an apology. My emotions were jumping everywhere.

"It was fucked up. I completely contradicted myself. I was the person who I hate, you know?" Skye felt bad about what she said in the cave. I wasn't even thinking about that anymore.

"Don't worry about it."

We walked a couple more minutes in silence.

"I live just up there." Skye said stopping and pointing down a block.

"I could walk you home." I offered.

"I can handle walking myself home, thanks." She sneered.

"You're right." I put my hands up defensively. "Why would you show a stranger where you live? Just show him your secret cave." I joked.

She actually laughed at a joke, *I made.* "You couldn't find that place again even if the path was clear!"

"I don't doubt that. I just thought you wouldn't mind the company."

She smiled. "Well, I am hungry." She began walking. "Let's go into town and get some food."

Like a date? I thought. I followed her. "I am starving. And you did put me to work."

"But it's getting colder, I want to stop home and get a jumper. And some shoes."

"Alright, let's stop by." I agreed.

"No." Skye interjected. "I'll go. You start walking. I'll catch up."

"I don't even know where we are exactly." I looked around. "I haven't been down at this end of town. And it's pretty dark." There were no streetlights, just the illumination of the moon and the light that spilled out from the houses that left their shades cracked.

"You'll be fine. You found your way all the way to here from America didn't you? Just walk down that way." She pointed ambiguously. "You can keep that headlamp for light."

She had reasons lined up for why I shouldn't walk her home. Sometimes it's easier not to argue.

"Alright, I'll see you down there if I don't get eaten by a dingo." I joked as she began walking away.

"Be the alpha male!" She called. I couldn't see her anymore. She wasn't using her headlight. Skye knew her way, even through the dark.

I couldn't read Skye's behavior. One minute she hates me the next she likes me. She trusts me with details from her personal life, but doesn't trust me to walk her home? Would she even meet me in town? ...If I even found where it was... Or would she desert me and completely disappear from existence? There was no way to predict her actions.

Walking alone in dark silence injects me with a compulsion of caution that straddles the line of fear. The longer I focus on it, the bigger it becomes.

I walked lightly because hearing my own footsteps made me paranoid.

Why did Skye insist on splitting up?

I had a bad feeling.

I began to walk faster, increasing my heart rate along with my paranoia until I was jogging.

I didn't know if I really heard something behind me or if it were my own steps echoing.

Lights from town became visible up ahead.

I turned to check behind me and I saw a hooded figure in the darkness. Immediately I began running.

The footsteps behind me quickened too.

It made me have a flashback to when I was fourteen...

It was my freshman year of high school and I was coming home late from a baseball game in the South Bronx. I didn't have my baseball bag with me, so all I had was my wallet in my pocket, my phone in my hand, and my headphones in my ears. I voluntarily gave up two of my most relied upon senses because I was watching a video on my phone.

My headphones were loud, so I couldn't hear them coming.

I was looking at my screen, so I couldn't see them coming. I was holding my phone, so I couldn't even defend my face as he came from the side and connected his fist to my jaw.

I hit the ground before my eyes could even adjust from the illumination of my phone. He kicked me twice, but not much more before he took my wallet and ran. To think, all that for fifteen dollars and a MetroCard that expired four days later.

My mom took me down to the police station as soon as I got home after I walked fifty blocks. The police officer who interviewed me said there was not much they could do if I didn't see anything. They told me to avoid distractions, be prepared to protect myself at all times, and always try to get a visual.

My mom hated that they couldn't do anything. Giving me advice for *next time* didn't make my mom feel safe. She didn't want there to be a next time. I'm convinced she told my dad to ask for a transfer out of the city because of that night. I was too embarrassed and angry to ever ask because that would mean we moved because of me, because I was distracted when I should have paid attention.

I ran with my hand in a fist, ready. I heard the steps getting closer. Town was still at least three blocks away. I needed to get a visual before I got attacked from behind.

I stopped and turned around, put my fist up over my face, and there was Skye, in a hoodie, meeting me like she said she would.

"I thought that was you, but couldn't see that far. Why were you running from me?"

Suddenly I felt stupid. "I didn't think it was you."

"I told you to be the alpha male if you ran into a dingo, Trip. And here you are running away."

We began walking, alongside each other.

"Where are we going?" I asked her, stopping myself. "Am I allowed to ask questions or is this an adventure?"

She laughed. She would laugh at me a lot. Sometimes I wasn't even sure why. Nonetheless, her laugh made me smile, so even if she was laughing at me, I was okay with it.

"It could be considered an adventure, depending on how versatile your taste buds are. What's the most exotic food you've ever eaten?"

"Aaaa... wild salmon."

"Well then yes, this is an adventure, so no more questions." She laughed and of course, I smiled.

We sat down at a place that just looked like a regular burger spot. *Burgeroo* was written across the wall. I profiled it for clues about what exotic food might be served to me. It smelt like *Shake Shack*, but still way different, and with a slight smell of burning. Most people had burgers and fries in front of them. I wasn't too worried about what Skye had cooking. We didn't even get menus, Skye just made eye contact with the waiter and held up two fingers; he nodded back in confirmation. Shortly after two burgers and fries came out and were served to us.

"What's so exotic about a burger?"

"See for yourself." She dared, taking a bite.

I was starving, so without hesitation I took a huge bite. Chewing, I realized it tasted different. Good. Great even, but different.

I swallowed my first bite. "It's delicious. What is it?"

"It's kangaroo." She said, taking her second bite.

I looked at it and pictured a kangaroo hopping around. I contemplated the difference between eating a kangaroo and eating a cow or chicken.

"Cows aren't native to Australia They were brought over on the First Fleet, so they're not in their natural habitats. Too many cows equals more methane gas in the air…" Skye stopped herself from what sounded like could have been a speech. "I'm a vegan. Well, half-ass vegan because of all the exceptions I have with that diet, including kangaroo. And special occasions…" She took another bite.

The burger was really good. Even better than a cow, but that could have just been because of how hungry I was. I took another bite. Skye nodded in agreement and we chowed down till we finished our food with barely another word spoken.

From dinners at home, I learned that silence during a meal could mean a few things:

1. Everyone is hungry

2. The food is delicious

and/or

3. Someone at the table is upset.

For almost every dinner I can remember since I moved to Connecticut I stayed quiet for all those reasons, but I let the last one take over and consume me. My permanent demeanor around my parents was upset because I always focused on the move I felt forced to do. I ignored the countless things they provided for me because I was too busy dwelling on the one thing they took away.

I was so upset about leaving the city, a place that would always be there, that I squandered the time with my parents, who I could never get back. I wondered what other enigmas would reveal themselves after it was too late. I wished for a way to realize these lessons beforehand. If only we could live life in reverse, to be fully equipped with life's lessons without the agony. But without the pain, would we even have a reason to listen?

Chapter 17: Secrets

That night after kangaroo burgers I went back to my hostel to relax with the book that Skye gave me. Initially, I began looking for reasons why the protagonist Pudge reminded Skye of me, but then I became oddly drawn to the girl in the book, Alaska. She reminded me of Skye; a beautiful mind, an adventurer, a smoker, a reader, a self-proclaimed badass. I saw why Skye liked the book.

I read on to find out what adventures Alaska led Pudge on, and therefore led me on. I was going from one adventure to the next. Ocean kayaking, surfing, climbing mountains, cliff jumping, to then climb into bed and go on any adventure I wanted through literature. I don't even remember falling asleep.

The following day I went down to the beach to catch an early surf again, hoping Skye would be there as well. A single day with her was more adventure than I've had in my whole lifetime. Her presence alone made my heart race.

I found Spigs, Coco, Budd, and Kenny sitting on the beach, sliding on their wetsuits, preparing to catch the morning waves. I didn't see Skye anywhere.

"I see that you too are now an addict for the ocean." Kenny said as I joined their group.

"Got to make the best of my time here, that's for sure." I told them as Budd tossed me a wetsuit and brought me out a board.

"Still an open ended trip?" He asked me.

I nodded.

"That's awesome. You learn a lot by traveling alone. Not just about how to get around and how to balance a budget, but about people, and mostly about yourself. How old are you, Lucas?" Kenny asked me.

"Eighteen."

"You look older than that." Coco commented. I shrugged as I slid on my wetsuit. I get that a lot. I'm very tall and have some facial hair. It usually makes me jump a couple years in people's eyes.

"I ran away from home and backpacked around Australia when I was your age. I lived out of my car." Kenny reflected with a look of nostalgia in his eyes.

"Homeless and backpacking are a little different, Kenny." Spigs said playfully.

"Hey, Roxxie was my home for that year. Home was where I parked her." He laughed and everyone joined him.

His story interested me. "Why did you run away?" I asked.

"Well I wanted to pursue surfing, get a sponsorship and hopefully go pro, but my parents were not a fan of my plan. They said I'd never make it especially with my leg... or lack of a leg." He laughed to himself.

"What happened?" I asked. He seemed pretty open and comfortable with the whole situation.

"Typical surfer boy tragedy. Shark got me while I was surfing when I was sixteen. My parents hated that I kept surfing. They wanted me to go to university and with them it was either their way or the highway, so I picked the highway. I haven't heard from them since my sister's funeral. That was a decade ago."

Kenny didn't see his parents in over ten years, by choice. I wondered how a relationship like that could falter to nothingness. I wondered if he ever thought of trying to reconnect with them. After all, they were still *somewhere*. He did have that choice.

"Now, don't let that scare you." Kenny added, picking up his board.

Scare me? Not seeing my parents? It terrifies me.

"This isn't really shark territory." He continued.

Oh.

Out on the water, I looked numerous times to see if Skye would appear on the beach to join us for a surf, but she never showed. I was pretty distracted out on the water and didn't surf very well. I felt a lot pressing in my mind.

My parents, of course.

The cave with Skye.

Almost dying.

And Kenny's story about his parents… who were Skye's grandparents.

It was so terrible that he just lost contact with them, but then I thought about it deeper. He'll never experience the hurt of his parents passing, like most do, like I did. Leaving enabled him to defy the dread of another's death. He didn't hear from them in over ten years. Something could have happened to them and he would have never known. He'd just continue on like any other day. Part of that thought made me sick, but another part of me felt jealous.

If there was a way to *never* feel the way I did a month ago when my parents died, I'd go that way. But that meant cutting all ties with those close to me and not letting anyone new get too close either. It meant trying to find happiness with myself and not with others. It meant I had to be okay with being alone. It meant never going back home.

The next day was July 4th. It was weird not having Fourth of July plans. Obviously, it's an American holiday, but it was always more than just Independence Day for me. It was a holiday that my dad took off of work for almost a whole week! It was a time I always looked forward to, with my family.

I can remember as a kid going to Lake Michigan. We would barbecue and rent a boat to go tubing and wakeboarding. The tradition started when I was eight and my dad said *money was good*. He was doing well at his job, which led to a lot of upgrades. Annual vacations, a new family car, we even moved to a different part of Brooklyn to an apartment with two bedrooms and plenty of space. My mom didn't have to keep her heels in the kitchen anymore and I got my own room. It was at that point my dad started working a lot more and coming home late. He was always exhausted.

It was just before high school when we moved into the Manhattan apartment, closer to my dad's job, closer to the high school I'd end up attending for only two years. It was in a really nice part of Manhattan, Upper West Side. Our apartment was down the block from Central Park. This worked out well because my mom didn't have to walk very far to see me play baseball. She always saw my games. Every. Single. One. Not only does she love me, but she loves baseball. She would get really enthusiastic and cheer me on in Spanish. Baseball really made my mom's Puerto Rican pride show.

My first year of high school I was the only freshman who made Varsity. I was even a starter. When I would get up to bat my mom would stand up, lean against the fence, and scream her throat dry. My cheeks would get red as I'd walk toward at the plate, resenting the very thing that deep down meant so much to me. During warm ups I'd always turn toward the stands to see when my mom would arrive. I wasn't completely focused on the game until I knew she was there, rain or shine. The other guys didn't have their moms in the stands every game and even though at the time I felt embarrassed, I now realize how lucky I was.

I knew if I even mentioned the Fourth of July to Skye she would get angry simply because it was an American holiday. She hated anything American. But I still wanted to find her to adventure with her for the day, even if she technically didn't know she was *celebrating* an American holiday with me.

Skye was out on the water shredding alone, so I got a board and paddled out to join her. It was weird though when I went to the Surf Shack to pick up the board. Budd seemed reluctant to give me a board when I mentioned I was going to join Skye.

Was he jealous?

Or did he get bit by the, I Don't Like Lucas bug that got Skye?

Did Budd like Skye?

Were they a thing?

I avoided his eye contact and looked around the shop at the gear and their Legend's Board. I noticed that Elsie's photo was included on the wall. That didn't surprise me. All the people I've met in this town have been kickass surfers.

It was high tide, so it took me more time to paddle out. Skye practically ignored my presence altogether, riding waves and paddling back out without so much of a glance, until I was ten feet away yelling her name. She gave me a half ass wave.

"What's up Skye?"

No response.

She began paddling, preparing for the next wave. I did the same to stay near her.

"You alright?" I asked while trying to paddle at her pace. She was fast.

No response.

The wave was right behind us. Skye popped up. I did the same, turning my focus to my form to avoid the embarrassment of falling. I kept my balance and then turned to look to Skye who was cutting her path away from mine. I still wasn't good enough to control the direction of my board.

I let the wave take me where it wanted to, riding it until my board began losing speed. I paddled back out, toward Skye's direction, but she already was shredding the next wave before I could set up to catch it. I waited for her to paddle back out.

"Did I do something wrong or did you just remember that I was American and you're supposed to hate me?"

She glared at me.

"Not in the joking mood?" I pointed out.

She sat up on her board.

"I finished that book you gave me."

Oh.

Her hostility was beginning to make more sense. I did warn her…

"So what did you think?" I asked.

"It was fucking sad, Trip. I don't blame you for crying."

"I wasn't- never mind." I mumbled under my breath. "So are you saying that you cried?" I asked.

"No, don't put words in my mouth. I said, I can understand why *you* would cry. Although, I'm still not really sure as to what issues you're dealing with…" She stated bluntly.

"Who said I'm dealing with issues?" I defended.

"It's pretty obvious that you have issues."

Ouch.

I wondered what Skye thought about me. Often the imagination can morph unknown realities into unthinkable nightmares. Yet, I doubted that Skye thought my reality was the nightmare it was. I left it to her wonder.

"Alaska seems pretty familiar." I commented, changing the subject.

"Oh yeah, can you relate with Pudge's hopeless loserness?"

"First off, loserness isn't a word. Secondly, no I think that Pudge is a lot smarter than I am. And thirdly, you act like Alaska. Don't you realize that?"

"You're right, Pudge is a lot smarter than you are." Skye replied, ignoring my question then paddling away to catch an incoming wave. I let it pass me by, and waited for her to paddle back out after she glided through the rip curl.

"I heard you went surfing with the guys yesterday." Skye said.

"Yeah, I'm trying to catch as much surf as I can while I'm here."

"You didn't tell anyone about my cave did you?"

"No. You said that nobody knew, so I figured you wanted me to keep it a secret."

"It's important that it stays a secret, alright? Nobody can know I go there or that you've been there, clear?"

"Why is it such a secret?" I asked to see what she might reveal.

"Because what's the point of a secret cave if everyone knows about it, Trip? Duh! You have to promise." She gave me a pouty face. This girl was manipulative. Turning the switch for whatever personality she wanted in that moment.

"I promise." That made her smile.

"I'm going up there tomorrow after the sunrise surf. Want to come?"

Even though I made it through the adventure the first time (barely), I was still reluctant to jump into the same waters that almost caused me to drown.

"What do you want to do up there?" I asked.

She gave me an annoyed face. "What do I want to do? Hike, cliff jump, dive, chill in the cargo net. So...?"

117

I shrugged. "Isn't it unsafe up there? Isn't that probably why no one but you goes there?"

"Are you scared? You said you weren't scared of heights. We are going during the day this time, so it can't be that you're scared of the dark, which you probably are after I saw you running away from me that night. You don't have to come, I'll go alone." She rolled her eyes.

"No, I'll go. Just don't disappear on me, Skye."

She smiled and let out a slight laugh.

"I mean it! You freaked me out last time."

"But it's funny when you panic." She laughed.

"Promise Skye! No disappearing and nothing stupid." I asserted. "I agreed to *your* promise."

"Define stupid." She smiled.

I splashed her.

"Okay, okay." She laughed. "I promise."

The next morning on the beach I felt bubbly inside. Part of it was nervousness about diving down into the cave again and another part was excited about sharing a secret with Skye, especially around the guys. I wondered where Kenny thought Skye went when she disappeared to the cave. It must have been difficult for Kenny to try to play the role of both parents when he was neither. I couldn't imagine taking on the responsibility of a teenager in my twenties like Kenny did.

Kenny had positive vibes and a glowing energy that radiated whenever I was around him. He was always offering to give me tips to improve my surfing. That morning he was helping me gain better control of the direction my board was going in.

"You're really good mate, you sure you've never surfed before?"

I smiled in appreciation of his compliment.

"Not before surf lessons at The Shack. My teachers deserve the credit." I said loud enough for the rest of the guys to hear.

"Thanks mate, but you have a persistence about you. That's why you're getting so good." Spigs smiled.

We all watched the way the waves curled in the distance, reading for perfect opportunities to catch one.

"Yo Lucas, your hair is getting wild. You going to take care of that?" Budd remarked as my wet curls flopped in front of my eyes.

I ran my fingers through my hair; water fell out of it like a sponge.

"I guess you're right... I need to cut it."

"No!" Skye exclaimed, suddenly interested.

Even Budd seemed surprised by Skye's sudden intrigue.

"Jade should braid it, I mean." Skye shrugged. "She's been asking to braid someone's hair, she loves it."

"I second that, she's great with braids. She's also done all the touch-ups on my dreads for years." Spigs added.

"What are you going to to do if they break up, bro? Shave your head?" Budd instigated.

"Don't put bad energy in the air like that Buddy. What if I said that about you and-"

"Alright, I'm sorry. I didn't mean it like that." Budd interjected.

Skye was into braids...

That thought kept a smile on my face as I caught the next wave. When I paddled back Budd, Kenny, and Skye were the only ones at the line-up waiting for the next wave. As I paddled up something smelled off.

"Do you smell something burning?" I said.

"We're in the middle of the ocean, what could possibly be burning?" Budd replied looking around.

"I don't see any smoke. Or even any boats out there." Kenny observed.

I looked toward the trees, in the direction of the cave, pensively.

"You're thinking too much about the surf Trip, your brain is fried!" Syke said as she began to paddle to catch an incoming wave. Budd paddled to catch it too.

"Maybe it's the salt you smell in the ocean." Kenny proposed.

"Maybe." But I knew it wasn't that. This was different than the smell of sulfur.
I put it out of my mind and caught the next wave.

For the rest of the surf I felt like I had Skye's secret sitting on my nose.

Spigs asked me what I was up to later on in the day.

"Just hilling out." I stuttered.

He looked at me confused.

"I was going to say hanging, but then I said chilling, so yeah..." I corrected myself awkwardly.

"You alright today, mate? You're acting funny." Spigs asked.

I nodded. "Couldn't be better."

I smiled and looked at Skye. She smiled back, but had her right hand on her forehead, her thumb and pointer finger up, shaped in an L and mouthed "loser." My smile faded, but hearing her laugh brought it back immediately.

She paddled over. "Never had a secret before, huh?"

"That's not true."

The cave was a happy secret, an adventurous secret, itching to be shared.

My secret was heart wrenching, dilapidating, meant to be locked up.

"Not one like this." I bit my tongue because the thought of that day alone choked me up.

Why didn't I just stop at the fucking light?!

I began to paddle away to catch the next wave because tears were forming in my eyes and I didn't want anyone to see, especially Skye. The anger that built up in my fists caused me to paddle faster. The wave was right behind me. I popped up on my board, so teary eyed that the shoreline was just a blur of blues and yellows blending together like watercolor paint.

I was going faster than ever. I felt like I was flying, yet my body felt like it was sinking. I shifted my weight, cutting into the wave as it curled, awwing at the water spiral as it passed through me. I was inside the wave. Gliding. Swallowed alive as I remained standing on my board.

I wiped my eyes to clear my vision from a mixture of salty tears and misty saltwater, focusing on my balance, and the mouth of the wave ahead of me. The inside of the wave was getting tighter; it was beginning to crash and I was inside of it!

I crouched down lower on my board and it sped up. The mouth of the wave was right in front of me, closing in. I got even lower, catching more speed, until the wave spat me out.

Behind me I heard whistling. It was the guys, cheering and going *crazy* behind me. I paddled back over to them.

"There you go, Lucas!" Kenny applauded.

"You're really controlling your board now." Coco complimented.

Even Skye was smirking.

"You got a lot more speed right before you popped," Spigs noted, "that's what you need!"

"Thanks guys." I smiled. "I couldn't have done it without your tips."

"I think that was a good moment to end on boys, we got to head in and open up shop." Spigs said to Budd and Coco.

"Yeah, let's ride the next one in." Kenny agreed.

Kenny headed to his car to head off to work and I walked with Spigs, Coco, and Budd to the shop to return the board. I've worked out a weekly package with them to take a board as much as I want during the week for only a little more than the daily rental rate. I probably wouldn't have been surfing as much otherwise. Skye told me she was going to run home to drop her board then meet me at the end of the beach like last time, so I walked to the rocks and waited.

I looked up at the mountain and the barely visible trail. I climbed it just days ago without a single fear in mind. But in that moment, I looked at it with hesitation and uncertainty about its safety remembering the feeling of being lost in the inky water without oxygen. I started to feel anxiety. I wanted to bail. I decided to walk back, so I diverged toward the first path leading off the beach.

"Hey!" I heard from behind me. I jumped.

Damn I thought, Skye caught me leaving. I turned around, but it wasn't Skye, it was Elsie.

I exhaled. Relieved. "Hey, what are you doing here?" Nobody is usually at this end of the beach.

"I'm always here. Were you writing down by the rocks again?" She asked. I realized that the last time I saw Elsie was down at the end of the beach as well.

"No, not writing, just waiting... for a friend."

"That girl you were watching surf?"

I nodded and tried to hide my smile.

"Skye. You like her, don't you?" Elsie smiled.

I shrugged. "Skye is like nobody I've ever met before. I don't think *like* is an accurate description of how I feel."

"Well, how do you feel?" She asked.

"Confused." I admitted.

"Well, that's normal, especially with everything going on."

I knew she was remembering what I told her about my parents. I wanted to change the topic.

"Have you ever hiked up that mountain?"

"That one?" She pointed. I nodded. "Yeah, plenty of times. Not anymore though."

"Is it unsafe?"

"Well anything could be unsafe if you're not careful. I wouldn't try hiking that mountain alone if that's what you were thinking."

I wouldn't want to hike it alone, Skye would have though. Guilt twisted in my stomach from my attempt to bail.

"You're right." I admitted turning back.

"Is that where you're headed?" She asked.

"Yeah, well, I'm not supposed to really tell anyone."

"Okay... but hey, if I don't see you around within the next couple of days, I'll have to call a search party." She joked. But part of me took her seriously. I felt better with Elsie knowing I was up there.

"Thanks Elsie."

"Anytime."

I walked back down to the rocks just as Skye came into sight in the distance. As long as we stayed safe, everything would be fine, I thought. I looked at Skye as she got closer. I knew *I could* rationalize safe from unsafe, but how was I supposed to control *Skye's* reckless behavior?

Chapter 18: Fears

I hiked alongside Skye, instead of trailing behind to inevitably get whipped in the face with thorn branches, like last time. We hiked while exchanging stories, Skye's *always* more intriguing than my own.

Skye had a way of making an adventure out of everything and having a story from every adventure. I tried to be funny, so I could at least make Skye smile, but she would usually end up laughing at me, not with me. I didn't mind, because either way I looked at it, she was smiling.

Along the hike, as I was trying to keep her pace, I tripped and lost my footing, but Skye grabbed my hand, keeping me standing. I squeezed her hand then turned my head to face her. Even her sweat glistened.

"Still haven't figured out the whole walking thing huh, Trip?" She was still holding my hand, but was beginning to let go.

"No, no I haven't." I moved my hand to lace my fingers through hers. "I need your help." I hinted innocently. I squeezed her hand tighter.

Her neck turned, only gradually, so that she could see me, but wasn't looking at me. She didn't let go.

"You're right, you do need me." She smirked. My heart sped up. "For more adventure in your life."

She pulled me toward her and we maneuvered off trail through some tree branches until a clearing opened up and we were standing overlooking the ocean.

I still had her hand in mine.

My heart was still racing.

She led me closer to the ledge. The drop below was about 20 feet, less than the ledge above the cave, but still pretty high up.

"How do you know the water is deep enough?" I asked. She let go of my hand.

"Because I've checked it."

"How do you know this is the spot you checked?"

"Because it is. Look," she pointed, "that's the way you climb back up. I've jumped from here more times than I can count."

I leaned over the edge, surveying the rocks below.

"Come on." I felt her fingers tickle my palm. "Loosen up."

I slid my hand back into hers then turned to smile.

She looked at me with her usual devious smile. There was so much behind her smile. I knew not to trust it, but always did anyway.

She turned to face me, our fingers still linked, her back to the water, heels teasing the ledge.

"How do-" I began, but she pressed her fingers over my lips, silencing me.

"Shhh," she whispered. "No more questions. Just enjoy the moment." She closed her eyes. I couldn't help but stare down at her lips.

She was standing right on the edge, which instinctively made me pull her closer to me, to safety.

Our hands were still locked, my lips inches from her forehead.

I think I even forgot to *breathe*.

I took my other hand and let my fingertips dance along the side of her arm. Then she grabbed it and opened her eyes.

"Ready?" Skye asked as if I could possibly object to anything she was about to do.

"Uhm. I-"

Her leaping backwards cut me off. She pulled me with her off the ledge. We squeezed each other's hands tighter and somehow that dissipated my fear of falling, like there was a dose of safety in Skye's hands.

I felt her try to let go, but I gripped tighter until we hit the ocean and water filled the spaces in between our fingers, slipping them apart. I let the coolness of the water refresh my limp body before swimming to the surface.

"Is it still too scary? Is the water too shallow? Should I check the depth again? Am I asking too many questions?" Skye mocked.

"Very funny. Sorry, I like to be cautious."

"When you live in caution, you die in fear." She declared as she began swimming over to the bank alongside the base of the mountain.

"Actually, I think I'm less prone to dying if I'm more cautious, just saying."

"You're also more prone to a boring life. Spice it up for once, Trip." She led the way climbing back up on the rocks. I followed, mimicking her steps, hoping not to fall.

We got back up to the jumping point. Skye's back was to me as she stood alongside the ledge and twirled her hair up into a wet messy bun, water still dripping. I couldn't help but stare at her as she stood there, taking pictures in my mind of beauty layered on top of beauty.

The light blue sky blanketed with cotton-like clouds that oversaw the vast ocean beneath seemed perfect enough, until Skye stepped into the frame and redefined my definition of perfection. Even the aspects of Skye I hated, I was growing to love. I forced myself to avert my attention and lingering thoughts.

Falling for Skye was falling straight into trouble, but how was I supposed to avoid falling for a girl who was literally pulling me over the edge?

"Again?" She turned around smiling. That smile…

I took a running start, grabbed her hand, and pulled her with me off the cliff.

This time I jumped first. This time I grabbed *her* hand. And this time, she didn't try to let go.

We jumped a few more times together before hiking to the summit to take a break. Climbing up the rocks was pretty tiring, but thankfully surfing had really built up my arm strength, so I didn't look like a wimp next to Skye's ninja-like climbing skills.

We sat together on top of the rock that marked the highest point of the mountain. Surfers in the ocean looked like tiny specs maneuvering in the waves. Their size made me feel small even though it felt like I was sitting on top of the world.

I thought about where I was: a paradise, a perfect place to be, it would seem, but I couldn't shake my lingering dejection. It wasn't enough to just change my environment and expect a resolution. I needed to have a shift in my mindset because my negative thoughts were still tearing me down. I went to Australia to escape, but that escape was more of a distraction from reality. Sitting atop the rock I realized I needed a fresh perspective. Feeling bad for myself wasn't exactly helping.

It's hard to look at my own life with a perspective different from my own, but being in a different place with new people does help. There are different lives with different experiences and different perspectives all around me.

I'm not the only one with pain.

I'm not the only one with secrets.

I'm not the only one searching for happiness.

Skye was able to get through her mom's death without even having a father. I wouldn't dare ask how she did it, of course. Facing abandonment twice. She was just a little kid with the weight of so much tragedy pushing down on her. I wondered if the pain subsided as time went on. I really, really hope it did.

I looked over at her. The sun was high in the sky, shining down in a way that made her golden brown hair sparkle. She looked back at me, but neither of us said a word. We just stared, arms slightly touching, lips speaking no words, but saying so much.

I wanted to kiss her and in that moment I'd like to think she wanted to kiss me too, but the moment was too flawless to be disturbed. I remember what she said back in the cave: *I like you Lucas, but everything I stand for hates you.*

I didn't want Skye to resent me in any way. I was enjoying my time with her and didn't want to ruin it. Although her adventures often made me uneasy and pushed my limits, they made my heart race in a way that reminded my body what it is like to feel alive. Breaking out of my comfort zone was the rush I needed to renew my sense of purpose.

I thought about kissing her... how perfect it would be... how it would overflow my expectations.

But what if it didn't?

What if it fell short?

Maybe the mystery was more of a rush. Skye loved mystery and I could see why. Because the imagination can be controlled, while reality is unpredictable, but even worse, it's irreversible.

I dismissed the temptation.

I watched the waves crash down into the rocks, some of which stood isolated like deserted islands away from the rest of the cliff.

"It's crazy the amount of corrosion the ocean can cause to the land." I thought out loud.

"What?"

I pointed out to the giant clusters of rocks that formed miniature islands off the shore.

"The weathering of the land over hundreds of years changes the shape of the coastline. Some parts of the land don't collapse with the rest and that causes those isolated rocks over there to form." I explained.

"It's amazing how some of them can stay standing with gaping holes going through the center." Skye noticed.

The boulders each had their own unique shape; some were wide, others tall, and as Skye pointed out, some had massive holes going right through them.

"Coastal erosion has been increasing due to rising sea levels." I paused for a moment. "Sorry, that sounded really geeky."

"Smart is sexy, Trip. Yet, you think it's a deficiency?"

My head perked up.

"I read how it's affecting different parts of the US, like Miami, Boston, New York..."

"Of course you don't know about anywhere but your own country." Skye rolled her eyes. "Why even bother caring about the rest of the world?" Skye's attitude was back without warning.

"I didn't say I didn't care, it's just the article was about the eastern seaboard of the US." I clarified.

"But see, you yanks only really know about yourselves and your own country. You don't know about things outside of your bubble, unless it affects you because you think *you're* the only important ones."

"That's not true."

"Oh yeah? How many stars are on the Australian flag?" Skye asked.

I didn't know.

"You got your 50 states, how many states are in Australia?"

I stayed quiet.

"There are six stars, Trip. One to represent each state."

"What about Australian independence day?" Skye continued.

"I don't know. Alright, you made your point." I admitted.

"You took no time to learn about the country you were visiting?"

"I said you made your point, Skye." I said, loudly as I got up and headed for the pathway that led to the backside of the mountain above the cave.

When we got there, Skye dove down right away, while I still felt a bit of hesitation. The water was certainly deep enough, so long as you jumped toward the correct spot. The right side was rocky, but on the far left there was a thorn bush growing outwards, which made it a tighter and more intimidating jump than the last ledge.

"Do I have to disappear underwater to make you jump?!" Skye called from down below. "Let's go!"

I jumped in beside her and grabbed her ankles before swimming to the surface. She squirmed to get away, but I pulled her under, just a little, for mocking me before. I felt her pull my hair playfully from above, forcing me to let go of her ankles and swim up toward her. When I got above the surface to take a breath she dunked my head back down. When she finally let go she laughed and splashed me.

"Ready to dive down?" She asked.

"Lead the way."

It was a lot easier to see where to go underwater during the daytime, but once we entered the underwater tunnel that led to the cave, everything went dark.

I felt Skye swimming next to me and tried to keep pace with her so I didn't end up in a drowning panic again. She grabbed my hand when she began swimming upward, so I kicked harder to reach the surface. I took a breath of air, indicating we made it in, except everything was pitch black and Skye was no longer beside me holding my hand.

"Not funny, Skye." My voice echoed throughout the cave. I heard her swimming.

"Should we have brought the headlamps?" But just then I heard a click and the cave lit up. Skye kept a big industrial light facing upwards. It provided an ominous illumination throughout the cave, enabling us to see. I swam over to the side and climbed up to the cargo net which remained intact from when we set it up last time. Weightless, I fell backwards onto it, ready to relax.

"This net was a good idea. Beats laying on a rock." I said.

Skye climbed on to join me, laying down. "That's the point."

The cargo net was tight, but our weight added enough give, forcing our bodies to collide at the center.

"Jump right on me why don't you." I teased. She tried to roll to the other side, but the net kept adjusting our positions for us. Eventually she stopped fussing and sat up, frustrated. I extended my arm out toward her.

"I think the net wants us to be close." I smiled.

She shook her head, as if to disagree, but her body language told me otherwise.

"What?" I asked.

"Nothing." She replied, as she rested her head on my bicep. I felt her body relax.

"You're going to have to get some pillows after I leave." I joked.

"Yeah, waterproof pillows."

"I wouldn't put it past you. Soon you'll hook up a fridge and start living here."

"*I wish.*" She sighed.

"What do you mean? I thought you loved it here. You said you'd never leave Byron."

"Well, the cave isn't exactly leaving Byron. It would just be nice to do my own thing, get my own place. Not be *in the way*."

"In the way?"

"Yeah. I always felt like I got in Kenny's way. He's never said anything, but I feel guilty that he gave up his dreams to take care of me."

"You shouldn't blame yourself for that. That was his choice. I'm sure he wanted to."

"For once it would be nice not to be someone else's problem." Skye sighed.

I didn't know what to say, so I just held her tighter and searched for the words that never came. We laid there, bodies pressed together on the cargo net. I had goosebumps, and I wasn't sure whether it was because of the cave's cool air or because of Skye's body so close to me.

She only had on her bikini.

I thought about the past week... How close I got with Skye, how much I liked her. Skye opened up to me a lot. Half of me wanted to hide my secret, while the other half wanted to vent it all to her. Putting together the right words was the toughest part.

I rehearsed what to say in my head until finally I said, "you know how you guessed that I had some *issues*. Well, I guess you're right." I took a deep breath. "See, it's hard for me to talk about, but you know how I said I really missed my parents?" I couldn't believe I got as far as I did. My heart was racing, faster than when I leaped off the ledge. It was racing so quickly that I didn't realize Skye's heavy breathing.

"Skye?" She didn't answer. I looked down at her eyes, which were closed.

Sleeping.

I exhaled. Her head was nuzzled on my shoulder. I couldn't help but smile because she looked *so* incredibly lovely, yet was completely unaware of it.

I wasn't tired enough to fall asleep, plus I couldn't let myself with such a beautiful girl so close to me; I wanted to be awake to actually experience the moment.

I laid with Skye as she began to twitch in her sleep. Her legs kicked, shoulders jumped. It wasn't a gentle twitch either. It seemed she was having a nightmare.

Did I kick in my sleep like Skye? Did I shudder violently? I wondered if Skye remembered her nightmares when she was awake.

She shook suddenly, her hand almost hitting me in the face. I hope she didn't remember her bad dreams. I did all I could do by just holding her tighter.

After a while Skye woke up, visibly dazed and confused.

"How long was I asleep for?"

"About an hour." I told her.

She examined the diamond shaped cargo net imprints on her back and legs.

"I look like a checkerboard."

I looked at my back. "Well, that makes two of us."

"Did you fall asleep too?" She asked.

"No."

"What did you do for an hour then?"

"Just laid."

She narrowed her eyes and gave me a questioning look. "Did I..." She began but stopped.

"Did you what?"

She shook her head. "Never mind."

"No, what?"

"Let's get out of here before someone thinks you kidnapped me."
Skye changed the topic. She was good at that. She rolled off of the net
straight into the water, splashing me from below.

"C'mon." Skye called as she flicked off the flood light, bringing
the cave to complete darkness. I couldn't see a thing, but listened to hear
Skye's movements and swam in her direction.

"Ready to dive?" She was right next to me.

"Just don't disappear please."

Naturally she laughed. "Let's go." And we both dove down. I was
beginning to get the hang of equalizing to relieve the pressure in my ears,
but still relied on Skye to lead the way through the darkness. How she held
her breath without panicking while navigating through pitch black water,
was beyond me.

I made sure to stay calm and close until we breached the cave's
opening and were back in the open ocean where sunlight enabled me to see
again. I rose to the surface, swam to the bank of the mountain, and climbed
to the trail that led us back to the beach.

I was hoping to hang out with Skye afterwards, but she told me
she had *stuff* to do. When I asked her what she was doing the following
day, she told me she was working. She said it in a way like she didn't want
to see me, which was really confusing because I thought we had a really
good time together.

I figured it was just Skye being Skye, moody and unpredictable. I
told myself not to take it so personally, but I couldn't help feeling
bothered. Getting attached wasn't a good idea; I knew it and she knew it,
so pushing away was probably for the best. I didn't go to see her at work
that next day because I respected the space she so obviously hinted. I knew
I'd see her around and that possibility alone was enough to keep me sane.

Chapter 19: Room Switch

Neptune's informed me that I needed to change rooms because of a conflict with prior reservations. It was the same type of dorm room with the same amount of beds, so I had no objection. I gathered all my stuff into my duffel bag and carried it to the new room on the opposite side of the hostel. Inside, everything was messy from the other guests in the dorm. Clothes and beer cans were scattered on the floor. I looked for the bed I was assigned, dropped my stuff on some empty space on the floor, and laid down, releasing a big exhale.

I looked up at the wood above my head and started reading all the writing and carvings that were left behind from travelers before me. My last bed barely had any writing on it, but this one was loaded!
K.A.S was here 14/05/13.

Even the dates are written differently! I read some more.
Blink 182 1998.

Could it be? I loved that band! It's probably someone just messing, but either way, I'm going to tell people that I stayed in the same hostel room as Blink 182. The wood was covered in so much writing it was probably impossible to read it all. I liked it, it aligned with the vibe of the hostel. People were given the opportunity to leave their own personal mark behind.

I reached into my bag to get a pen. I contemplated what I was going to write on the wood. My initials and the date? Do I write the date the way they do in America? Will that single me out as the backwards American? I thought of the judgement that Skye would have. I clicked my pen and began scribbling. I was getting pretty focused, considering whether I should use block letters, but worrying I would just mess it up.

Suddenly the door swung open and I heard a man say, "Excuse me, there will be no vandalism in this room. We try to keep this place clean and respected," he exclaimed as he walked in, kicking a beer can and tossing his stuff in a locker on his way. Instinctively I jumped, bumping my head really hard on the top bunk as I rushed to my feet. Three guys trailed in behind him and they all laughed at my panic.

"Sorry." I said, as if *I* should be apologizing.

I rubbed my head where it was now throbbing.

"Where you guys from?" I asked to take the awkwardness out of the room.

"You know… here and there, but mostly there." One said. It was the same guy who tried to reprimand me before.

"How long you in Byron for?"

"Just tonight." Another answered.

I sat back down on my bunk and stopped asking them questions. They clearly weren't too friendly.

After a few minutes they left again.

I turned back to the wooden post and finished leaving my mark right above Blink 182.

Lucky to live.

I went down to the beach for a rest day, which I felt I really needed after the past week of adventure. It was good that I was able to keep my body and mind active. It was the best I've felt since The Night My Life Fell Apart, but as soon as I began to watch people on the beach, I started to feel down.

There were a few families there together. Watching them made me jealous of them and angry at myself. They reminded me of how fortunate I was and how I just threw it all away. I ran a red light. The biggest mistake of my life so easily solved for most by paying a ticket. But there's no going back. I am tarnished for the rest of my life by the haunting truth that *my selfishness* killed my parents.

I'msorryI'msorryI'msorryI'msorry. Yet no sorry will ever mean a thing because they're not able to hear it. Actions cannot be reversed. Apologies cannot be heard.

As I buried myself in sand and sadness I remembered how down I felt after the move to Connecticut. It wasn't that I didn't like having a nicer house, with more space, and the ability to see so many stars from just outside my window. Thinking back, there were actually a lot of things about moving that I loved, but I wouldn't let myself admit it because I would constantly compare it to what I use to have.

"Isn't this huge backyard incredible, Lucky!?"
"I like Central Park better."

"There's a nice shopping mall a short drive away."
"There's better shopping in SoHo."

"It's nice to be able to find parking so easily."
"I rather be in the city taking the subway."

My mom would respond by telling me a quote by Theodore Roosevelt, "Comparison is the thief of joy." Mom was right. Any opportunity to appreciate our new home was stolen the moment I compared it to New York City. Part of me even thought that if my parents saw how much I *hated* it, we would move back. Reflecting, I realized that Connecticut was better for my parents. Mom could run daily errands so much easier. Dad's commute to work was cut in thirds, enabling him more time with the family and to relax. People were even more welcoming and hospitable. I probably came across as a stuck-up city kid who was too rude to socialize with everyone else.

I looked around at the families enjoying themselves on the beach. Comparing myself to them was causing me such pain. There I was, sitting in paradise alongside them, complaining yet again. If I always focus on what's missing in my life, how will I appreciate the things I already have?

I needed to shift my perspective in order to realize the many wealths of life. I was rushing past so much so quickly, without being present in that moment. I couldn't keep waiting until things were *gone* to finally appreciate them. Would I appreciate being in Australia more after going back to the states?

I went to bed early because I felt mentally drained from thinking so much and my head still hurt from knocking it on the bed from earlier that morning. A bump was beginning to form. I was restless that night, carrying a lot on my mind. I tossed and turned until I woke in the morning much later than usual to an empty room with no one in it. The bunks occupied by the guys I ran into the day before were stripped, and their clothes and garbage picked up.

Groggy, I hopped out of bed and went into my duffel to get my toothbrush. To my surprise, my bag was zipped open. When I looked inside my clothes were clearly rummaged through. I panicked and looked at the "hidden" pocket of my duffel, where I kept my passport, debit card, and extra cash. It was already open. I reached inside and pulled out my passport which had my debit card between the pages. I released a big sigh of relief. I looked further for my cash, only to discover it was gone. Those fuckers stole my money!

Immediately I ran down to the breakfast area to see if they were still around, but I didn't see them anywhere.

"Excuse me!" I said running to the front desk. "These guys who just left this morning stole money from my bag."

The swivel chair turned around to reveal Creep, the receptionist from the night Ana wandered into my bed.

"Did you see them steal it?" He asked.

"No, I was sleeping."

"You sure you didn't put your money in another place? Or spend it?"

"I'm positive. My bag was open and all messed up. I didn't leave it like that."

"Your stuff wasn't locked up?"

"No…" I admitted.

"Well, there's nothing we can do if you just left your stuff out."

"But you must have their information. What time did they check out? Where are they going next?"

"That's none of your business, mate. That's personal information."

"They stole my stuff! And you're not doing anything about it!"

"Don't be yelling at me with your stinky morning breath, mate. You should have had your belongings in a locker." He said pointing at a sign on the wall that said: *We are not responsible for any lost or stolen items. Please use the lockers provided to keep your belongings safe.*

"We have locks for sale if you need one."

I thought back to day one in Byron when Bradley asked if I wanted to buy a lock. I really wished I got one.

I was so angry for getting played like that, but even more angry at myself for not being more cautious with my belongings. I left it sitting out in a room with people I just met; people who didn't even give me a good vibe to begin with. I shuffled back to my room knowing Creep would only get me more agitated. Focus on the positive: I was lucky they didn't steal my debit card or my passport.

Chapter 20: Zane's Birthday Bondfire

I was eager for Friday because I knew it guaranteed seeing Skye at the Bondfire. It was going to be an even bigger crowd than normal because it was Zane's 20th birthday and they were hosting a bash.

I went over to the guys' place early because Zane personally asked me to help set up. I assumed the role as the fire starter, mainly because it sounded like a cool job. They had wood chopped for days, ensuring that the fire could burn the whole night, so all I had to do was get it started.

I cheated a bit by using some lighter fluid, yet still managed to get covered in black cinder. Ash and sweat drenched my face, arms, and T-shirt. I looked like a coal mine worker. I needed to look presentable before the party began. Thankfully I brought a change of clothes.

The fire was up and roaring by the time Skye arrived. She was wearing a coral print sundress with a matching flower in her hair. As usual, she didn't have any shoes on. I froze at the sight of her when she walked into the yard. Her beauty radiated, even over the growing flames. Caked in filth with a bumpy bruise on my head, I couldn't have looked any worse. I attempted to hide from her line of sight, but the blazing fire beside me was hard to miss. Our eyes met. I gave an awkward half-wave. She walked over. My heart raced.

"You look amazing." I smiled.

"Thanks. You look..."

"...Like I'm about to head to the shower."

"No." She laughed. "I like it. You have a scruffy-homeless-traveller look going on."

She reached up and grabbed one of my greasy curls.

"Homeless is not what I'm going for." I replied. "But if you like it, I can skip the shower and jump right to a hug." I joked, opening my arms.

"No, no, no." She said backing away with her hands defending herself from my sweaty embrace. "By the way, I spoke to Jade and she's pumped to braid your hair. And I know you didn't really say you wanted to braid it…" She twirled my locks in her finger once more. "But you totally have to because she will do an *amazing* job."

It was funny to see Skye being so nice to get what she wanted. Especially when she was convincing me of something I already wanted to do.

After a shower, I was changing in Coco's room when Jade walked in without knocking. I only had a towel on. Budd already seemed to hate me and I didn't want Coco to as well if he saw me half naked next to his girlfriend.

"Once you're dressed I'll braid your hair. I was telling Skye how badly I wanted to braid someone's hair. I learned some designs that I can't quite get right on myself, but know would be dope on someone else's head."

I managed to fully dress myself in 30-seconds or less.

"Well, I'm glad to have a professional braid my hair. It will bring me back to when I was a kid."

"I'm no pro, but I do what I can."

As Jade pulled and weaved my hair in criss-cross designs, I told her about my elementary school braids and the first love of my life, Kendra. Jade told me how she was studying business marketing and planning to help Coco and the Surf Shack expose their business and expand their merchandise better. She was done braiding faster than I would have expected for such intricate designs.

"I love them! These are amazing!" I said admiring myself in the mirror. "Thank you!"

I flashbacked to my kid self watching a movie with Kendra as my mom passed me a hand mirror to show me the art she twisted from my curls. I looked in the mirror and imagined my mom smiling in the background watching me, watch myself.

By the time I got back out to the yard, a good amount of people had already showed up. It felt comforting being able to recognize people and have them recognize me back. People complimented my braids and said things like, *it's great to see you.* I was beginning to feel like I belonged with these people, in Byron.

I saw Zane, so I went over to give him some birthday wishes and a gift I picked up. He was surrounded by a big group of people, who were smoking, drinking, and laughing around the fire. He was sitting on the floor leaning against Budd.

"Happy birthday, Zane!" I leaned down to say.

He jumped, turned around with a big smile on his face, stood up, and threw his arms around me.

"Lucas!" Zane squeezed me so hard I couldn't even hug him back. I was taller than him, but he was clearly stronger than me. The beer bottle pressed he into my back could make an imprint. Then he chugged the rest of the bottle and tossed it not-very-gently to the side.

"This hair! It's fabulous." Zane grabbed my head with both his hands. "Lucas, you somehow got even sexier."

"Thanks..." I said awkwardly as I caught Budd's eyes grilling me.

"Thanks for coming mate!" Zane slurred, hugging me again.

"Of course." I lifted the bag with his present inside. "I got you something." I pushed the gift forward.

"Woah, mate *you* got me a present!" He exclaimed, taken back.

"Yeah, but you've really welcomed me and all. You didn't have to do that, but I'm thankful that you did." I handed him the bag. "Open it."

He grabbed the bag and reached inside.

"Mate! I'm stoked!" Zane said tossing the rugby ball up into the air and showing it to Budd. Budd unenthusiastically nodded his head.

"Ey, Finn, catch." He called over to someone on the other side of the fire. Finn caught the ball and checked it out.

"This is a quality ball. We need to give it a go out on the beach this weekend."

"Too right." Zane replied. "Thanks mate, really. You got to play with us tomorrow!"

"Sure."

Zane paused. His face lit up, an idea visibly popping into his head. "Do you like brownies?" He asked me. I thought it was kind of a random question.

"Yeah... Who doesn't like brownies?"

"Someone made me brownies for my birthday. You have to have one, as a thank you." He insisted.

"Sure." I said and he grabbed my arm pulling me toward the back door eagerly.

We shuffled through the crowd and went into the kitchen where Spigs was digging through the cupboards.

"Woah, mate. What happened to your head?" Zane noticed. The lighting was much better in the kitchen and the bump was pretty obvious.

"I knocked it on the bunk bed at Neptune's." I told him.

Spigs turned around. "I thought you said you knocked it surfing."

"No... it was from Neptune's." I confirmed.

"I'm almost positive you told me surfing, mate. You said the board whipped you right in the head."

"I don't remember saying that."

"Hey Spiggle, where are those brownies I had in the fridge?" Zane interrupted.

"On the bottom shelf. I had to make room and move things."

"Found them!" Zane exclaimed retrieving a piece on a napkin and handing it to me. I took it from him.

"Thanks." I took a bite, and another bite, and another, and another, until the brownie was gone and I was left licking my chocolatey finger tips clean.

"They're good, right?"

"Yeah. It's good."

"Here, have another!"

I ate it as we walked back out toward the yard. The yard was more crowded than I had seen it before. It was so loud, Zane had to lean on my shoulder to talk to me.

"Let's go get some grub from the grill. I'm hungry!" I was actually still hungry even with the brownies, so I followed.

There was a lot of food cooking. They even had two grills going! I grabbed a cheeseburger and Zane loaded his plate with a hot dog, grilled chicken, a burger, ribs, and three slices of watermelon; it was piled on. Nobody could judge though because after all, it was his birthday.

After I finished my burger, I sat back and focused on the heat waves from the fire that were blanketing my face against the cool crepuscular air. Like the suns rays that warmed my back as I paddled out to surf, contrasting the cool water that splashes me; it put me at ease. I relaxed to the sound of the fire crackling under the stream of music flowing from the speakers on the roof. I tried to focus on the part of the fire the crackling was coming from, but it was too hard to track. So, I decided to focus on only the sound of the crackling and just watch the fire dance in the center of all those gathered around it. I looked around at all the people. Everyone was smiling, and realizing their smiles, made me notice the smile on my face. I felt like I was being lifted off the ground like the ashes from the fire that rose straight up toward the stars.

I closed my eyes and pictured my body floating. Suspended in the air, floating up, like gravity gave up. I floated next to the rising ashes from the embers and didn't even think about if they would burn me, like we agreed to float in harmony. After The Night My Life Fell Apart I had a nightmare about falling into an endless black hole of smoke. It was the only nightmare I could really remember, thankfully. Burning was all I could remember smelling after the crash. Burning coated in shame from my swallowed screams. I was spinning out of control with a heavy pit in my stomach, dense chalky air in my lungs, and a pounding drum in my head. Floating up to the stars was a pleasant change. I didn't even care that I couldn't control where my body was floating because I just let it take me. Drifting. Rising further and further up, up.

I felt soft hands rest over my eyes. They pulled me down from the stars and back toward the crackling fire below. Back to the Bondfire. I opened my eyes to turn to see who it was. Skye.

"You can't seriously be sleeping. Like are you serious?" She chided, her eyes squinting in disapproval.

"I wasn't sleeping. I was floating" I told her.

"Floating?" She looked at me puzzled. "Well welcome back to Earth. Get up, we gotta wake you up." She grabbed my hand and led me through the party. I bumped into people like I was inside a pinball machine. I felt Skye squeeze my hand tighter. I needed to keep up.

She led me through the hole in the bushes out onto the beach where the sound of crashing waves began to replace noises from the party.

I began to laugh uncontrollably, grabbing Skye's shoulder to keep my balance.

"Woahh, Lucas. Okay, okay. Someone had too much to drink." She stated.

But I didn't. I barely finished a single beer. Why was I stumbling all over the place?

We walked·to the log further down the beach. I sat down on the sand, using the log as a backrest. Skye joined me. My eyes began to droop again.

"Oh no you don't. You can't fall asleep. It's barely even eleven o'clock."

"I'm not falling asleep. I'm just thinking." I plopped my head down on her shoulder. "What's that smell?"

"The party, the ocean, the fire."

I sighed, "no…"

"No, no. Don't fall asleep. Tell me what you're thinking about. It'll keep you awake. And pick your head up. Otherwise you'll definitely fall asleep."

"The sky." I said flopping my head to look up.

"What about the sky?"

"How pretty she is tonight." I turned to face her and smiled.

"Very corny. Thank you." She laughed.

"What's the story of your name?" I asked.

"My mom thought nothing was more intriguing than the sky. Its beauty, its depth, its complexity. She would tell me my possibilities were as high and wide as my name. It's because of her I'm an astrophile… and a selenophile… and a heliophile." Skye went on.

"I'm sorry, *what* are you talking about?" I was dragging my words.

"An astrophile is a lover of the stars. A selenophile is a lover of the moon. And a heliophile is a lover of the sun."

"So are you a word-ophite too?"

"A logophile?"

"Seriously? Let me guess, a lover of words?"

"Correct." She smiled boastfully. "What's the story of your name?"

"My name? Hmm... Well it's not poetic or anything but it was my dad's middle name."

"Was?"

I didn't even notice I said *was*. Hearing her repeat and emphasize the past tense was an anchor pulling down my chest.

"Yeah. Uhmm... My dad... my parents, they just recently passed away." I managed to say.

Skye jaw dropped. "Both your parents... What happened?"

I dug my fist into the sand. "I... There was... It was a terrible car accident." Accident. Saying that word felt deceptive. Accidents are spills that can get cleaned up. Accidents are bumpers that get smashed. Accidents can be repaired. My parents can't be repaired. There are no undos or backspaces or amends. Can death be an accident?

"Do you want to talk about it?" She asked and I felt like I did, but I was feeling a lot of things I didn't normally feel. I told her about the crash and waking up in the hospital. I told her how I ran away and went to the airport. I told her how I found my way to Byron.

She didn't say a word the whole time; she just listened closely, without ever looking away, even though I sat with my body turned away from her, barely looking up. As the words poured out, I experienced a cathartic cleanse.

"It was the worst day of my life. It ruined my life. It ruined me. I ruined me."

I was livid, and punched my fist to the ground.

Skye put her hand over mine to try and calm me. "It's the hardest tragedy ever, I know. But you're not ruined." She tried to comfort.

"Skye don't say, *you know* like you know everything."

Although she experienced a lot, she wasn't responsible for her parents' death. Their blood was still stained my hands.

"I don't know everything, but I do know you're not ruined." She said firmly. "You made it this far. Across the globe after something like that happens. It has to be for a reason."

My breathing calmed as I listened to her voice. Her eyes, bright as a blue flame in total blackness, warmed my angst away.

"A reason? Like what?"

"Like a purpose."

"What do you mean?"

"Everything doesn't need to be a question."

"But I've been here a month, what am I am supposed to be looking out for?"

"Shhh..." She put her fingers over my lips. "You don't have enough time to hear the answers if you're always asking questions." We were facing each other. Her ocean blue eyes were like waves after a storm.

"Just enjoy the moment." She whispered.

I still had a weird feeling in my head and throughout my body and it was only intensifying with Skye's flirting. My senses felt overloaded. My heart was racing and my palms were beginning to sweat. My body felt light and heavy at the same time, like a two hundred pound bag of feathers.

Skye was so close, I could feel her breath falter against my forehead. She reached her arms around my shoulders and I felt the warmth of her body comfort mine. I moved my chin up further towards her and closed my eyes.

I felt the space between our faces shrinking. I stopped myself just before her lips, imploring her to continue moving forward, *to me*. I felt her inhale upon my exhale as our breaths became one, until our lips finally met.

I thought kissing Skye would be like fireworks exploding, but it wasn't like that at all. We kissed slowly. Gently. Perfectly. Fireworks were too assertive. Kissing Skye was like running on a misty summer night, after the rain had just stopped. It was a feeling I wanted to have forever, but knew I could never capture. The best moments are the smallest slices of my life, yet they take most of the space in my soul.

Our lips parted and Skye even cracked a smile.

"Remember the first time I saw you here? At this very spot." I reminisced.

"Yeah, I do." She laughed.

"Back when you judged books by their cover and thought you were the coolest person to walk the earth." I joked.

"I still am the coolest person to walk the earth." She tried to push me but I moved away, grabbing her hands. "And that book you gave me was really depressing also. I can understand why you were crying."

"I wasn't-"

"I know I'm just fucking with you." She said, which made me smile because Skye's playful aggressiveness was cute.

Suddenly, in my peripheral I saw a figure down by the shore. I looked over to see what it was. It was a person, a woman. She was walking toward the water in her clothes. The waves were crashing aggressively, but she seemed to be unfazed by the angry ocean.

"Hey! What are you doing?!" I yelled, loud enough that she should have been able to hear me, but her stride continued. The water was up to her knee, but she continued moving forward into the dark sea.

"What's wrong?" Skye asked turning around.

"What is she doing?" I jumped to my feet and began to hustle towards the water.

"Who? Where?"

"Heading to the water!"

As I got closer I realized I knew who it was. It was Elsie!

"Stop! It's too dangerous! Don't go any further." I yelled as I approached the shoreline, but Elsie continued on as if she was in a trance.

"Don't go in there Lucas!" Skye called as she ran in my direction. I could only see Elsie's head hovering above the water. Was she sleep walking? I paused where the seafoam met my toes to contemplate my next move. I looked back at Skye who was running toward me, then at Elsire out in the water. A wave curled, crashing down hard, bringing Elsie under, out of sight. I had no choice. I ran as fast as I could into the freezing cold water. Immediately my skin got goosebumps, but I was sweating. I swam in the direction that I saw Elsie last.

I heard a woman screaming. A voice I knew.

"Where are you?!" I dove under water below a crashing wave but could only see complete darkness under the surface.

None of it felt real. It was more like a dream sequence. I rose to the surface to meet a jolting wave as I attempted to take a breath. I toppled over and struggled to retrieve my perception of where the shore was, nor less where Elsie descended beneath the sea. By the time I secured myself above the surface, another wave was crashing down above my head. I swallowed some water and felt my legs get thrown above my head, like involuntary somersaults underwater. I knew I had to get out, but my body wasn't mine.

My limbs were too heavy, and my head was too light, and the water was too strong. I swallowed more water. I remember thinking that I couldn't die because I needed to find Elsie. I needed to save Elsie.

I swallowed more water and it all went from the dark deep blue of the ocean to the quiet blackness of the insides of my eyelids. Silence and darkness. It felt peaceful compared to moments before of being tossed like a rag doll underwater. I wondered if mom and dad felt peaceful at the end or...

I was glad that I was not conscious long enough to finish that thought.

Chapter 21: What do you think you saw out there?

I woke up to voices around me. I was lying on the sand. The waves crashing in the background was an immediate reminder of the last moment I remembered. Only, I couldn't open my eyes. I couldn't move my body. There was only the voices.

"Why did you let him go swimming while he was stoned?"

"Let him? He just ran for the ocean! And how was I supposed to know you gave him a special brownie?"

"Two…"

"That thing was potent!"

"At least he's breathing now."

"No help from you."

"We need to get him off the beach and dried off. Let's carry him to the house."

"Because what, a raging party is a better spot for him?"

"Kick everyone out."

"Do you know how long that will take?"

"Bring him to the hostel where he's staying."

"And just drop him at the doorstep? We can't just leave him alone."

"Maybe we should call 000."

"You know that will end in Spiggle getting fined or worse, remember when-"

"Will you quit arguing? Just help me get him to your car, I'll bring him back to my place."

"You sure?"

"Yeah."

"I'll drive the car up to the beach."

"I'll get him a towel."

"I'll stay here, with Lucas."

Skye grabbed my hand and then everything faded away again.

I woke up to the smell of the lavender sea breeze scent of her sheets. I inhaled deeply, filling my lungs with her familiar smell before opening my eyes to greet the sun peeking in through the window. I knew it was Skye's room right away because I recognized her surfboard by the door. The room was pretty small, barely any space to walk between her bed and the huge bookshelf, which was loaded with books and surf trophies. There were beach posters on the wall and another surfboard hanging from the beams on the ceiling above her bed with a name engraved in huge letters I couldn't miss, Lessie.

Pinned on the wall alongside the bed was a photograph. It was a woman and a little girl with their surfboards in one arm, while holding hands. They faced the water and I could only see their silhouettes, but I just knew it was Skye and her mom. There were no posters on that wall, just that one picture.

"Water?" I heard Skye say from the doorway. She walked into the room in an oversized T-shirt which made it so that I couldn't tell if she even had shorts on or not.

"Thanks," I said taking the glass from her hand as I sat up.

There was an awkward silence as I gulped the glass to empty. I could still taste saltwater in my mouth.

"How do you feel?" She asked.

"Thirsty."

She smiled. "Even after that entire glass you devoured?"

I nodded.

"There's a jug in the kitchen. Come on, brekkie is ready."

"Brekkie?" She was already out of the room. I threw back the covers and trailed behind her. I walked out of her door frame and was immediately in a very small room that had a pull out couch, pulled-out. There was a surfboard on two buckets that was used as a table. Skye was in the even smaller kitchen pulling out a jar of Vegemite from the cupboard before placing two pieces of toast on the table. I stood in the doorway.

She peeked up. "You can sit, you know." She pointed to the chairs beside the surfboard-table, then filled up my glass of water.

"Thanks."

"Sorry my brekkie isn't as exciting as at Hideaway."

"No, it's great, thank you." I said taking a bite of my toast.

"Vegemite?" she asked.

"No thanks, too salty."

Her jaw dropped and she put her head down like I just kicked her non-existent dog or something.

"Typical American," she mumbled.

I glared up at her as she took a sip of tea. With her face half hidden behind the mug she looked at me and winked, and I can tell by her eyes that she smiled too.

"I'm joking... I just making sure you have your senses about you after last night. How about some Nutella?"

My eyes lit up. "I love Nutella."

"You yanks got this idea from us, just to be clear."

"We'd be lost without you, thanks." I answered, sarcastically.

She passed me the jar and I smeared a generous amount onto my toast.

After a little while, she finally asked, "What did you think you saw out there?"

I stayed silent, chewing.

"In the ocean," she continued.

I swallowed.

She waited.

"I thought I saw my friend."

"Your friend? Who? Someone from the party?"

"No. Maybe. Someone I met on the beach a few times. I saw- I thought I saw her going into the water." I paused pensively. "Did you see anyone?" I asked.

"No, but to be honest my eyes are terrible…" she shook her head. "Maybe you saw shadows or something because you're the only one who was in the water."

"Maybe." But it looked too real to be a shadow.

"I have to find her down at the beach." I suddenly realized, shoving the last bite of the toast into my mouth. "Just to be sure."

"Who is she?" Skye asked, as she continued sipping tea.

"Her name is Elsie."

"Where's she from?"

"Here. Byron. She's a local."

"Local? I don't know any local by the name of Elsie."

"She's older than us."

Her eyes narrowed, "still."

"Maybe you don't know her. She seems to be pretty to-herself."

"Maybe."

"Do you want to go down to the beach?" I asked Skye as I stood up.

"You seriously are looking to go to the beach? Are you not even impacted by what happened last night? You drowned! And it looked like you almost did it on purpose."

"On purpose? What are you trying to say?"

"I'm just saying what I saw. You had some heavy weight on your mind and you were clearly tightly wound from it. It seemed like you just snapped."

"I thought I saw her..." I defended.

"Yeah, part of this is Zane's fault. That brownie he gave you had pot in it and knowing Zane, laced with who knows what else." She began bringing the dishes to the sink to wash. "I punched him in the gut pretty hard for not warning you."

That would explain why I was feeling so different that night. Like I was floating.

"I have to go to work in a bit. You should probably chill the rest of the day, take it easy. I don't think going to the beach is a good idea, nor will it solve anything because nothing was there in the first place, Lucas. Nothing." She stopped washing the dishes and looked sternly at me.

"Okay. You're right, I'm going to get going. I'll probably go back to my room and nap."

"Do you know how to get back?" She dried her hands and walked over to me.

"We walked this way in the pitch black when you scared the shit out of me before kangaroo burgers, remember? When you forbade me from walking you home." I recollected.

"Yeah, well... This place isn't exactly one I like to show off." She shrugged. "You're only here because you drowned and I needed to look after you." She said, which made me smile on the inside and probably on the outside too. She needed to look after me.

"Oh yeah? That's what I have to do to get invited over, drown?" I joked.

She went to push my shoulder, but my reflexes caught her hand, which I grabbed and pulled toward me slightly.

I may have imagined Elsie in the ocean, but I know my kiss with Skye was real. I saw flashbacks through her eyes as she looked at me.

"I'm glad you're okay."

She still hadn't let go of my hand and adding that comment made me sure that she had those flashbacks too. I took it as an invitation to kiss her, again. Our lips touched for barely two seconds until

"Ahem. CPR is only necessary when someone is unconscious." I heard from behind me. I pulled away from Skye quickly to see Kenny on the porch with his surfboard, returning from sunrise surf. I didn't know how to respond, but saw he was smiling and figured that could mean he wasn't too upset that I was trying to make out with his niece.

He leaned his board against the side of the house. "So you're feeling better, I see?" He asked.

I nodded, still a bit embarrassed that he caught me kissing Skye.

"How were the waves?" Skye asked Kenny, nonchalantly changing the topic.

"Pretty weak to be honest. You didn't miss much." He peeled off his wetsuit, came into the kitchen, and grabbed an apple.

Skye continued washing dishes.

"I'm going to Coral's in a bit if you want to come." Kenny said taking a bite of the apple.

"It's open this early?"

"It's Saturday. *Beer and Brunch*." Kenny went into the room that had the door closed. The room I assumed was his.

"What's Coral's?" I asked Skye.

"It's a pub that Kenny lives at because he's in love with the bartender."

"I'm not in love with the bartender!" Kenny yelled from his room then popped his head back into the kitchen. "We're friends."

"I think she's beautiful and you shouldn't be ashamed that you love her."

Kenny rolled his eyes dropped the apple core into the garbage. "Are you going to come?"

"No, I have work."

"Lucas?"

I was surprised Kenny invited me, but I had another plan in mind for the day.

"Maybe another time." I said.

"Alright. Just me then." Kenny opened the bathroom door.

"You and Daisy." Skye smirked.

"And all the other people in the pub." Kenny turned to say.

"But you're going for Daisy."

"I'm going for *Beer and Brunch.*"

"Tell Daisy I said *hi!*"

Kenny closed the door. I could tell he was smiling too.

"I better get going. Thanks for breakfast and well, saving my life." I lingered by the door hoping Skye would come over to finish our kiss.

"Don't make it a habit." Skye said drying off her hands. She stayed where she was. Too far for a kiss or even a hug.

"Will I see you again?"

"Probably." Skye shrugged. "You always seem to find me."

It was true… I did gravitate toward her.

Skye stayed across the room, leaning against the sink.

"Well, thanks again." I turned and began walking out of the door. I was past the porch when I heard Skye say, "Wait, you forgot something."

I paused on the road in front of her house.

Skye came out with my wallet in her hand.

"Oh wow, thanks." I was surprised my wallet survived the night before.

"You're welcome." Skye kissed me on the cheek just as I was putting my wallet in my pocket. I didn't even expect it, but before I knew what was happening, it was over.

"See ya when you find me." Skye snickered walking away.

I know I told Skye that I wouldn't go to the beach, but that's exactly where I wanted to go and exactly where I headed. I knew Skye wouldn't be surfing or anything because she had work. I needed to find Elsie to be sure the night before was just my imagination. It couldn't get it out of my head.

I got down to the beach to find Zane and the other guys playing rugby with the ball I got him for his birthday. He stopped the game immediately when he saw me.

"Lucas!" He called from afar and ran over to me. "Mate, how you going? You had us going troppo last night."

"I'm good now, I think. Just a little tired."

"You were out cold. I was shit scared. I'm glad you're alright though."

I nodded.

"Ropeable, mate?"

"Huh?"

"Are you mad at me? I'm sorry I didn't tell you about the brownies. I thought you knew."

"No, I'm not mad." Should I have been?

"Good mate. I really am sorry, truly. Listen, do you want to get in our rugby game? The ball you picked up is bloody awesome." Zane was very animated when he spoke. Budd stood ten feet behind him, grilling me as usual.

"Thanks, but I'm not really up for it."

"Yeah that makes sense. You're probably beat." He patted me on the back. "Hooroo!"

I waved and continued walking toward the far end of the beach. Zane was an interesting character.

I figured I could walk down to where I usually see Elsie and wait for her to pop up. It was the only plan I had and once I started getting impatient waiting after fifteen minutes, I realized it wasn't the best plan. What would I do if Elsie never showed up? Did that mean I did see her in the water? Does that mean she may have drowned? Or does it mean she just didn't come to the beach today? Should I be worried?

I was really tired and these questions bounced around my head. I watched the guys finish up their rugby game and leave the beach. I watched the beach slowly empty as lunchtime passed and the air got cooler. I watched the sun move across the sky. I waited as I battled my eyelids to stay open.

I was startled when she sat down next to me. I didn't hear her walk over, but sure enough when I turned my head, there Elsie was.

"Woah. You scared me."

She laughed. "Were you sleeping?"

"Maybe." Then I processed the reason why I was waiting for Elsie in the first place.

"What did you do last night?" I quickly asked. Rubbing my eyes as if to ensure she wasn't simply a mirage.

"Nothing much, you?" She calmly shared. It must have been all in my head.

"I was at Spigs' party. Do you know Spigs?" I was curious to see who Elsie actually knew in town since Skye didn't know who she was.

She nodded yes.

"It was kind of a crazy night."

"Why?" She asked.

I didn't want to tell her that I thought I saw her drowning, "I told Skye about my parents." Which was true, but only part of the reason why the night was crazy.

"Are you happy you did that?"

"Looking back, not really. The whole point of coming to Byron was to escape. Telling Skye is like inviting my problem to continue following me around."

"Or helping you get past it…"

"It just makes me feel like less of a person in her eyes. It makes me feel weaker."

"You're allowed to show emotion, you know. It's what *healthy humans* do."

I shrugged. There was a long pause where we both just sat there, thinking, looking at the ocean. A million things were running through my head, but they all brought me to the same solution.

"I think it's time for me to go. You know, get out of Byron. It's been great here, but I think I'm getting too close to people. The last thing I want is to get attached and well, hurt." I was kind of embarrassed about admitting even more vulnerability.

"Ready to go home?"

"Well, no. I can't do that either. I haven't even contacted anyone from home in a while and I just dread having to explain myself. I feel like I need to start over somewhere, fresh."

"Isn't that what you tried to do here?"

"Kind of. But I messed it up as soon as I started getting close with Skye. I need to go some place and not get attached to anyone."

Elsie looked at me in clear disagreement. "You can't run away from every person you're close to. A life of running away is a life of loneliness." She stated insightfully.

I thought about my parents, and how painful it is to even think about losing them, still.

"If I don't let people get too close, I won't have the pain of loss. And nothing feels more lonely than that," I replied.

"Nothing?"

I shrugged.

"I'd rather have a life full of heavy and hurtful loss than a life of loneliness. A life of loss is a life full of people who may not be there any longer, but when they were there they filled your life with the very reasons you laughed and learned and lived and loved. And in the end when life hits you with their loss, it may hurt, but the heavier the hurt the greater the love that once was."

I thought of the heavy pain on The Night My Life Fell Apart and how much love I had *and still have* for my parents.

"What is the point of laughing if there's no one to share it with? What is there to learn about the world if you don't go out and experience the people who make it what it is? And really, what is the meaning of life without people you love? Although loss leaves you with a hole in your heart, you should be thankful that you had people to fill those holes in the first place. Running away more will just leave those holes in your heart."

"Then filling those holes is like, replacing them. I can never replace them." I felt my fingers tense into a fist.

"Your parents wouldn't want you to live a life of loneliness and seclusion. They'd want you to fill those holes with fresh relationships and new love. It doesn't mean you're replacing them, you're just living on, the way they'd want you to."

I sat quietly, processing her words.

"Do you think I should stay here then?" I asked.

"I'm not telling you that's what you should do. But what you shouldn't do is make a choice with the mindset of escaping relationships that make you happy."

Her words trudged in circles around my mind, but all it led me to was: Skye made me happy.

Chapter 22: Stay?

I felt anxious after my conversation with Elsie. The different possibilities of where my life would lead overwhelmed me. Staying in Byron would be a huge decision. What if living in Byron wasn't as exciting as visiting? It was way different than anything I was used to and really far away from anyone I've ever known. Elsie urged me not to run away from relationships that made me happy. There were a lot of people in New York who still made me happy, I just ran away before I gave anyone the opportunity to help me deal with The Night My Life Fell Apart. Just the thought of my friends and family members made me miss home. *But it wouldn't be the same without Mom and Dad.* I said to myself. *There would be too many reminders of their absence.*

My mind was going a million miles an hour, so I walked toward the Surf Shack for a distraction. Behind the counter I saw Spigs fixing his dreads with a crochet hook and Budd organizing surf wax.

"Hey guys."

"G'Day Lucas." They said stopping what they were doing to turn their attention to me.

"How you going?" Spigs asked.

"Good. How are the waves?"

They looked at each other and shrugged. Their demeanor changed.

"Not the best honestly," Spigs responded.

"Can I grab a board?"

They looked at each other again in a peculiar way.

"Not today, Lucas."

I didn't understand. "What? Why?"

Budd continued organizing the pile of surf wax.

"I don't want you to take this the wrong way, but I heard about what happened during the Bondfire and... well, maybe you should hang back from the water for a bit." Spigs said.

I thought of Skye. She must have told them.

"Seriously? I'm fine."

They both stared at me.

"We know, but just to be safe."

I didn't want to argue with them. I wondered what they heard.

"Alright guys, I'll catch you later." I said with my head down.

Spigs apologized and I began to walk away.

"Catch you later, Lucas."

I was pretty bummed that the guys thought I was too unstable to ride on my own.

I wandered over to HideAway bothered that the guys wouldn't let me surf. I was tired, but I wouldn't be able to nap back at my hostel with a full mind and an empty stomach.

"How are you feeling? Were you able to sleep?" Skye asked concerned. It was the first time she stopped what she was doing when I walked into the cafe. I was a bit annoyed at the thought of what Skye might have told the guys, so for the first time ever, Skye was actually more excited to see me than I was to see her.

"I'm good. Just hungry."

"Should of had the vegemite." Skye winked. Without responding, I just put my head down to face the menu.

I ordered an omelette and a coffee. Skye tried to convince me to get Her Coffee, but I learned from the first time not to trust her barista judgement. The tension I was causing between me and her was growing, so I finally decided to address it.

"So, I was wondering, did you tell Spigs to not let me surf or something like that?"

She shot a glance at me. "No, why?"

"He wouldn't let me take a board today."

Skye narrowed her eyes at me. "You went to the beach?"

I kind of forgot she told me not to do that. *Oops.*

"Being active usually helps me feel better. Especially with surfing lately. I thought it would help." It was true.

"Whatever you say. " She rolled her eyes. "And Budd must have told Spigs because I didn't tell anyone except Kenny because well, it was his house you crashed in. Budd helped me after I saved you. Him and Zane were on the beach and saw the whole thing. They helped me drag you out of the water."

Budd told Spigs, and whatever he told him, it was bad enough for them to think I was too unfit for the water. *Damn, I must have looked crazy.*

"Since I can't surf, you want to go to the cave after your shift ends?" Skye looked around to see if anyone was listening.

"I think it's better if you stay on land for a little."

"You think I'm crazy too?"

"I didn't say that, but you were knocked unconscious, so you should take it easy for the rest of the day."

I put my head down, defeated yet again.

"It doesn't mean you have to sit and do nothing." Skye smiled. "There's a new moon tonight, so the sky will be really dark. Perfect for stargazing."

My head perked up.

"Is that a date?" I asked her.

"Ha! You wish."

Chapter 23: Stargazing

We planned to meet near the log, the same spot we kissed at the last Bondfire. It made me smile to think that Skye and I had *a spot*. When I got down to the beach she was already waiting for me wearing baggy sweatpants, a cozy long-sleeve, and of course no shoes. She was sitting on a tapestry that was laid out over the sand. When she saw me, she moved over to make room beside her.

"How are you feeling?"

"Fine." I sat down.

"It's a clear night, not a cloud in sight." Skye said looking up and leaning back to lay on the tapestry.

I followed her lead, and laid down too. The sky was the darkest I've ever seen it, floating with thousands of crystal stars. There wasn't any moon in sight.

"Have you ever seen a shooting star?" I asked.

"Oh yeah. Almost every time I stargaze on a good night. It's pretty clear out here. The best is when there's a meteor shower. Then you can see a hundred shooting stars in a single night. Have you ever seen one?"

"No, never."

"Seriously? Well, then we aren't leaving the beach until you see one."

Although I wanted to see a shooting star, part of me hoped it would take a while to spot one, so I could spend time with Skye under the moonlight all night. She pointed out different constellations in the darkness as if she had a space map memorized.

"How do you know so much about the stars?" I asked her.

"When I was a kid, stargazing was just about the only thing I loved doing that involved staying still." Skye laughed to herself. "It was the only way my mom could keep me entertained without having to chase me around. It was always a reward for her to let me stay up late enough to stargaze. My mom taught me about the constellations and I always stayed interested in it."

"Well, when you have a view like this…"

"You didn't watch stars as a kid?"

"Couldn't really. Unless we left the city. There was too much light pollution to see more than just a couple stars. Nothing like this, ever in my life!"

"I never realized that." Skye said.

"What?"

"It may sound stupid, but I just assumed everyone could look up and see the stars each night. Like, there could be a meteor shower right above your head and you and the millions of people in New York wouldn't be able to see any of it. That's crazy."

"More than half of the world's population live in a city. Which means more than half of the world won't have a stargazing view like this closeby. What you have here is something really special."

It's easier to appreciate things that aren't a part of your routine.

"If you think this is amazing, you should see what the stars are like in the outback, where there's *nothing* around for miles and miles."

"How far away is that?"

"Well, it all depends on how deep you want to go. Australia is huge, but for the most part, people live along the coast. Over here on the east coast is the most popular. Everything in the middle is outback. Thousands of kilometers of desert."

"How far do you usually go?"

"I've driven out ten hours, but I have a good spot about two hours away- *over there!!*" Skye's arm shot up to point at a shooting star that had just sailed across the sky.

"Did you see it?"

"Sort of. How did you see it so quickly all the way over there?"

"You kind of got to scan the sky. You'll see one."

We laid quietly for a few minutes, until Skye said, "I can take you there one day if you want."

I had to backtrack in my mind as to what we were talking about until I realized. "To the outback?"

"Yeah."

"Really?" I didn't expect Skye to invite me to a trip like that.

"Yeah, I'll drive you out there and you can borrow my tent. I'll pick you up like a week later. It will be your ultimate survival test." Skye laughed to herself.

As her words faded into silence, she slid her hand into mine. I swear Skye would have been able to hear my heartbeat if the waves weren't crashing in the background.

"You know if my mum was alive, I probably would have lived in America." Skye shared.

"Really? Where?"

"Somewhere in southern California."

"Was your father over there?"

From my periphery I saw Skye look at me with a disgruntled expression. "No, fuck him. I've never heard from him in my life. It was because my mum's sponsorship wanted to transfer her to California."

"That would have been cool."

"No way! I hated the idea. I got so upset at my mum when she told me we had to leave Byron. *Everything* I loved was here."

"Did your mom want to go?" I asked.

"I think so. She would have had a better shot over there... they said." Skye hesitated. "I didn't understand that when I was ten though. I was so angry I didn't talk to my mum for four days. And then the next two days, I'd talk to her, but with such an angry tone... She died with me angry at her." I felt Skye's fingers tighten in my hand.

"The last time my mum told me *I love you* I just kept playing. I ignored her. How was I supposed to know she would never come back?"

Her words suspended in the air in front of me.

"What happened to her?"

"She hit her head in the ocean. No one was around to help her. And you know if I wasn't so mad at her, I could have been there. *I* could have helped her."

"Skye, you were only ten years old."

"So? I could have swam, or gotten help, or done *something*. But karma came back around. I had to go to foster care for a while until I was able to live with Kenny. It took a couple years until he was able to get his shit together enough for him to be my legal guardian. So I got in the way of *his* dreams of going pro too."

"Skye that's not your fault either."

"Kenny had to pick up two jobs when I came along. I always just got in everyone's way. It makes me wish my father never went to Australia on holiday, never knocked-up my mum, so that I could have never been a thought nor a problem."

She had let go of my hand.

"You don't think you have a purpose, Skye?"

She looked at me, quiet for once.

"Remember what you told me? That even after all that I went through, I must be here for a purpose."

"Yeah, well you traveled across the world. I haven't been anywhere, but here. Just taking up useless space."

"Are you kidding me, Skye? It's not about where you go, it's about what you do. And look at you, you're the most amazing surfer I've ever seen. Better than anyone out on those waters. And if you want to go places, I'm sure you can get there with surfing."

"Why? So I can chase the same invisible dream that my mum had and Kenny had... it all ends the same, failure."

"Why do you think that way? Your mom wasn't a failure. She was pro. And you're really going to call Kenny a failure? That's harsh."

"I didn't mean it like that."

"You can't think that way though. You're just pulling yourself down by doing that."

"I guess... have you been thinking about your purpose?"

"Yeah." I knew Skye was just trying to change the topic off of her, but I let her because she seemed a bit overwhelmed.

"And what did you come up with?"

"I need to use these rough times to become stronger, and focus on the things that make me happy."

"Oh yeah, so what makes you happy?"

"Well... these stars are making me happy, surfing for sure, meeting new people, exploring... spending time with you."

"Are you happy in Byron?"

I smiled. "Yeah."

"Well, I guess I'm happy that Spigs invites tourists to the Bondfire after all."

"So are you saying that I make you happy?"

"Maybe. But-"

"Over there!" My hand shot up to point at a shooting star that raced across the sky. "That was huge!"

I could sense Skye smiling. "Told you you'd see one."

"Do I get a wish now?" I said sitting up with eagerness.

"What are you five-years-old?" Skye rolled her eyes.

"Wishes are not just reserved for five year olds."

"Alright, alright. What's your wish." She said moving to sit up.

"To take you out on a date."

Skye rolled her eyes and laid back down. "You're so corny."

"But wishes on shooting stars are supposed to come true." I flirted.

"Wouldn't that be nice. But I've tried that and sorry to break it to you, they don't come true."

I laid down again, gazing at the sky anticipating another flash. I was focused on what was above me, so I never expected Skye to lay her head on my shoulder.

As usual, Skye's words said one thing and her actions said another. I put my arm around her. She laid next to me as the sand hugged our bodies from below. We watched the stars, moving closer as the night brought a crisp chill. Skye used me as her pillow, moving to get comfortable however she pleased. Of course, I didn't mind.

After a while I let out a yawn.

"Tired?" Skye asked me.

"A little. More hungry than tired to be honest though."

Skye moved her head up toward me. "Want to get something to eat?"

"Sure"

"I have a perfect spot."

We walked into town and as always, Skye led the way. Most of the shops were closed so I was surprised to see a little white storefront with its lights shining bright. As we got closer, I recognized a sweet and familiar smell.

"Best ice cream you'll ever have." Skye said as the door opened to the sound of a wind chime.

"We're closed!" I heard immediately, but then the voice continued. "Oh hey, Skye. Alright one more."

"Two more," she replied.

I walked in behind her.

"Everything is put away besides Cheeky Chunky Monkey and Triple Fudge Cookie Dough." Budd was standing behind the counter looking at Skye like he didn't even notice I was there.

"Cheeky." Skye replied.

"I'll take the cookie dough."

Budd scooped two cones, handed them to us, and went back to cleaning behind the counter.

Skye grabbed a napkin. "Want one?" I shook my head.

"How much Budd?" I asked while reaching for my wallet.

He peered over the cake display. "I'll add it to Skye's tab."

Skye was on her way out the door. "See you Budd." She blew him a kiss. Budd winked and blew a kiss in return.

"Thanks Budd." I said trailing behind Skye.

We went outside and indulged upon our ice cream.

"Thanks Skye."

"For what?" She asked me.

"For the ice cream... and the stargazing and well, saving my life."

"You're welcome. I'm good at that."

"At which?"

"All of the above." Skye grinned.

"Wow!" I said after a huge bite. "This is amazing. What is a lover of ice-cream? Ice-creamophile?"

Skye laughed so hard she almost choked on her ice cream. "I'm not sure, but it's definitely not that."

I took another bite. "I always used to get ice cream with my parents. It always followed an accomplishment though."

"Well then congratulations on your accomplishment."

"What did I accomplish?" I asked.

Skye thought for a moment. "A little late, but congratulations on catching your first wave." She reached her ice-cream cone out as if to call a toast. I put my cone against hers.

"To catching waves and shooting stars." I said.

"To secret caves and healing scars." Skye replied.

I wasn't sure if she was referring to my scars or hers. Maybe both... but I don't think there's possibly enough ice-cream to do that much healing.

"You know, if you close your eyes and smell that particular ice cream, it will smell just like the cookies were baked fresh out of the oven." Skye told me.

I closed my eyes and inhaled the fudgey-cookie-goodness.

Suddenly I felt the ice cream press up against my nose, mouth, and cheeks. All I heard was Skye laughing. She pushed the cone into my face.

"Do you have that napkin?" I asked.

"No, you said you didn't need one." Skye mocked.

"You're right I'm all set." I just continued eating my ice cream even though my face was covered in chocolate. Not the worst problem to have.

We walked another block.

"You got something on your face." Skye teased.

"Yeah, I know." I pretended it didn't bother me. "I'm saving some ice cream for later."

I took a few more steps. "You want some?" I asked pointing at my face, jokingly.

I never know what to expect with Skye, but right then she leaned in to my chocolate covered face and kissed me, licking the ice cream clean off of my lips.

She got some caught on her nose. I pointed to it smiling.

"I'm saving it for later too." She responded.

We walked through town with ice cream on our faces until we got to the block of my hostel.

Skye stopped walking. "I'll see you around."

"Let me walk you home." I said.

"Why?"

"Because-"

"You need to protect me in the town I know better than you?"

"No... but it's just courteous to walk someone home."

"Yeah, that's why we're here. I walked you to your Australian home. Goodnight."

We both still had chocolate on our noses. Skye turned to leave.

"Goodnight." I replied standing in place, watching as she walked away.

"Hey, Lucas." Skye turned around. "You know that wish you made? Well, I'm free Monday night."

"Really?"

"Yeah." She said, while I walked in her direction. "Don't follow me. Or I might change my mind."

Chapter 24: Date, Finally

I slept in and took it easy until Monday came. I spent Sunday researching where to take Skye to dinner with help from Bradley at the front desk. I laid out my shirt, a button down my mom got me for graduation. I looked at the shirt resting on the bed.

I remembered when Mom got it for me.

"Do you know what you're going to wear for graduation?" My mom asked me at breakfast one morning.

"No." I responded without looking up from my homemade banana chocolate chip pancakes. I knew mom made breakfast special because it was my last day of school. My mom always tried to make things extra special. The chocolate chips were even shaped into a smiley face.

"We could go shopping after school if you'd like," my mom offered enthusiastically.

"Yeah Lucky, a new button-up would be nice, wouldn't it?" Dad agreed enjoying his pancakes as well.

"I don't really get why what I wear matters. I'll be wearing a gown over it anyway. People will only see my shoes."

"You'll take pictures with and without the gown, Lucky." Dad pointed out.

"Why do we have to take so many pictures?" I groaned.

"It's an important day."

"Then I'll just wear what I wore at Uncle Will's wedding. I only wore that shirt one time."

"A fresh new shirt would be nice." My mom persisted.

"I have plans after school, so I won't have time to shop."

"I could pick something up for you."

"No, thanks." I said coldly.

I loathe how I was responding to my parents.

"Okay, well, let me know if you change your mind. I could certainly pick something up while I'm out."

"Okay I'll text you."

I never texted my mom.

My mom picked up a new shirt for me anyway. It was placed in my room wrapped beautifully with a green and white bow. Those were my school colors. The shirt fit perfectly. *I never said thank you.*

Beside it was a note, in my father's handwriting:

Dear Lucky,

Words nor gifts could ever portray
how much we love you
each and every day.
Happy graduation
to the light of our life.
You're the reason we shine,
for your soul is so bright.

Love always,
Mom & Dad

Dad always had a special way with words. He could recite a poem on the spot if you asked him to. From memory, or make it up right then and there. He proposed to my mom with poetry. They were in a rowboat out on Central Park on a crisp autumn day when the park was full of brilliant foliage. It had begun drizzling, so my parents took cover under a tree with wide, dense branches.

From what my mom says, my dad was making a poem out of everything he saw: the rain making dimples in the peaceful water, the way the clouds glowed from the sunlight pressing behind it, the way my mom's smile warmed the whole boat. Once they were protected from the rain under the tree, my dad held my mom close and continued pulling poetry out of the autumn air.

The rain can fall
the air can chill
the world could collapse and crumble,
but I know
I still could find shelter in your arms
and warmth in your heart.
I could be saved by your sweet soul,
whom I never wish to part.
Madeline, you are the
strength that paddles me back to shore
and the water that keeps me alive.
You're the reason in life I strive for more
and the propeller of why we thrive.
I've never been so sure
so happy...
so in love...
Baby, will you marry me?
I swear I'll place no one above.

Obviously my mom said yes to that!

I shook myself out of the trance and smelled the shirt my mom spent her precious time picking out, for me. It still had a trace of the laundry detergent my mom used. I closed my eyes and inhaled deeply. It had the smell of home, which warmed my soul and wrung my heart. *Thank you mom,* I whispered aloud. *I love you.*

The shirt was wrinkly from sitting in my duffel for over a month, unused. I remembered a tip my dad taught me. I hung the shirt up in the bathroom while I took a shower to get the wrinkles out with the steam. Dad told me his dad taught him that trick when he was a teenager. When I put the shirt on all the wrinkles had fallen out. *Thank you dad. I love you.*

I was ready to go, but wanted to wrap a gift I got for Skye first, so I went to the lobby to see if they had anything. I didn't want to give her the gift till after dinner, but I had nowhere to hide it, so wrapping it was the only way to keep her from seeing what it was upon seeing me. The front desk didn't have any wrapping paper, but the woman was really clever. She took out a fold-up map of Byron.

"Use this as the wrapping paper. Here's some tape."

I thanked her for her great idea and the tape and got to wrapping. I hoped Skye would like it.

As I turned down Skye's block I saw that she was already walking towards me. She floated in a sea blue sundress as bright as her eyes. Her hair rested on her left shoulder in a long beautiful braid and for once, she wasn't barefoot.

I smiled as soon as I saw her. "You look stunning," I told her when she was near enough to hear me.

"Thank you," she smiled. "You look…" Skye paused a moment and tilted her head just slightly. "OK," Skye teased me (I think) and continued walking. There was no getting rid of Skye's sassiness. But didn't want to. It's what made her Skye.

As we were walking she noticed the gift in my hand.

"What's that?" She asked.

"Just something I got for you."

"Why'd you get me something?"

"I saw it and it reminded me of you."

"Well, what is it?"

"You'll find out later."

She rolled her eyes, which made me smile.

"Where do you want to go?" Skye asked.

"I made reservations at Vinchetti."

Skye looked at me with wide eyes.

"What?" I asked, unsure of what her reaction meant.

"Fancy," she replied.

"Have you ever been there?" I asked.

She shook her head. "No."

When we sat down at the table for dinner I suddenly felt really nervous. I had spent more days than I could count with Skye, yet I started feeling as nervous as I did the first night I met her in Spigs's kitchen, when I fell over the stool and earned myself the nickname Trip. Thankfully that name faded away… and soon enough the feeling that my heart was going to jump out of my throat faded away as well.

I think Skye was even nervous at some point too, especially in the beginning. When we were first seated, she looked around silently at the decor around us, like I took her to the MoMA for the first time. Once Skye and I started talking to each other, our nerves calmed and everything just flowed, the way it normally does, except even better. The surroundings seemed to blur once I focused on Skye. I couldn't have wished for a better focal point.

We walked to the beach after dinner where I gave Skye the gift.

"Now you can open it." I handed it to her.

"It's a book." She said, judging by its shape.

"I figured you were a bibliophile based on the amount of books in your room."

Skye narrowed her eyes at me.

"A lover of books." I clarified, although I knew she already knew that. I googled it at Neptune's before I left.

Her eyes were still narrowed, but her lips grinned.

"Well, open it!" I urged.

Skye peeled back the tape that joined together the map-turned-wrapping-paper revealing a brand new *Looking for Alaska* by John Green.

She looked at it musingly. "Why'd you write L. Catano on the side?"

"Because Carter is written on your book, well *my book* now, and so I put my name on this one so, well, you'd see it and maybe remember me." I stumbled through the statement.

"You know I've read it four times?" She smirked at me.

"I heard the fifth read is the best." I smiled at her, bringing my face closer to hers.

"It just gets better and better each time," she replied, closing the gap so that our noses touched.

I couldn't keep my lips so close to hers without moving to join them. Like magnets pulled together, unable to split. Perfect physics mixed with an entropy of chemistry. I held her cheek in the crevices of my palm as I kissed her.

"You're out of this world." I whispered when our lips parted, beside the sound of waves crashing and hearts pounding.

"That book is for keeps, not for trading." I told her.

"Of course."

We sat together on the beach gazing up at the glowing moon.

"Looks like there will be great surf tomorrow." Skye commented.

"How do you know?" I asked.

"Based on the moon, or lack thereof."

"You can tell by the moon?"

"Yeah, the moon has gravitational forces that pretty much control the tides. That's why surfers, well real surfers, are selenophiles."

"Fascinating."

"So study the moon a bit and then you can be a real surfer."

"Deal."

"And you got to get your own board."

"Eventually."

"Plus maybe a few more years of practice."

"A few? I've been killing it in the last month."

"Killing it?" Skye laughed. "Don't let your confidence supersede your ability. You're improving, but surfing takes a lot of practice, a lot of patience, and a lot of commitment. Over a lot of time."

"I respect that. And I'll get there. You'll see." I put my arm around her then saw a bright flash of light in front of us. A shooting star that flew like a baseball across the sky. Huge! It stretched longer than the one we saw the other night.

"Woah! Did you see that?" I perked up in excitement.

She nodded, "Yeah that one was massive."

"A wish on a star like that has got to come true." I said.

"You only get one wish on a shooting star. You wasted it on me."

"That wasn't wasted, Skye. Tonight was amazing. You're the most enchanting person I've ever met."

"Not when you *really* get to know me."

"What are you talking about? You get more spellbinding *as* I get to know you."

Skye sighed. "What do you want from me, Lucas?"

"What do you mean?"

"Why'd you want a date? Why do you even want to hang out with me?"

"Because you're exciting and smart and extremely talented... do you not see any of that in yourself?"

"I mean, I'm a good surfer, but that's about it."

"Seriously? Why are you so hard on yourself?"

Skye rolled her eyes. "I'm a realist. I analyze what's in front of me and don't believe in fairy tales."

"So you don't believe in happy endings?"

"What do you want, Lucas?" Skye asked louder, almost yelling.

"*This*. To spend time with you."

"You just want to get with me."

"Is that what you think? That's the kind of person you think I am?"

"It's not *you*. It's just the way guys are."

"And you think all guys are the same?"

"Well, with sex, yeah."

"Not every guy is like your father, Skye."

"This isn't about him."

"Then why do you think that way?"

"Because that's what people *like you* want on holiday. To have a good time, and find a good fuck, so you can tell your mates back home all about it."

"So, this *is* about your dad."

"No Lucas, it's about the people I've met passing through here. Don't play games with me."

"I'm not."

"Then just tell me the truth. Fucking admit it."

"Okay, the truth is, I'm a virgin."

"What?"

"You heard me. I've never had sex. And I didn't come here looking for that. Out of anyone here, *you* should know that. I didn't come here looking for anything to be honest. I especially didn't expect to meet someone like you."

Skye stayed quiet.

"You know, for a person who says she hates when people judge, you do a lot of judging."

Skye kept her eyes to the sand.

"I'm sorry... I'm being hypocritical again... I just have a guard up, you know?"

"Yeah, I do." I took her hands. "Can't you just accept that I'm not the American asshole you paint up in your head?"

"I guess you're not an asshole. So are you sure you're American?" She played, so I jokingly pushed her hands away knowing she would grab them back. She did.

"I want to kiss you right now, but I don't want you to think it's 'cause I want to get some." I moved my face closer to hers. "It's because you're the most mesmerizing person that has ever caught my eye. When I first saw you, *nothing* stood out more. Not this paradise beach or the most perfect sunset. *You.* Floating on the waves. Even from so far away I knew I wanted to be close to you. And here we are. I'm close to you and you're even more dazzling than I could have imagined. Just sitting here makes my heart race more than when we jump off the cliffs." I put her hand on my heart to prove it. "Because of you Skye... You spark this life in me every time you laugh, even if you're laughing *at me.*"

"You're a smooth talker, Lucas." She said.

I would have preferred she phrased it with, *you have a way with words,* but that wouldn't be Skye.

"I meant every word."

"But you're just going to leave, so really what's the point?"

I let her words dangle in silence for a moment. "I might not leave."

"What do you mean?"

"I don't know what my plan is yet. Staying here has crossed my mind."

She narrowed her eyes at me. "Staying longer or like moving?"

"Well, I wouldn't go back to New York to move anything here technically. I guess I would just... stay."

"I better not be a reason for that decision."

I didn't answer her and just looked up at the sky above as the Skye to my side glared a hole right through me. As if she was offended that I care for her.

"Let's just focus on right now."

I was surprised she dropped the conversation so easily. She rested her head on my shoulder and we kept watching for shooting stars. When we'd see one I would always get excited, but knew not to mention another wish. I got my wish. And I wouldn't want to have another one because I know it couldn't come true, like Skye said.

Of course I would wish to erase the night of the crash, I would wish my parents were alive and well and by my side. But making that wish would only leave me disappointed.

I thought about what would be different if that wish could come true. I wouldn't be sitting on a beach with Skye. I wouldn't be in Byron. I would be back in Connecticut preparing to move back to New York City for college. Everything would be different. Well, everything would be the same as it once was. Now, I didn't even know if I would go back for college. And for the first time, I felt okay with not knowing.

Chapter 25: Helping Her at HideAway

The next day in town I ran into Kenny.

"Hey, Lucas! How you going?"

"Good, just on my way to get something to eat."

"Have you ever had Burgeroo?" He asked motioning to the place he just walked out of with a huge cartoon kangaroo in the window.

"Yeah, I have. Skye took me there. It was great."

"You two seem to be spending a lot of time together."

Kenny always gave me good vibes, but he went into protective mode in a second just by the shift in his tone of voice. After all, Skye is his niece.

"You seem like a good guy, mate. So that's fine with me, but there's something you should know." Kenny continued. "She's known to be a little unpredictable."

That's pretty apparent, I thought.

"She's just like her mum and... that didn't end well for Lessie."

The name was familiar. I saw it on the surfboard hanging above Skye's bed.

"I don't know what Skye has told you Lucas, but my sister died on the beach down there. She was cliff jumping off the mountains down by the rocks."

I pictured the spot in my head. That's exactly where Skye took me to for the cave.

Skye's mom died at the very cliffs we were jumping off of. The thought alone ran chills throughout my entire body.

"Wow... I didn't know that."

"I'm not surprised she hasn't told you. She doesn't really talk to people about her mum."

I thought about all the details Skye revealed about her mom. She trusted me with those secrets. She trusted me with many of her secrets. Though, it seemed pretty obvious as to why she didn't tell me *how* or *where* her mom died.

"It's hard for me to look out for her. She's so independent and secretive. She tells me she's working all the time, but sometimes I go into the cafe and they tell me she doesn't work that day. But she's not surfing, or in town, or at home, and the car isn't gone. I think she's getting herself into trouble. I think she might be going up to the cliffs."

I didn't know what to say. Skye made me promise not to tell anyone about the cave, but that was before I knew about the cause of her mom's death. I stayed silent.

"Do you have any idea where she goes?"

I thought about how dangerous it was to get to the cave. Then my thoughts shifted to how close I became with Skye because of that cave. How would she react if I revealed her secret?

"We get food sometimes. And watch stars." I told him. I wasn't lying. I just wasn't telling the whole truth.

"You seem to treat her well. I hope she does the same for you," he laughed, which lightened the mood.

"Listen the Bondfire this Friday is a special one. It's the ten year memorial since Lessie passed."

"Oh, wow."

"Skye will need your support that day," he said.

"Are you sure you want me there? That seems like it should be an exclusive group."

"I'd like you to be a part of that group."

I smiled. "I'll be there."

"Thanks Lucas."

Kenny gave me a fist bump and we parted ways.

I went to HideAway for lunch because I knew Skye was working. She makes the best paninis. All she does is take it from the chef, put it in the panini press, and push ON. So, maybe I give her more credit than she deserves, but there's no doubt I've had breakfast and lunch at HideAway more than any other place in Byron. I sat at one of the barstools at the counter instead of grabbing a table. She glanced past me and kept cleaning spilt coffee from the counter. She seemed annoyed. Her mood was high-stakes roulette every time I saw her.

"How's the day going?" I asked her, her back still turned away from me.

"Good. Busy."

I looked around at the barely half full cafe then back to the counter where my eyes landed on a freshly baked apple pie, untouched. "I could eat somewhere else if you're too busy. I only want a panini. And a coffee. And a piece of apple pie."

Skye grabbed a carton of milk from the fridge and walked across to the espresso machine. "If you get the apple pie, I'm having half." She said sternly.

Her seriousness about apple pie made me laugh. "I'll take two slices of apple pie then." Her eyes moved over to me for a moment.

"I don't want to have to spoon fight you for the best apples." I clarified.

She finally cracked a smile. "Because you know you'd lose in a spoon fight with me."

"That sounds like a challenge."

"No, that's just a fact. And no challenges while I'm at work, especially today."

"What's up with today?"

"The barista who was supposed to work called in sick and the other three baristas are on holiday together in the Philippines, which is sweet for them, but pretty shitty for the rest of us. So now I'm down a barista. Either Jade or Kelsey will hopefully come in soon to at least help me waitress, so I can focus on this barista thing."

"Well, congrats on your promotion."

"Yeah, I'm not counting on a pay raise or anything, but I do like making the drinks."

"Who taught you if none of them are here?"

"I've just watched them for so long. And, I watched a YouTube tutorial, which filled in some gaps."

"Self-taught barista over here." I applauded.

"Yeah, well a few were already sent back for being too strong, but really, it's just that those people are too weak. I don't wanna dump it, do you want it? It's a caramel latte." She put the mug in front of me. "Otherwise you'll probably have to wait like 20-25 minutes for a fresh one."

"I'll take it."

"Let me know if you think it is too strong."

I took a sip and tried to hide my cringe.

"Can I add some more milk?"

"You're weak too, huh? Here." She placed the carton in front of me. "Go ahead, ruin the perfect ratio of coffee to milk."

"You've been a barista for less than a day. How could you know the perfect ratio?" I pointed out as I poured the milk.

"I've drank coffee for a decade. I know."

"Whatever you say." I said as I took another sip. It still needed more milk.

Thankfully the kitchen was not as overwhelmed as Skye, so I got my panini pretty quick. Skye made me get up and put it in the panini press myself because she was *too busy* with the rest of the drink orders.

"And what about those pieces of pie?"

Skye was fumbling with the espresso machine again.

"Cut your own piece."

I served two slices on one plate and fed Skye bites when she'd pass me at the counter.

"This is really good pie." I indulged.

"Right? I made it."

"Really?"

"No... but I did take it out of the oven." She laughed.

"You took a badass pie out of the oven, Skye."

"I try."

As we finished the slices of pie, a few more tables filled up.

"I'll be right with you!" Skye called as she filled an espresso cup.

I looked back at the tables, which were now *all full.*

"Do you want me to help you? I can go take some orders."

Skye looked at the tables then back at me pensively. "Could you?"

"Yeah, sure."

Skye handed me a notepad and a pen.

"We're out of sweet potato fries."

"You have sweet potato fries? I've never seen them on the menu."

"They're not on the menu. But locals just know. Go. There's more people at the door."

I walked over to a table of two and introduced myself, trying to mimic the servers I've had in the past. I could tell by their accents that they weren't from Byron.

"What do you recommend, the pesto turkey or the smoked caprese?"

Luckily I've had just about every sandwich on the menu, so I was actually prepared to answer that question.

"The smoked caprese with chicken is one of my favorites, but you can't go wrong with HideAway's pesto."

"Could I get the smoked caprese with chicken and pesto?"

I didn't know if they could do that, but I couldn't see why not. "Sure, and for you."

"Just a coffee for me, black no sugar. I'm not that hungry."

"Well, if you want something small to go along with the coffee, maybe you'd be interested in a slice of apple pie that came out to the oven this morning. I just had a piece and it's insanely delicious."

"That does sound good. I'll take a slice."

"Ooo… I'll have a slice too please."

"Would you like the pie before, during, or after the caprese?"

They glanced at each other, "before."

I put the caprese order in before going to the next table. After I got the next table's order I cut the slices of pie and poured the coffee. I was happy it was just a plain coffee because Skye was backed up with the espresso orders, because of the send-backs that were too strong. She seemed to finally adjust the coffee ratio to the customers' needs. Skye thankfully took the large group while I struggled with writing fast enough at a table of four. Soon enough, the chaos reached a more manageable pace. It was then another waitress showed up.

"Hey, Marcos called and said you needed another hand over here." She said while putting on an apron.

"Hey Kelsey, yeah there's no barista today, so I've just been figuring it out."

Kelsey looked around at the tables. "You seem to have everything pretty handled for a packed place."

"Lucas helped me. He even sold an entire apple pie already." Skye said. She even seemed proud.

"Impressive. You should totally work here. Marcos needs another server. Especially since half our staff is on holiday for another week and a half." Kelsey rolled her eyes. "You know, they should really make a rule that more than two people can't go away on holiday at the same time."

"You're right, they should." Skye agreed.

"Thanks for helping out, Lucas. I'm sure you'd rather enjoy the beach then be bossed around by Skye."

"It is a beautiful day out." I smiled, but the truth was I liked it. I liked talking to the different people who I'd probably never talk to otherwise. I liked seeing people enjoy something I suggested. But most of all I liked working alongside Skye. Kelsey was right though, she *was* kind of bossy, but I was used to that.

I went to pay for my check, but Skye told me no. "You worked off that bill."

"You sure?"

"Definitely. But I gotta get back to work, the orders for the big group are ready."

"Alright, I'm going to go surf, but do you want to hang out tomorrow?"

"I can't, they need me to work." She answered, beginning to grab plates from the window and load them on a tray.

"Okay, how about after work?"

"Probably not. Kenny needs my help with some stuff, so I'll be busy." She stated dryly, and continued working.

"Okay, I guess I'll see you around then?"

Her vibes kind of flipped on me, but I didn't really know why.

"Yeah." She responded, more invested in her actions than she was in her words. I didn't want to bother her, so I turned to leave.

"Lucas." I heard her call after a few steps.

I turned around.

"Do you want to go to the cargo net on Thursday?" I knew she referred to the net rather than the cave because there were people around, people who would probably wonder what "cave" she meant. My bones stiffened thinking about what Kenny had just told me….

I didn't want to go to the cave, but I did want to spend time with Skye.

"Do you want to surf instead?"

"You can go surf if you want. I'm going to go to the cargo net."

Skye was the type to do what she wanted even if no one else was.

"Fine." My heart agreed as my head filled with anxiety.

I never felt so excited to return to a place that made me feel so uncomfortable.

"I'll see you at the rocks at nine."

Chapter 26: Closer in the Cave

The beach had more people than usual that day. I was nervous that someone would see us climbing the rocks that led to the trail on the mountain, revealing the path to Skye's hideaway. I worried someone would see me with her and it would get back to Kenny. But whether I was with Skye or not, she would take the risk of climbing the mountain, jumping off of it, and diving to the underwater cave. Skye could relate to the cliffs, the jagged rocks, and the underwater cavern... she was just as dangerous as they were.

"Leading the way this time?" Skye asked me as I powered through the trail, ahead of her. I wanted to get out of sight quickly.

"It's the only way to make sure you won't whip me with thorny branches."

"Oh please, you walked into them," she claimed.

I pulled the next branch and released.

"Ouch!" Skye yelped.

"Did you walk into a branch? Be careful." I laughed, playing Skye's game.

I felt her throw a small rock at my back.

"Oh, it's like that!?" I exclaimed, stopping on the path and turning to face Skye. I was extra tall, standing on the higher part of the trail. She looked up at me with a face of confidence, daring me to Do Something About It.

"Would you like to lead the way?" I asked.

"Why? You seem to know where you're going."

We both stared at each other sternly. I felt a smile building behind my teeth, but kept a serious stare. Serious, but flirty. Skye stared back. It's so hard to read her eyes because it's so easy to just get lost in them.

"Well, if you're going to just stand there," she said pushing past me, "then I'll lead."

She strutted ahead of me and I couldn't tell if she was being her usual self or if she was actually upset. The silence continued as Skye weaved through the branches and shrubs, letting none fly back my direction. I guess I proved my point.

"The Bondfire on Friday will be a bit different," Skye said suddenly, still keeping a steady pace forward.

"It's not just open invite and well I guess," Skye seemed nervous with her words. "I wanted you to know that you are still invited."

A smile grew on my face. There I was, thinking that Skye was upset because I gave her a piece of her own medicine and she was thinking about the Memorial on Friday. She was making sure I was going. I suddenly felt important in Skye's eyes.

"Of course I'll be there." I promised her. "Kenny actually invited me on Tuesday," I told her. She turned just before reaching the summit. I was smiling, but she wasn't.

"I'm happy that I have a direct invite from you though," I added.

She turned and continued to climb to the top of the mountain.

The breeze was refreshing after the sweaty climb to the peak. I closed my eyes and let the misty wind cool me. When I opened them Skye was sitting atop a boulder beside the cliff. I went over to join her, thankful to take a break while I could before the inevitable exhausting swim to the cave. Skye's arm was against mine and even though I was extremely uncomfortable with the way the rock was against my back, I stayed still. I knew before long Skye would want to leap off the edge and I feared any sudden movements would make her jump away from me.

We watched the water for what felt like only a few seconds before she began getting up and as her arm grazed away from mine, I caught her hand with my fingers and pulled her back. I sat up from the rock and looked at Skye whose eyes were perfectly aligned with mine. I saw storm clouds in her irises. Her face looked heavy, and not from the barriers she tried to hold up; Skye looked sad. It looked like those storm clouds were ready to rupture. She looked down and squeezed my hand. She pushed the pebbles at her feet around pensively.

"Do you have other family? Back in New York." She asked.

"Yeah, some. I haven't talked to anyone since I left though." I admitted, feeling guilty.

Skye reminded me that I no longer had that privilege of a welcoming home. I would go back to a house full of memories and reminders of how different life was. There was no more home without my mom and dad. There was no more banana chocolate chip pancakes for breakfast or ice cream sundae rewards. There was no more Lucky. That part of me died beside my parents. I felt the tension building up in my head as my face got hot.

"Are you crying?" She asked.

"Yeah, are you going to make fun of me? Go for it." I turned my head away from her, angry that she evoked those emotions.

"No, Lucas. I'm sorry. Maybe I shouldn't have brought it up."

"I just miss them so much." I bawled carelessly.

Skye put her arms around me.

"Does it get easier? Ever?"

She squeezed me tighter.

"Yes." She started tearing too.

"No... sometimes." Her warmth felt so comforting I didn't want to move even in the slightest. I squeezed her back. "I got used to the routine of my mom not being here, but sometimes I feel like I need her more than when I was just a little kid. Sometimes I feel like she's all around me and I just can't hug her or see her."

She cried and I held her tighter. "I'm sorry... I'm sure that's not what you wanted to hear." She said, lifting her head from my shoulder.

I had no words to produce. It wasn't her fault. She was hurting too. I felt helpless.

In one moment I feared the vacancy of my happiness and in the very next I experienced a strong reminder of the excitement that still exists. I was surprised when she kissed me. Probably the best surprise of my life. The way her hand moved my chin toward her complicated my whole mood. She shot a surge through my distraught heart. Even if it was only just for that minute, her kiss relieved my pain and I didn't feel guilty about my own happiness.

"Can I walk you home tonight?" I asked.

She paused as if she was thinking about it.

"Yes." She responded looking toward the cliffside. "But only if you jump first."

There was never just a simple answer from Skye. I always felt the need to impress her. I turned to look at the cliff and without looking back I took a running start and leaped off the ledge, already aware of my surroundings as to which way to jump. Midway gliding through the air I thought about how cool it would have been to do a backflip or something like that. I'm glad I got the idea when it was too late because just thinking about it was intimidating enough and cliffs were not a place for tricks or stupidity. Plus, I've never even tried doing a backflip before. It would be a disaster.

Skye came splashing into the water shortly after me, laughing.

"Wow, you want to lead into the cave too?"

"Do I get to walk you home?" I asked.

"Yes."

"Then, no." I said as we laughed together.

The dive down into the cave was a bit less nerve wrecking than last time, even with the information Kenny told me. I felt like I remembered the way, so diving into the darkness didn't seem as daunting. As we descended the tightness in my ears reminded me to equalize and as the pressure intensified, so did the darkness. Once we turned into the cave's underwater entryway, there was absolutely no source of light from the sun. All that glowed in the inky water was Skye who led the way with a headlamp. I kept pace, swimming fast, scared I would lose her like the times before. She began swimming up, which was a relief because the oxygen in my lungs was running out. I stayed calm. Panic would only make it worse. Finally, when it felt like my lungs had nothing left, Skye breached the surface and I kicked extra hard to make it up there too. I gasped for air and swam over to the shore to catch my breath.

Skye switched on the industrial light that lit the whole cave with an ominous glow. I collapsed onto the cargo net before Skye could even get on it and purposefully laid sideways to take up most of the net. Skye looked at me with narrow eyes and a half smile. She climbed on the net and used my stomach as her pillow, letting her feet dangle off the edge of the net.

"You hungry?" She asked. Which I thought was an odd question considering there wasn't anything to eat either way. Unless Skye added a snack pantry behind the stalagmites.

"I'm good. Why?"

"Your stomach is growling," she laughed, mortifying me.

"Well, then maybe just a little, but I can wait."

We started playing a game finding different animals or objects in the stalactites, kind of like cloud watching, but with rocks. I found an alligator head and a wishbone. Skye saw a surfboard and claimed she found a kangaroo, but I didn't see it.

In the middle of the game she said, "Can I show you something?"

Skye got up from the cargo net and went over to a crevice of the cave and knelt down.

She pointed to the rock. LC was carved into the wall of the cave.

"That's my mom's initials, Lessie Carter. They're a bit faded, but for being at least ten years old, they're pretty distinct."

"How do you know they're your mom's? Did she… take you here?" I asked.

"No. I found her initials a few weeks ago. But I know she's been here."

I watched Skye as she traced the letters LC with her finger.

I thought about her mom swimming in that very cave over a decade ago. Would she go alone like Skye? Would she have wanted Skye to discover the cave?

The cave kept becoming more and more creepy to me. Thinking about what Kenny told me about Lessie's death made me get bad vibes. She died in these waters, not far from where we were, on the same rocks that helped to build these caves. The thought alone gave me chills down my spine.

Chapter 27: Boarding with Budd

After the caves we got something to eat. Afterwards Skye was asked to go help out at HideAway, so she left, but I went back down to the beach to do some thinking. Byron Bay had become a place I could see myself living a happy life. It felt like a fresh start. To my surprise I saw Elsie out on the water surfing. The waves looked incredible and Elsie tore them up effortlessly. Shortly after she saw me she rode the next wave in.

"I didn't want to interrupt your surf!" I told her.

"No, I was out there for a while, I'm exhausted."

She placed her tricolored surfboard onto the sand and we sat.

"I was thinking of staying in Byron, for even longer than I thought."

"That's great, Lucas. I think you really need that." Elsie said. I was slightly surprised by her reaction.

"Me too. And to be honest, you've really helped to steer me in the right direction."

"I'm flattered, but I just listened to you sort out your thoughts."

"Yeah, but without someone to talk it out with, I would be lost in my own mind."

Suddenly from a distance I heard someone calling for me.

I turned to see Budd waving at me down the beach.

"I'm going to get going." Elsie said grabbing her surfboard and getting up.

"Wait." I said, but she was already walking away.

I got up too.

"Bye Lucas," she said hurrying her pace.

"Lucas!" Budd called, from a bit closer.

I turned around to face him. "One sec!" I yelled, waving my pointer finger up.

I turned back toward Elsie's direction, but she was already gone. I sighed and started walking toward Budd.

"Hey mate. How you going?" Budd said.

"Alright, you?"

"Just finished teaching some grommets out on the water. Ten to twelve year olds, really getting ripper." Budd said, in seemingly another language. "I saw you sitting there and I wanted to ask if you wanted to surf."

"Yeah, for sure." I was surprised Budd wanted to surf... with me.

I walked with Budd down to The Shack and grabbed my usual rental board.

"What have you been up to today?" Budd asked.

I froze at the question knowing how bad I was at lying. "Just chilling with Skye."

"I didn't see you two out on the water."

"Yeah, we weren't surfing. We got some food."

"Did she take you to Burgeroo?"

"Yeah, that place was delicious."

We paddled out on our surfboards. I wondered what Budd had on his mind.

"You must be some sort of special, Lucas."

"What do you mean?" We sat on our boards anticipating the right wave in the distance.

"Skye is usually not very friendly with people who aren't from here. Or with many people at all to be honest." He laughed to himself. "Skye's very... picky about who she wishes to spend her time with."

I didn't know how to respond to his statement, so I was glad that a good wave was forming. I started to paddle to catch it. Budd did too, and of course he was faster. He sped out in front of me, cutting so close that it made me lose my balance right as I was popping up. I bailed. The worst thing about bailing, even more than the embarrassment, is having to paddle all the way out again. Especially when the current is strong. It's exhausting.

I was already pretty tired from the hike to the cave with Skye, so that first bail hit me pretty hard. Budd had already caught another wave by the time I finally got all the way out again.

"You're not going to catch a wave with the way you're paddling." Budd pointed out.

"Yeah, I know. I'm just tired."

"You can't be tired on the first wave, c'mon shark biscuit." I liked that Budd was pushing me, but part of me was annoyed by it. The guys have always given me tips and it's only helped me, but I just wasn't feeling any sort of criticism. As we paddled toward the next wave, I still had Budd's comment about Skye floating around in my head. I paddled harder this time and just barely caught the wave. My mind felt too preoccupied to focus on the surf.

"How did you meet Skye?" I asked Budd.

"We met in primary school. Year 4. Skye was a new student and she was so quiet and didn't talk to anyone for the first week. I saw she had a surf folder and I showed her my cool surfboard pencil erasers and after that we were always tight."

"Skye was shy? I can't imagine that."

"She was shy up until her mom passed away. After that she was *always* getting us into trouble. I'd go along with her crazy ideas until Spigs and Kenny made me stop because they said *I made her* more defiant. Which is totally bullshit because Skye was defiant on her own. I always followed her lead."

That all sounded familiar… I wondered if Budd had ever been to the cave. "What kind of *crazy ideas* would she have?"

"One time she disappeared for a week to camp in the outback. She hitchhiked there and back… alone. But most of the time it was just cutting class to skate or surf."

As the word surf left his mouth Budd began propelling himself toward a wave that I already decided I was going to skip.

It's like Budd had webbed fingers or something because he moved through the water so quickly. It didn't even look like he was trying very hard. He cut his own path through the wave and paddled back to where I was.

"Did Skye finish school?" I asked.

"Yeah, top of our class. She always got good grades and never even had to study. I don't know how she did so well with all the class she'd skip."

"Skye always seems to find a way." I said.

Budd looked at me pensively. He was probably wondering what I meant by that.

I moved the conversation along. "All you guys seem really close."

"After Skye lost her mom, the surf crew became her family."

"Is this the first Memorial Bondfire?" I asked.

"You're going to that?" Budd seemed surprised.

"Skye and Kenny invited me."

He nodded and turned to look at the next wave, which was on its way. Again like lighting he was gone.

Budd's tone and the way he moved away so quickly made feel like he did not want me at the Memorial. I was happy that Kenny invited me because at least I knew *he* wouldn't be bothered by my presence. I caught only a few more waves, while Budd had more runs than I could count. I didn't mind when he suggested riding the next one in.

"So when do you plan to head back to the states?" Budd asked me.

"I'm not sure."

"You been here for a while, mate. More than a month, am I right?"

I nodded.

"I wish I could take a holiday that long. That's pretty spiffy. Where you say you're from again?"

"New York."

"Oh, New York. I always wanted to go to New York. It gets really cold there though right?"

"In the winter. Now it's even warmer than here."

"That's when I'd go… in July or August. But I don't think I'd ever be able to leave."

"Why not?"

"Well, I've never left Australia, so I guess I can't really envision it for myself."

"Just 'cause you've never left doesn't mean you can't one day."

"I know, but I'm not like you. I'm not a traveler."

"Neither was I two months ago. This trip kind of just happened. That's why I don't have a plan or a ticket back."

"What made you just get up and leave?"

I thought about how to answer his question.

"I needed to get away."

It sounded like such a cliche answer, but the truth was not something I was prepared to reveal.

Thankfully waves continued and Budd was off. This went on for a while until we finally paddled in.

"Sorry I was so out of it today. I hope I didn't hold you back." I said as we arrived back at The Shack.

"You gotta quit snaking. You got to get control."

"Snaking?"

"Cutting people off."

"Oh. Sorry."

Budd took my rental board and put it on a surf rack to rinse it off.

"See you at sunrise surf tomorrow?"

"Definitely." I said pleased that Budd invited me. "Thanks, I'll see you." I began to walk away.

Budd put down the hose. "Hey, Lucas, hold on real quick."

I turned back to The Shack. Budd stared blankly at me. "Yeah...?" I asked.

He stood tall like he was about to make a speech. "Be respectful of Skye. She may seem really tough, but..." His sentence faded off.

"Of course I respect Skye." I replied. "You don't even need to tell me that." What did he think of me?

"Yes I do. You're spending time with her and she deserves the best." He raised his voice a bit.

Was Budd jealous?

"I respect her." I stared back at him.

His eyes were intense. He was clearly trying to intimidate me.

"I'm not trying to start any problems, we just hang out sometimes." I tried to diffuse the tension.

Budd still had that glare in his eye.

"Do you have a thing for her or something?" I finally said.

"Is that what you think this is about?" His reaction made me wish I never asked that question. "Skye is like my sister. You're just some guy coming through so no, I'm not just going to assume you're going to be thinking about what's best for her."

"I respect that." I said. "And I respect, Skye. Don't you know by now that Skye can handle herself pretty well?"

"She seems tough, but it's not always what it seems."

I nodded as if I understood, but most of me had more questions I decided not to ask.

"Thanks for the surf, Budd. I'll see you around."

I began walking away.

"Lucas." Budd said.

What now?

I turned around again.

"Don't fuck with her *feelings*, mate."

I stared at him, unsure of how to reply.

I wanted to promise Budd that I wouldn't fuck with Skye's emotions, but if she was feeling the way I was, *feelings* have already been fucked with.

Chapter 28: The Memorial

I went to bed early to make sure I was well rested. It was emotional for a lot of people. When I woke up that morning, I felt a bit anxious just being a part of it.

I got to sunrise surf right as Spigs, Coco, and Budd were opening up The Shack. It was still dark outside. We were going extra early to ensure we had enough time to use the rest of the day to set up for the Memorial. I greeted the guys and helped them finish setting up shop, even though they told me I didn't have to. As soon as the last rack of boards were out on the sand, Budd took out a box of Tim Tams and turned on a pot of tea with the electric tea pot. Coco took out four mugs, tossed a tea bag in each, and filled them with the boiling water.

I could get use to this...

I looked down the beach to see if Skye was coming, but there was no one in sight, only the candy corn sunrise beginning to peek out from the horizon. The orange and yellows beamed to awaken the whole beach.

"Sun is here. Let's get out there." Coco suggested. The guys finished up their tea and began putting on their wetsuits. I wanted to ask about Skye. I wanted to know where she was. I wanted to wait for her.

"Are we expecting anyone else?" I asked, in attempt to not be as obvious as to who I was insinuating.

"Jade can't make it because she has work." Coco said.

Where's Skye?

"Kenny said he'd see us later on."

And Skye?

"Zane opted to sleep in." Budd said as he tossed me a wetsuit. "It's just going to be us four."

We surfed all morning as the sun climbed its way up the sky. Spigs and Budd had already surfed in to manage the shop, but Coco was still out on the water shredding with me. Eventually hunger set in and my stomach's growling got in the way of my focus on the waves. The guys offered me some snacks that they had at The Shack, but I passed to get a real meal at HideAway. I knew Skye didn't work Fridays, but hoped that somehow someway she'd be there.

She wasn't, but I sat down for food nonetheless. HideAway was packed, as always, but I managed to grab a stool at the counter. Kelsey and Jade were both waitressing.

"Hey Lucas! How you going?" Jade said enthusiastically when she saw me.

"Good, just got off of surfing" Her long dark brown braids tempted me to ask if she does them herself.

"I'm jealous! Busy over here as usual. Do you know what you want, or do you need a minute?"

I figured it was not the time to distract her from her job. "Lemme get scrambled eggs with bacon. A chipotle turkey wrap. A side of sweet potato fries."

"Really hungry?" Kelsey said with wide eyes.

"Yeah... is there any pie?"

"Half of a blueberry."

"I'll take that too."

"The rest of the pie?"

I laughed. "No, just a slice."

"To drink?"

"Orange juice." Coffee has been a bit unpredictable.

"You got it."

While I was eating my eggs I heard, "You're Lucas, right?" From over my shoulder

There stood a bearded man, about 6 foot 5 with a bald head and glasses.

"Yes." I nodded.

The tall man extended his hand, "I'm Marcos. This is my cafe, welcome."

It was my hundredth time at HideAway, but I still embraced his welcome.

"Thanks." I thought it was weird that I've never seen him before. Yeah, I was mostly focused on Skye, but this is the kind of guy who is hard to miss.

"The girls were telling me that you gave some much needed help the other day when we were short staffed. Thanks for that, mate."

"No problem."

"I like that initiative, Lucas. Listen, anything you get today is on the house." I wanted to stop him and tell him that Skye already gave me a free meal, but I didn't want to get her in trouble so I just kept quiet about that.

"Thank you. I appreciate it." Then I wished I ordered the whole other half of the pie.

"I also wanted you to think about working for me as a server for a few days since we a short staffed. I've been meaning to hire someone, but the last couple months have been crazy because my wife and I just had a baby. Do you know how much attention a baby needs?!" Marcos took off his glasses and rubbed his face. I wasn't sure if his question was rhetorical or not.

"Anyway-" he interrupted his own apparent exhaustion. "Think about it. We'd love to have you. Just until my staff gets back from Singapore, or was it Malaysia? Oh I don't know!"

Philippines. I thought to myself, remembering what Skye said.

"Their Instagram says they were in Indonesia this morning." Kelsey commented as she walked by with a tray of food, that wasn't mine.

"Tell them to bring back Indonesian coffee!"

Marcos reverted his attention back to me.

"Thank you for the offer sir…" I wanted to tell him I would be ready to work again as soon as he needed, but he jumped into talking about Skye.

"She was raving about you, you know? I've never heard her talk so nicely about someone." His words shocked me. "How did you meet her?" Marcos asked.

"Through surfing, pretty much."

"You must be really good to go surfing with Skye."

"No, I'm still just learning. Skye just shreds through and around me."

Marcos looked at me surprised.

My wrap and fries came out through the kitchen window.

"I'm not much of a surfer, mate. I'm not very coordinated and try to stick to the land."

I took a bite of some fries as he poked a message into his phone.

"Marcos, when can I start the job?"

His face lit up. "Well, how about… right now?"

"Aaa.. today I'm busy." It was the Memorial.

"What about tomorrow?"

"Yeah, I could do tomorrow."

"Great, come in around ten.

I hoped it was okay with Skye that we were coworkers.

Later, I ran into Kenny after lunch when I was walking back to Neptune's.

"Lucas! Have you seen Skye?" He asked me in a hustle.

"Not today, no."

"I can't find her. She said she would be around today to help set up for the Memorial, but I haven't seen her at all. I'm kind of nervous."

"Is there anything I can do?" I offered.

"Do you have any idea where she might be?"

I thought about his question and the cave immediately jumped into my head.

"No, but I will go look around."

"Today is a crazy day for me, for all of us, especially Skye. I thought this Memorial was something she wanted, that's why I've put so much work into it. I'd do anything for that kid." Kenny began to choke up. "Even if she doesn't want to come, can you find her and make sure she is safe?"

"Yeah, I'll try. What time does everything start?"

"Right at sunset, five o'clock. It's almost 2:00 now."

"I need a waterproof headlamp..." I mumbled under my breath.

"What?" Kenny looked at me puzzled.

"Aaa... never mind."

I had three hours to hike to her, *hopefully* find her, convince her to come back and get ready, and bring her to the Memorial. *Assuming* she was in the cave to begin with. *Where else could she be?*

I headed straight to the rocks after speaking with Kenny. I never thought I would have to do that hike again, and sure enough I was doing it, alone. I walked at a quick pace, but didn't want to go too fast because I knew the trail wasn't completely cleared and didn't want to make the wrong turn. I thought about what I would say to her. How would she react when she saw me? What I would do if she wasn't there...?

When I got to the jumping point, I stood on the edge and looked down. Standing over the jagged rocks and choppy waters after such a strenuous hike had me breathing heavy. Adding the pressure of making sure Skye was safe put an extra weight on my chest. I began to question myself. Is this the jumping spot? Was I in the right place?

I scrutinized the rocks that curved to form the cliff I was standing on. I looked at the other ledges within my range of sight, which looked extremely similar to the one I was standing on. They all looked the same. I turned around to observe what was behind me. I looked at a boulder that looked like the one Skye kissed me against. This had to be the spot. I peeked over the ledge again. I was almost positive. *Pretty sure.* Was *pretty sure* enough to plummet into rocky, possibly shallow waters?

I took a breath. I looked to see if there was any way to climb down, but that seemed even more dangerous. I thought about waiting until Skye left the cave, but then what if she wasn't there at all; how long would I wait for? I was upset that I made myself so paranoid. I walked over to the rock I was *pretty sure* about and sat down. I tried to picture what was around me when I was sitting with Skye on Wednesday, but all I could picture was what Skye looked like and what Skye was doing.

My eyes fell in frustration onto some pebbles on the ground. That's when the memory clicked in my head of Skye pushing pebbles with her feet. That's when *pretty sure* turned to *certainty*. Without wasting another moment to possibly psych myself out again I took a running start and leaped off the ledge.

I dunked down into the water and opened my eyes to see if I could find the entryway to the cave. Similar to at the summit, everything looked pretty similar. I rose to the surface to take a breath to see if I could recognize anything from above the water. I saw a curve in the rock of the mountain and followed my intuition to dive down in that direction. I've done this before and stayed confident that I could do it again. I kicked deeper to where my ears began to feel the pressure, flashing back to previous depths where I've had to equalize.

Keep swimming, I hummed to myself, grabbing and pulling my way through the water. Darkness set in and I felt it was time to swim horizontally. I propelled myself straight into the daunting black crevice of the rock and let my instincts fill the absence of a headlamp. I began swimming up when I saw a light above my head. The light in the cave! It was on!

I pushed my head above the surface to see the illuminated cave.

"What are you doing here?" I heard her ask. Skye was sitting up in the cargo net glaring at me with puffy eyes.

"I saw the light on from the beach." I joked. She wasn't having it.

Skye rolled over on the cargo net to put her back to me. I needed to cheer her up.

"Guess what, Skye?"

"What?" She sniffled.

"I got a job."

"Where?"

"We're coworkers now."

"Really?" She turned to face me. "When did that happen?"

"Today. Thanks for recommending me to Marcos."

"I didn't recommend you. I just said you helped out a bit."

"Well, whatever you said, thank you."

"He trained me as a barista now, so we'll probably work together." She dangled her feet off the edge of the net.

"You won't make all the drinks so strong that they get sent back, right?"

Skye rolled her eyes. "That table was weak. I refuse to serve them again."

"Weren't they on vacation and that was their last day?"

"Good. They gave a terrible tip. I'm glad I don't have to see them again."

I walked over to stand beside the cargo net. Skye looked so so sad.

"Kenny is looking for you." I said taking her hands in mine.

"Tell him not to worry, that I'm fine." She kept her head down.

Kenny did say that he wanted to confirm her safety, not necessarily force her to attend the Memorial, but Skye not attending seemed so wrong to me. Selfish even.

"Kenny put a lot of work into tonight. He's doing this for you, you know?"

Skye sat silently. She let go of my hands and laid back down onto the cargo net.

"This isn't just about you Skye. It's about your mom and the respect and appreciation you should have for your uncle and his sacrifices. He would do anything for you, even mold his dreams and aspirations for you. You can't just let him down. He's hurting today too." I felt a bit bad throwing guilt onto Skye, but we didn't have much time and I knew how stubborn she could be. A few seconds passed and I could hear her crying.

"What would your mom want?" I challenged Skye to think about. "I'd think today of all days, she'd want you to be with those who care about you, remembering her and smiling, not crying."

I could still hear her sniffle. I recalled the conversation when I asked Skye if it ever got easier. She couldn't really give me a straight answer and I see why. All it takes is an off day or a nostalgic memory to make the whole world feel like it was collapsing all over again. Because the ground can still tremble weeks, months, and years after the same formidable event. The pain may still remain heavy, but the strength and the growth that has been acquired can stretch beyond, and overpower it.

"Let's go back, Skye. There's still time." I implored her. She wasn't crying anymore, or at least from what I could see and hear.

Skye sat up on the net, still avoiding eye contact, and nodded in agreement.

She moved past me and walked over to the corner that carved her mother's initials. She grazed her fingertips to trace over them. She stood there a moment, took a breath, and turned to face me. "Okay... alright... Let's go."

Getting out had much less pressure than navigating into the cave, especially with Skye leading the way. We hiked back in a comforting silence, with staggered conversations along the way. Skye never takes her phone to the cave and neither of us had a watch on, so we weren't sure of the time. Skye estimated that we had over an hour based on how close the sun was to the horizon, which left enough time to shower and change. I didn't really want to show up in our bathing suits, so I was glad that we had the extra time to spare.

Initially, I was nervous that Skye and I would split up to get ready, me at my hostel and Skye at her home, and then Skye wouldn't show up. Leaving me to stand there like an idiot, waiting for her. I didn't want to obsess over it. If my words got her out of the cave, they must have gotten through to her, and resonated enough to bring her to the Memorial, on her own. I'd just have to wait and see.

When I walked through the front door, Jade was fixing Spigs' dreads on the living room sofa. Zane was sitting cross-legged on the floor solving a Rubik's Cube.

"Ey mate, good to see you. Those braids are really holding up."

"I can fix them up whenever you need it." Jade added.

Walking into that house always gave me a breath of fresh air. "Thanks."

Jade was telling me about the process of fixing dreads when Budd and Skye began walking down the steps with their arms around each other's backs.

Jealousy bubbled inside of me. "Do you know what's up with Skye and Budd?" I whispered to Zane. "Are they like, a *thing*?"

"No," Zane laughed, slapping his hand on my shoulder. "They're just really close, always have been. Shit, it even gets me jealous sometimes."

Did Zane like Skye too? Was she messing with all of our minds and hearts?

Skye was resting her head on Budd's shoulder and I felt the blood boiling in my veins. I've never been a jealous person, but for some reason… lately… I've gotten so worked up, very easily.

They hugged at the landing of the stairs. And then I truly felt like I wanted to hit Budd. *What was wrong with me?* Part of me wanted to push him off her, tackle him to the ground, while my rational mind told me to look away… walk away… go outside. So I did.

I walked straight out of the living room, through the kitchen and into the yard, which was decorated to celebrate the life of Lessie Carter. Surfboards were lined around the edges of the entire yard, creating a fence-like appearance, tables were set up for a sit down dinner, and there was a table near the back door with photo albums and framed photographs. I walked over to take a look. A big sign in the center read,
Lessie Carter: mother, sister, friend, pro-surfer, inspirational human being.

You will always be in our hearts LC.

I looked over to see the photographs. I glanced at the first and froze where I was standing. I looked at the next photo and felt my bones

tingle.

I know her, I whispered to myself in pure bewilderment.

I looked at more pictures. One photo had a gold frame around it that read Legend of The Surf Shack. A picture I've seen before…

It was Elsie.

In all of the pictures.

I felt my heart racing and my palms sweating.

Elsie. How? *What is going on?* I mumbled to myself.

I felt the blood rushing out of my face.

I was overwhelmed.

I needed to get out of there.

I walked quickly through the yard and stopped before exiting through the gap in the bushes.

I took a deep breath and turned around.

I looked over at the photographs again.

It was definitely the same person.

I sprinted to the sand.

I needed to walk to the end of the beach.

To the rocks.

Where I always found Elsie… LC…

How was I talking to someone who has been dead for ten years?! I felt weak in the knees and dizzy. It felt like I would collapse, so I sat down on the sand.

"Lucas, are you alright?" I heard a voice call from down the beach. Elsie?

I turned to see Skye walking in my direction. "Why did you run away when I came down the stairs?"

I remained sitting and tried to gather my thoughts. To somehow organize the last month of conversations into any sort of sense. If Elsie is LC, then how did I possibly see her, talk to her, cry to her *multiple times?* Nothing made any sort of sense.

"What's wrong?" I heard Skye say from behind me as she placed her hand on my shoulder.

"Nothing, nothing." I tried to pretend.

"Lucas, you don't look good. You're really pale. What's going on?"

"I'm fine, go inside. I just want to be alone for a little."

"You're worrying me. What happened?" She kneeled and grabbed my hands.

"I don't feel well. I think I ate something that got me sick."

"What did you eat?"

"Fish tacos on my way over. It was probably bad."

"Do you want me to get you anything?"

"No. I think I need to go back to Neptune's though." I got up onto my feet, semi-stable.

Skye looked at me with sadness in her eyes. "Okay... do you want me to walk with you?"

"No, you go inside."

Skye looked at me with heavy eyes.

"I'm sorry."

"Just feel better." She kissed me on the cheek and wrapped her arms around my shoulders.

"Thank you for getting me. Thank you for caring." Skye said into my ear.

I squeezed her tight because she was the only thing I knew to be true and real.

Skye pressed her lips against my neck.

"Go inside, Skye. They need you." I said kissing her forehead.

"They're expecting you as well." She said looking at me.

"Your presence is far more important on this night." I told her.
"I'm not feeling well. I'm sorry I can't stay." My body suddenly stiffened at the reason why I couldn't stay.

Skye took a few steps backwards but still held both of my hands.

"I'll see you tomorrow?" Skye asked, pausing for my answer.

"Okay."

I let go of her hands.

Skye turned and walked away from me. I wanted to follow her, but I was too scared to. My fear paralyzed all the questions that overflowed my mind at realizing that Skye's dead mom was someone I had countless conversations with.

On my walk home, I was paranoid. *What was real around me?* I analyzed people as if I expected to see them flicker like a mere computer projection. I touched fences, trees, cars, and everything that I *believed* to be real. I contemplated if I ever felt Elsie; a hug or a hand on the shoulder. The more I thought about it the more paranoid I got. I quickened my pace and basically jogged the rest of the way to Neptune's.

The bar was full of people and the music was bumping. I went around the side to avoid it. I fumbled in my pockets and quickly realized that I couldn't find my keys. I groaned in frustration and headed back toward the lobby checking my pockets again and again as I walked.

Maybe all of this is just a dream. I said to myself walking up to the empty reception desk.

When did the dream start? I backtracked my day in my mind.

"Did you come to report another girl in your bed?" I heard from behind me.

"Aaa... No." I turned around. It was Creep, the front desk guy.

"Are you here to complain that there's no girl in your bed?"

As usual he was annoying me. "I just realized-"

"That your bunkmate stole your unlocked possessions?' He cut me off as he walked by me.

"What is wrong with you?" I said.

His eyes were drooping a little. I could smell alcohol on his breath.

"I lost my keys."

"What's wrong with me? Nothing. What's wrong with you? You lost your keys. You bring the problems, mate."

I glared at him and he took a sip of his beer.

"Should you be drinking?"

"You should be drinking. Come on let's get a drink." He put his arm around my shoulder.

"No, I'm good." I said firmly, pushing him off of me. He stumbled into the wall.

"Let me into my room. Please."

"I don't know mate, I really like this song." Creep said motioning toward the DJ at the bar.

I wanted to jump behind the counter and strangle him, but thankfully he handed me a key. "A fee will be charged."

I took the key and left.

Nobody was in the room and I was thankful because I felt like crying. Just when everything felt like too much, more hit me. I rubbed my eyes and ran my fingers through my hair hoping this all was just a terrible dream. That I would wake up to that morning's sunrise surf. Or to the morning of the last day of school when mom made homemade banana pancakes with chocolate chip smileys.

I felt the tears scrambling down my cheeks. I closed my eyes and imagined crying in my parents' bed. Not in our house in Connecticut. In our small apartment in Brooklyn. When we all shared one bedroom and mom kept her heels on top of the kitchen cupboards. Once we moved out of there everything got complicated.

The first weekend we left that small Brooklyn apartment and moved into a new place, something interesting happened. It was something that reminded me of this situation of seeing Skye's mom...

For the first time I had my own room and my parents made sure that it was all set up before we moved into the new place. But on that first night, I still wanted to spend the night in their room. So I slept on the floor on the new carpeting that was just installed.

I remember waking up that first morning feeling heavy in the head. Like I had a stuffy nose, but I wasn't sniffling. I remember my thoughts being very loud. Almost like someone else was in the room yelling at me. My parents were unloading boxes in the living room and I began to help them, but my head felt so loud, I just went back to sleep.

I woke up feeling worse from bad dreams that seemed as real as Elsie. I was confused about what was real and what was in my head. I was hearing voices. My parents took me to the doctor who determined I was home sick, so my parents decided I would have a sleepover at my cousin's house for a couple nights while they finished setting up the new place. I was comfortable in their house because I've slept there before. It did help me feel better. But when I went back into our new home I felt that heaviness and yelling in my head again.

My parents took me to a different doctor who said it was the carpet. I was breathing in the chemicals from the new carpet, which were causing me to hear things that weren't there. It was why my head felt so heavy. It was why I was confused about what was real.

"How can we be certain it's the carpet and not something else in the apartment?" My mom asked the doctor.

"I'm almost certain it is the carpet, but even if it wasn't, he needs to leave the place that's causing the hallucinations."

It was summer, so it worked out that I went away for two weeks for a baseball camp. By the time I got back, the carpet was taken out and there were two air purifiers in my bedroom. My parents insisted I sleep in there from then on. No more sleeping on the floor in their bedroom. After that, everything just seemed to go back to normal. The days where I heard voices only felt like a dream.

Even though the carpet was gone and I never heard things in my head again, we still moved out of that place pretty quickly. I left the memory of those hallucinations at the apartment we never visited or ever really talked about again. I never thought about those voices until I realized that I might be hallucinating again. I looked around the hostel room. It had no carpet. None of the furniture was new. It's all been there. Aired out. I even changed rooms at one point. So what could I blame this on?

I laid on the bed in a daze. It felt like some sort of dream sequence that I couldn't make sense of. I attempted to play back all the moments I spent on the beach with Elsie. Over and over and over again. When I fell asleep I knew, none of it was a dream, it was all real. I just didn't know what real meant anymore.

Chapter 29: First Day of Work

She cuddled up against my back, which scared me at first because I didn't know who it was, or *where* I was. *Did Ana the drunk girl after karaoke wander into my bed again?*

It was when I inhaled that I realized whose smell nuzzled up on my neck. I turned to face her, under the covers, and wrapped my arms tightly around her.

"Good morning." I heard Skye whisper.

"Hey." I opened my eyes. My body felt achy. "How'd you get in here?"

"Well, you left your key down at the beach. Coco found it and I recognized it was yours."

"Yeah, I had a little trouble getting into my room without that last night."

"How are you feeling?"

My body still felt the rollercoaster of emotions that started the night before.

"I don't know. Not good."

"Still? What's wrong?"

I took a deep breath. "I think I'm going crazy."

Skye laughed. "Fish tacos don't make you go crazy." She shifted her body so her head rested on my chest and looked up at me. "What do you mean, *you're going crazy?*"

"You wouldn't believe me if I told you."

"Try me."

"No."

Skye moved her hands under the covers and started tickling me. I pushed her away. She sat up and looked at me.

"Do you want to go to the beach?"

"No." I sighed.

"To the cave?"

"No."

"Well, you need to eat something at least. Let's go to Burgeroo."

Then suddenly I realized. "I gotta go to work my first shift today at HideAway!"

"Do you want me to tell Marcos you are not up for it? I can cover you if you want."

I thought about what I wanted. "No, I should go in. It might help."

"Help what? What is wrong with you in the first place?"

"I just feel off."

"You don't know why?"

Of course I did, but I told her no anyway.

"Well, go get ready then." Skye pushed me up and toward the bathroom, then she got comfy in the cozy bed I just forfeited.

I stumbled into the shower trying to process the previous night, but yet again there was nothing I could make sense of. Was it something I could just ignore? Trying to force answers out of thin air was causing my head to spin all over again. I decided I would try to forget it all. Pretend that night didn't happen. This way everything could feel calmer again.

Running away had worked this far…

I finished my shower and went to my duffel to get dressed.

"Budd said you two went surfing a couple days ago and you seemed off. Have you felt off for a while?" Skye asked still laying in my bed.

"No." I pulled a shirt out of my bag. "What does he mean, I was off?"

"He said you weren't yourself."

I was kind of annoyed Budd said that.

"I'm fine." I put my shirt on. "To be honest, I think he has a crush on you."

Skye shot a sharp look at me. "Budd is like my brother."

"But he's not your brother. And he has a crush on you. It's obvious."

She sat up. "When did you become so jealous?"

"I'm not jealous of him." Which was a lie. "I'm just telling you what I see."

"And there's plenty that you don't see." Skye stated firmly as she stood up.

I leaned down to put my sneakers on in order to break away from Skye's stormy eyes that shot lightning at me. Obviously she was aggravated.

"Do you want to come by HideAway to eat?" I asked to change the topic.

We walked toward the door.

"I think I'm going to just head home to get my board to surf."

"You gotta eat something." I reminded her.

"I have vegemite and toast in the pantry."

We walked outside to discover it was raining. Skye continued walking unfazed.

"You're going to surf in the rain?"

"Absolutely. It makes it even better. Plus I'm a pluviophile."

"A lover of...?"

"Rain." She opened her arms as the rain soaked her face, hair, and clothes.

Just the sight of Skye *soaked* raced my heart so fast that I couldn't speak for the entirety of the way.

We walked together in silence until we had to turn in different directions.

"I'll see you." Skye said. Then quickly kissed me. I wanted it to last longer, but she moved away so fast.

"Have a good surf." I said as she walked away.

I wondered what Marcos was going to say when I showed up soaking wet and late. I hoped he would still let me work so that I didn't walk all that way in the rain for no reason. When I walked inside I saw Kelsey behind the counter.

"Hey, Lucas! I heard it's your first day." She said enthusiastically.

"Yeah." I said standing in place because I didn't want to soak the whole floor. "Do you think there's a towel I could use to dry off?"

"Gimme a sec." Kelsey ran to the back. I felt awkward standing there sopping wet. I waited for her to return, as I inhaled the smell of fresh brewed coffee beans, fresh baked pie, and *something* slightly burning. Kelsey returned with a towel and a T shirt in her hand. "Dry off and put on that shirt. I'll tell Marcos you're here."

"Thanks."

There were a couple customers at the tables, so I went back outside to the porch to change. I wrung out my shirt and hung it on a hook away from the rain. I dried off and put on the white T that Kelsey gave me. It said HideAway on the back and had a wave behind the text. Somehow a simple T shirt lifted my spirits, even if just a little. My shorts and sneakers were still soaked, but at least half of me was dry. When I walked back inside Marcos was there with a big smile on his face.

"Hey Lucas! You look like you work here already." He waved me to come behind the counter. "Let me show you a few things in the back and then Kelsey will help you work the front."

He led me through the doors of the kitchen. He didn't seem upset about my tardiness, which was a relief.

"This is Bolivar. We call him Boli. He's three people in one and makes all the delicious food." Boli was short and plump with a bright white smile that contrasted his skin. His hands were kneading dough.

"I keep telling Marcos that my paycheck should be multiplied by three because of that, but I'm still waiting."

"You are an amazing chef." I said basically bowing down.

"Thank you. What did I make you?"

"Uhh… close to everything on the menu. I come here a lot."

"Well, welcome to the team. Don't slack off."

Marcos introduced me to the rest of the kitchen staff and showed me where they kept different supplies. I got a tour of the walk-in freezer and the basement.

"If there's something you forget, just ask someone." Marcos assured. "Now go to the front and check in with Kelsey. I have to run home to my wife and the baby. He's sick and not sleeping… anyway, you got this Lucas!"

When I returned to the front more customers had arrived, including Coco and Jade. I was kind of nervous seeing them at first because I didn't want them to ask why I missed the Memorial the night before.

"Do you want to pick a table to serve or do you want to run the food to all the tables?" Kelsey asked me.

I liked talking to the customers last time. I definitely wanted to do that again. It would help me get my mind off of things.

"I'll grab tables. Did you get that table over there yet?" I asked her, motioning at Coco and Jade.

"Nope. All yours." Kelsey smiled walking over to the booth in the corner.

"Hey, Lucas! Are you working here now?" Coco asked as I walked over to them.

"Yeah. You're actually my first official customer." I added the word official because technically I helped Skye wait tables before.

"Oh really? We'll try to be as difficult as possible then." Jade joked. I thought.

"Do you have vegan chicken?" She asked.

"Aaa… I'll have to check on that."

"What about walnuts?" Coco asked. *Walnuts?*

I didn't know if HideAway had walnuts either. I looked at both of their faces as they wore smiles that held back laughter.

"Are you just messing with me?"

"Yeah." Coco laughed. "I don't want walnuts… and Jade isn't even a vegan."

"Vegan chicken is good though. But we don't have it here, just so you know." Jade added.

"Thanks for the heads-up."

"I'll have the steak quesadillas."

I took out the notepad and began writing.

"I'm going to have a BBQ Chicken wrap and an apple juice." Coco ordered.

"Ooo me too!" Jade's eyes lit up.

"You also want an apple juice?" I asked.

"Yeah and the BBQ Chicken wrap."

"So, no more quesadillas?" I wasn't sure.

"No, I'll still take those."

"Are you sure?" Jade was about 5'3" with a small waist. I couldn't see where she was going to put all that food.

"She'll surprise you, mate. We just surfed all morning. She always eats double after a gnarly surf."

Jade leaned back proud that her boyfriend knew she could and would eat both meals.

"How was it out there?"

"Awesome." Jade replied.

"Yeah. Jade was shredding her cutbacks." Coco smiled at her.

"Did you see Skye out there?" I asked. I was just with her and she was already back on my mind.

"She was just about to paddle out when we got back in. The rain just started. We wish we could have stayed but you don't want to get in Jade's way when she's hungry.

"Let me put those orders in for you then."

I walked away already feeling kind of exhausted. The shift had just started. I was just happy that they never brought up the Memorial, at all. Maybe Skye told them. But told them what?

The rest of the shift went by pretty quickly. Kelsey said I didn't need to stay until close, which I was glad because my legs were already sore from being on my feet all day. I don't know how Skye can do double shifts.

I left HideAway and wanted to find Skye. She was on my mind all day. Like when someone would order a coffee, especially a caramel macchiato. When the cups needed stacking, or even when they didn't. Even when someone would let the door slam, she hated when it'd do that.

I felt bad with how we left off the conversation when I told her that Budd liked her. I didn't think she'd get so upset about it. I honestly thought she could tell that Budd was into her.

The rain had stopped. I walked down to the beach, without even thinking... There were a lot of people out on the water. I squinted to see the surfers in the distance.

"Hey." I heard from behind me.

When I turned around, there she was. Elsie. *Again.* Standing right in front of me.

I rubbed my eyes. She was still there. I looked at her closer, as if expecting to see right through her or something.

"Why do you look so freaked out?"

"Because. You're not real. This cannot be. I should not be able to see you." I backed away quickly.

"Did I do something wrong?"

I just need to ignore her. She's not there. I said out-loud to myself.

"Yes I am. I'm right here. Lucas, are you alright?"

I ignored her and contemplated to myself.

I need to ask someone else if they can see her.

"Excuse me! Excuse me!" I yelled to the closest group of people I could see. They were about fifty feet away. I took a couple steps into their direction and used my hands to project my voice. Two people turned to me.

"Could you come over here please? I called.

They pointed at themselves to confirm I was talking to them.

"Yes!" I nodded my head. They didn't move.

"Am I standing here with someone?" I called as I turned to look at Elsie. She was gone.

"What?" The people moved closer to me.

"Was I standing here with someone just before?" I asked.

"I don't know, mate. You just called us over now."

"Was there anyone with me?"

The guys looked at each other confused. "No one is with you."

"I know, but *was* anyone with me?"

The guys looked even more confused.

"No, mate."

I stood there embarrassed. I just made myself look like a complete idiot.

Chapter 30: Hot in the Freezer

I was so thrown off after seeing Elsie again on the beach that I just headed back to Neptune's without looking for Skye anymore. I dragged my feet the whole walk back. *What was happening to me?*

I was happy to share a shift with Skye the next day. When I walked in, she was already there sipping on her usual: quad shot soy upside-down caramel macchiato iced with two straws.

"Hey." She said in between slurps.

"Hey." I walked behind the counter toward her. Skye was making a latte for a customer sitting at the counter.

I wasn't sure of how I was supposed to greet her *at work*. So that was it. *Hey*. Did that mean she was still mad at me, or is she treating me like a co-worker because we're at work...? I comforted myself by deciding it was the latter.

It was pretty calm at the cafe that day. But Skye kept us *busy* anyway. When there were no customers, she'd show me how to refill condiment dispensers. It was kind of gross seeing a *ten pound bucket* of mayo. I wasn't good at aiming into the dispensers with the spoon so it got all over my hands. I don't think I'll ever order mayo again.

"Boli, keep an eye on the front. I'm going to show Lucas how to set up the bread for tomorrow. We're running low."

"Alright. I'll holler if someone comes in."

Skye led me down to the end of the hallway and into the walk-in freezer. Marcos showed it to me the day before, but we didn't go *in*. Skye walked inside the ice box and turned to me. "Close the door behind you. We don't want to let the cold out."

"But won't that lock us in?"

"You think the designers of a walk-in freezer made it automatically lock people on the inside?"

I shrugged my shoulders. "Better safe than sorry."

I shut the door. It was heavy. The cool air felt good. Skye's hand grabbing mine felt even better.

She looked at me with the eyes that gave me both comfort and nervousness in the same glance. I wanted to kiss her, but we were at work.

No one can see...

I leaned my chin down and brought my lips toward hers. I could see her breath in the cold as she exhaled. She kissed, bit, and sucked my bottom lip all in one swift motion. I leaned toward her wanting more, then she turned.

"The dough is already kneaded and made into rolls. Boli did that this morning. We just have to get the tray ready for the oven, so whoever opens in the morning tomorrow can just pop them in and turn it on."

I nearly fell over from that kiss while Skye decided it was the right time to give directions about bread preparation.

I nodded my head. I tried to play it cool like Skye, but after a kiss like *that*, I was sweating. Even in a freezer.

"Grab this tray." She directed passing it to me. "And this one in your other hand." I took both trays. They weren't heavy, just big and bulky. I made sure not to drop them.

"Bring them to the counter next to the oven."

I carried the trays while reaching to open the door with my foot.

"Oh, and one more thing." Skye said from behind me. But I didn't think I could carry anything else.

I turned around and she placed another kiss on my lips, almost as electrocuting as the first. I balanced the trays while leaning into Skye's trance.

"Skye!" I heard Boli call. "You got customers up front!"

I jumped when I heard him call, but Skye drew me back in for the kiss, as if Boli, the customers, and *time itself* could wait. I was still awkwardly balancing trays of dough. It was almost like Skye was *trying* to get me to drop them. When she pulled away, she brushed her thumb over my lip.

"What are you trying to get me in trouble?" She said, winking.

We walked out of the freezer and put the trays down on the counter, then Skye rushed to the customers in front.

I was trailing behind her with my head down, making it as obvious as I could that we were just up to something.

"Lucas," I heard Boli call from behind me.

Oh no… he knows… we're both going to lose our jobs… Skye needs this job… She LOVES this job…

I turned around guilty as can be.

"Can you take this rubbish to the dumpster out back?" Boli asked. I exhaled in relief. "Sure."

I carried the garbage out and looked down at the beach that was not too far away. Even though I promised myself to *stay off of the beach*, I would still tempt myself by looking down to see if I saw Elsie anywhere. It's like my curiosity, not my sense of reason, controlled my steps because I walked over to take a peek at the rocks. I knew I should get back to work, but the beach was so close. Peeking would only take a minute.

I didn't see Elsie anywhere… *thankfully*, but I did see Budd leaning over someone who was pressed against a tree. Both their shirts were off and they were kissing. I looked closer. He was kissing Zane. *Budd and Zane? I thought Budd liked Skye…*

I walked back to HideAway before giving them the chance to see me. I began cleaning the counter while Skye prepared a latte.

"Is Zane seeing anyone?" I asked Skye.

"Yeah." She replied, looking up from the espresso machine. "Why?"

I didn't know how to explain why I wanted to know. "I'm just curious." I lined up some mugs on the shelf. "Who…?" I dug further.

Skye narrowed her eyes at me. "What did you see?" Skye said like she read my mind.

"Zane and Budd kissing."

"So…? Do you really need me to answer then?"

I shrugged. "So, Budd is with Zane?"

"Yeah, they've been together for almost two years. Since we graduated school. He practically lives at the guys' place."

The order bell rang. Boli had plates ready.

"Why didn't you tell me that before?"

I loaded a tray with the orders that just came through the window while Skye poured the latte into a mug.

"You mean, when you accused him of having a crush on me?"

I nodded my head in embarrassment.

Skye put the mug on my tray. "Whether Budd is in a relationship or not, our relationship is platonic. Stop being so *paranoid.*"

We left HideAway after our shift was over. I stayed to the end to help Skye close.

"So, since I have a job now," I said to Skye, "does that make me a local?"

Skye rolled her eyes. "You got a long way to go to be a local."

"What if I order sweet potato fries *all week.* Then am I a local?"

Skye laughed at me.

I *love* it when she laughs at me.

"By the way, we both have off the next two days. HideAway is closed because Marcos has to repair something with the plumbing, so the water will be shut off. So I was thinking... we should go camping."

"Where?"

"The outback."

That sounded perfect. Spending time with Skye. And it would keep me away from the beach.

"How would we get there?" I remembered Budd telling me how Skye used to hitchhike.

"I'm sure Kenny could let me borrow his car."

I smiled big and couldn't help it.

You're perfect. I thought.

"That's perfect." I actually said.

It's like Skye could read my mind that I really wanted to get away.

"Let's go to my house and pack some gear. We'll grab your stuff at Neptune's when the car is all packed.

"Oh, you mean right now?"

"Yeah. Why? You busy?" She put her hands on her hips.

"Yeah, I already planned to spend the rest of the day with you." Her glare morphed into a smile.

And then she read my mind again and kissed me.

Skye sent a text to Kenny as we picked up a bag of ice on our walk back to her place.

"He said we could use the car. And that he's at the house so we'll talk about it there."

I suddenly felt nervous to talk to Kenny about going to the outback with Skye, even though I've talked to him so many times before and he was super chill. Did he know it would just be the two of us?

When we got to their house, Kenny already had some gear laid out on the porch. A tent, sleeping bags, a lantern, and cooler were sitting in a pile.

"Thanks for pulling it all out." Skye thanked Kenny as we walked inside.

"Yep. Where are you planning on going?"

"The outback."

"Well, yeah. That spans over six million square kilometers. Which campground?"

"I have a spot." She said as she sifted through the fridge.

"You should stay on a campground. Not just in the middle of *nowhere.*"

"Everywhere is nowhere out there."

Kenny had arms crossed. "Skye, I'd like to know where you are."

"I'll have my phone." She threw some things into the cooler followed by the bag of ice we carried home.

"Yeah, but with no signal."

"Good." Skye said sharply.

"So how will I know where you'll be?"

"I'll be back on Tuesday."

"Skye…" Kenny groaned. Besides the day of the Memorial when Skye went missing, I've never seen Kenny in parent-mode.

"Kenny, I'm not a little kid anymore. You have to give me space."

"You turned 20 two months ago, but I still worry Skye."

"We'll be fine. Lucas was a Boy Scout back in the States. He won the medal for building a fire the quickest." Skye blurted out.

I did?

"Oh yeah, you like to go camping, Lucas?" Kenny asked.

I wasn't ever a Boy Scout and I've only been camping twice. But Kenny asked if I *liked* camping and while it sucked sleeping on the floor with bugs, I did like my two camping experiences.

"Yeah, it's great." I said. I could tell Skye was just trying to change the topic, but I didn't want Kenny starting to ask me about my *memories from the Boy Scouts* which didn't exist. So instead I changed the topic again.

"What should I expect camping in the outback?" I asked him.

"It'll be hot when you wake up, but not as hot as in the summer months. Lots of dry desert, tons of stars, kangaroos..."

"Kangaroos! Really?!" I exclaimed.

"You haven't seen a kangaroo yet?" Kenny asked in disbelief.

"Only on his burger." Skye added. Which for a moment made me a little guilty, but only for a moment. What makes eating chicken more acceptable than a kangaroo? It's all what your culture gets you used to.

"There haven't been any kangaroos on the beach..." I joked.

"Well, then Skye definitely has to take you to the outback. Just don't go too far off the road."

Off the road?

"Distance is perception." Skye stated, making Kenny roll his eyes.

"I trust you to be safe." Kenny said with a stern face.

What did he think could happen?

What was going to happen?

We were on the road quickly. When Skye had a plan, she was full speed ahead in executing it. After about an hour of driving, I lowered the radio.

"Where are we going?"

"You know my rule about adventures and questions." Skye said. I managed to avoid any question asking for quite some time, but hoped we would arrive soon because the sun had already set and it was only getting darker and darker.

"Is it far?"

Skye kept her eyes straight on the road and didn't answer.

"Are you kidnapping me?"

"I believe *the victim* would need to show resistance in order to be considered a kidnapping."

"I thought you weren't answering questions." I grinned.

"Clever." She said in a monotone, but then broke a smile.

"You know, I'm glad you finally figured out Budd and Zane on your own."

"What do you mean, *finally?*"

"Well, it took you weeks of paranoia to realize what I was saying had been true all along: Budd does not have a crush on me."

"Just because he's dating Zane doesn't make him immune to your beauty and charm."

"Ha! You won't give it up! He's gay, Lucas. He's known that since he was twelve. Whatever… I wonder who's more jealous, you or Budd."

"What do you mean?"

"Budd gets pretty jealous of you too."

"Because he likes you!"

"No, because Zane likes you!"

"Zane doesn't…"

"Zane doesn't really curb his thoughts… Budd overheard Zane say to me *'kiss him for the both of us,'* which was a joke, but Budd didn't find it very funny."

"So he got mad because of me?"

"It was more jealousy than anger. Which is funny because when you and I are together, you act jealous of Budd."

"Well... you two get really close sometimes."

"Because we are really close. He's my best friend."

I shrugged. I knew it was an argument I would not win. Skye was correct that I was jealous, but who determines what is too close for a *friendship*? Even Zane mentioned he felt jealous of Skye sometimes. Or was he joking? I don't know... but jealousy is a powerful emotion that really has the potential to fuck up a good thing. But trust should have the ability to overpower it. Right?

Suddenly Skye cut the wheel to the left and we were driving off the road and onto the dirt.

"Woah! What are you doing?!"

"Finding our campsite."

"How can you see anything?!"

"The car has lights, stop freaking out. It's called off-roading, city-boy." Skye said nonchalantly.

Skye always took the road less traveled... actually there usually wasn't even a road at all, I thought, thinking back to the way to the cave. Skye really went out of her way to find an adventure. And even with all my questions, nervousness, and skepticism, I was glad that she took me along.

Chapter 31: The Outback

Setting up camp took no more than three minutes. Skye had a tent that popped up before I could even attempt assisting her. She said it would be a clear night and we didn't have to worry about rain. We didn't put the rainfly on the tent which was perfect because we could see a zillion stars all around us.

"Grab the lighter on the dashboard." Skye told me.

"Are we going to make a fire?" I asked, sighting firewood in the trunk of the car.

"Tomorrow."

"What do you need the lighter for?" I asked tossing it to her.

Although it was already getting dark, she caught it effortlessly. Then, pulled a joint from her ear and lit it up.

"Why do you smoke those things?"

Skye exhaled a huge puff of smoke into the darkening night. "It depends. Sometimes for stress. To ease my anxiety. Sometimes for allergies. Sometimes to help me sleep."

"But right now, are you stressed?"

"No."

"Well, you don't seem to have any allergies and I don't think you want to go to sleep just yet."

"You're right. Right now it's more to open up my mind. The same way it eases my anxiety, weed eases my mind and opens it up. I see the stars with more detail and can envision these alternate universes that might exist out in space. Thinking about how vast the universe is makes my problems seem a lot less… significant." She took another hit.

"Do you want some?" She asked.

I shrugged. "I've never smoked before. What if I don't like it?"

"You don't have to. It's not for everyone. That's for sure."

"Yeah.. I mean, I've heard of people freaking out or passing out or dying."

Skye laughed as she inhaled. "First of all, nobody *dies* from smoking weed. Or ingesting it at all for that matter."

Exhale. "If anything they'll fall asleep and wake up groggy if they have too much THC." Skye ashed. "See, it's all about your environment. Where you are. Who you're with. Your mindset. If you're not comfortable, it won't be good."

Inhale. "Are you comfortable?" Skye asked.

"Yes."

"Good." Exhale. "Stay comfortable. Let's get more comfortable." Skye walked over to the car and pulled pillows and sleeping bags out of the backseat.

"Help me bring these into the tent." Skye directed.

I placed the pillow inside the small two-person tent.

"Could I try it?" I asked her.

"I don't know, you seem pretty hesitant. I don't want you *freaking out* on me like down at the beach."

Don't remind me. I thought.

"But those were edibles, which are *much* stronger. That's a whole body high. I *still* can't believe that Zane gave you that shit without *warning* you first." Skye shook her head.

"I think this is a better environment. Just you, me, and the stars." I pointed out.

Skye shrugged and passed me the joint.

I put it to my lips.

I inhaled.

She walked away

Where are you going?

and opened the car door.

I started coughing. Hard.

My throat was on fire.

Then I felt her slip a bottle of water into my hand. "You'll want this."

Skye was always predicting the future.

I chugged the water, then took another hit.

Slower.

I passed it back to Skye. She did smoke tricks effortlessly as I watched her, mesmerized.

She took one last hit, then leaned in to kiss me.

With her lips against me, she passed the smoke from her mouth into mine.

After that hit I was on cloud nine. A happy place. Where I couldn't stop smiling and giggling.

"Come on," Skye took my hand. "Let's lay and watch the stars."

Skye was in astrophile heaven. She led the way into the tent.

"Thanks for bringing all this gear." I followed her, collapsing on one of the pillows face-down.

"Are you tired from that strenuous set-up?" Skye teased.

"No, but I am from following your orders at HideAway." I said with a pretend grumpy face.

Skye kissed my grumpy lips and turned them into a smile.

"Have you even looked up yet?" She said into my ear.

I turned onto my back to view the sky with endless stars, glistening gloriously.

"Incredible." I laid back, astonished.

"Are there more stars in the universe or grains of sand in the sea?" Skye asked.

I contemplated her question as I tried to estimate the amount of stars twinkling in the darkness. Then I thought of all the beaches and even more than the beaches, *all the sand at the bottom of the ocean. After all, the earth was like 70% water, so that was a lot of sand. But the universe is an even more massive, stretching lightyears... How big was a lightyear anyway? Must be pretty massive. The earth is only a spec in the universe...*

"Stars in the universe." I declared.

"I agree." Skye said as she moved her head to use my stomach as her pillow.

"I can't believe you couldn't stargaze as a kid. That's even worse than not surfing as a kid." Skye said, keeping her trance up to the stars. "You're losing points here."

"Losing?" I challenged. "I'm doing them now aren't I? I should be *gaining* points."

"Yeah, you're lucky I saved you from a star-less and surf-less life."

"Lucky." I repeated. I hadn't heard someone say *Lucky* around me in a while.

"Yeah... lucky."

There was a silence that we filled with stars as our hands linked together. Fitting perfectly.

"My parents used to call me Lucky." I told her.

"Really?"

"Yeah. It was like a nickname."

Skye's thumb was tracing circles in the palm of my hand.

"Lucas, what were your parents like?"

"My parents?" Her question took my by surprise. "Why?"

"Well all I know is what you've told me... about the crash. But what were they *like*?"

"Incredible." My mind drifted to some of my happiest memories of them. "Kind, loving, thoughtful, hardworking… real life superheroes." I smiled at the thought of them.

"Mom was really good at arts and crafts. The first apartment we lived in was really small.

"Every month, we would decorate the living room with different themes. Mom always had the most creative ideas and knew exactly how to use recycled things from around the house to transform that room into a whole new place. It was a family project on Sundays when we lived there. We had a pirate theme and a baseball theme. We did an underwater theme where we made paper-mache fish and hung them from the ceiling! That was when my dad brought home our first pet fish."

"What was his name?"

"That fish was named Poseidon. You know, *God of the Sea.* Then there was Billie Jean- my dad loved Michael Jackson. Billie Jean came on the radio in the car when we were trying to figure out the name." I could feel Skye giggling against me.

"The most recent fish is Sushi." I missed Sushi… who was now staying with a neighbor.

"Your fish is named Sushi?" Skye laughed.

"Yeah."

"Did you ever eat sushi around him?"

"Yeah, we did." I laughed. "But he never said he minded."

We laughed even harder. We couldn't stop shaking in hysteria.

"What was your dad like?" Skye asked.

"He was always challenging me. Making sure I stayed persistent in anything and everything that was important to me. We would play baseball together. He played through college. Actually, he met my mom at a baseball game."

"That's sweet. Would you all play together?"

I nodded my head in delight. These memories felt good to recollect.

"We'd go to the park, my mom would pitch to me, and my dad would go deep in the outfield. I'd hit for hours. Mom would pack a whole cooler of drinks and snacks."

"That's amazing." Skye marveled.

"It was. I never really realized how special those family practices were. I can't get out of my head how we'll never share that together again…" My tone drifted to sadness.

"It sounds like you had an outstanding childhood." Skye said sincerely as she tightened her hand in mine.

I did. I truly did. It occurred to me that Skye didn't have parents *or* a good childhood. She dealt with the grief of her mother at such a young age then was passed from foster home to foster home until Kenny could get custody. I couldn't even imagine that type of pain as a child. In that moment I understood why my parents called me Lucky for all those years. I had everything I could need with heaping portions of my parents' love. I was beyond fortunate…

I pulled Skye closer and she wrapped her arms around me. I saw her glossy eyes look away from me, hoping I wouldn't see her tears. But there was nothing she should have to hide. I kissed her cheek right where a tear was falling.

"You know you consume too much caffeine when your tears start tasting like coffee."

Skye pulled away and wiped her eyes. "Seriously?"

"No, but it made you smile."

"You always make me smile, Lucas." Her raincloud eyes looked at me, thankful.

"Because I love your smile." I kissed her.

"And your laugh." I kissed her again.

"And your mind." I grazed my hand along the side of her head, pushing her hair back slightly, letting the moonlight illuminate her face.

"And these lips…" I kissed Skye extra long.

"I even love your craziness." I kissed her nose.

"Normal is completely overrated. And boring."

I nodded. "You make things that use to hurt, feel… good."

I kissed her again. "I haven't been able to talk about my parents and feel… happy… in so long."

"That's good. You should remember them and feel happy."

"You're right."

"You know, we still haven't seen a shooting star tonight." Skye said as she laid back down on my stomach.

"Hmm… that's true. We can't fall asleep until we see a shooting star." I declared.

"Did you know that even the stars that die keep glowing? They don't need to be alive to shine."

I shook my head. Skye taught more facts than I could keep track of.

"In the meantime, do you want to learn some constellations?"

"Yeah." I said taking advantage that Skye was basically like an astronomer.

"So, starting with the basics. That's the big dipper, and then over there is the little dipper." Skye was pointing up.

"How am I supposed to know what you're even pointing at?"

"The dippers!" She exclaimed. We both erupted into laughter.

"Okay look." She got closer to me so that her perspective matched mine and pointed up again. "Look at those stars in the row, beginning with that *really* bright one right over there."

I saw what she was referring to, but suddenly became far more focused on how Skye was so close to me, in a pitch black tent, with not a soul for probably a hundred miles. I inhaled her scent and tried to keep my cool. She showed me Jupiter, which I didn't even know could be seen from earth with the naked eye.

Skye was so knowledgeable about stars, planets, and constellations. She's absolutely brilliant.

In the middle of tracing the stars that made up the Milky Way, a massive shooting star jetted across the sky like a firework exploding from outer space.

"Woahhhh!" We both exclaimed in unison.

Skye's arms wrapped around me tighter as I made a wish.

"That one was amazing." She awed.

"*All of this* is amazing, Skye. You. These stars. This moment. *Everything.*"

She buried her face in my neck and started kissing me, moving up to my cheek and nibbling on my ear. She sent a surge through my entire body. I held her as close as I could, imagining how to possibly get even closer.

Skye moved on top of me, kissing me deeply. I wrapped my arms around her waist, letting her skin warm my body against the cool night breeze. She took off my shirt and I took off hers, breathing intensely, quickly heating up the small tent. I traced her bra with my fingertips letting temptation get the best of me. With Skye, I felt strong and powerless at the same time. She made my heart race faster than the speed of a falling star...

and it felt as if stars were falling *all night*, until we drifted asleep in each other's arms.

I woke to her kisses on my chest under the sunrise as the outback breeze turned from cool to warm. Our skin pressed against each other, tangled legs replacing blankets.

"Good morning." She whispered when my face couldn't help but smile.

I kissed her forehead. "Good morning, beautiful."

Skye's eyes were like high tide as they looked up at me and pulled me under her swell's spell.

"How'd you sleep?" I asked.

"Like a koala." Skye snuggled deeper into my arms.

"Thanks for taking me out here. It's so good to *get away.* "

"Thank you for reminding me that I needed to come out here. It's been *too* long."

"By the way, I hope you don't think I'm a champion fire starter from the Boy Scouts, or whatever you told Kenny."

"Yes you are. I saw that fire you made for Zane's birthday Bondfire."

"*That's* where you got that idea?" I laughed.

"Starting fires won't be a problem. I just said that to make Kenny quit questioning me."

I knew it.

"Besides, I'm a pro fire-starter."

"Let me guess, a pyrophile?"

"No, a pyromaniac." She corrected.

"I actually knew that! But all your suffixes got me thrown off!"

Skye sat up. "Although, I'd love to sleep 20 hours like a koala, we need to meet the other marsupials out there. We should get going to be back before the hottest part of the day." She unzipped the tent. "I brought bread and vegemite for brekkie."

Eh. I thought.

"But I brought you peanut butter because you Americans go bonzer for peanut butter."

I smiled big. I did love peanut butter.

We packed a bag of power bars, water, and a boomerang.

I inspected the boomerang with eagerness to throw it as hard as I could into the flat, empty outback.

"Slow down… don't just throw it with all your might, unless you're looking to play fetch with yourself."

I scrutinized the boomerang as if it was going to start dictating directions. Skye took it from my hands.

"This is the handle where you hold it. You have to throw it at *this* angle." Skye began to demonstrate the angle of a proper throw.

"What if I was a lefty?"

"Well, then you'd need a different boomerang because this one is to be held with the right hand."

Skye handed it back to me. I gripped it in my hand just like she showed me then slow motion mimicked a throw without letting go.

"Like this?"

"Yeah, but open up your body. I thought you said you were a baseball player."

Skye's comment dropped me back into a pitcher's pose, like I was ready to strikeout a homer hitter. I gave a wind-up and released. The boomerang somersaulted through the air cutting first to the right then changing direction and dipping left, until finally it began speeding its way back to our direction. I realized that unlike baseball, the person who throws it, must also get ready to catch it. I hustled forward a bit to intercept where it was landing. I couldn't let it drop if I wanted to impress Skye. Like I was charging at a popup in center field I snatched the boomerang, then ran it back to Skye.

"Pretty good, but let me show you how it's *really* done." Skye took the boomerang from my hand.

She whipped it in the same direction as my throw, except her's arched much higher and moved *much* faster. It came speeding back in our direction and Skye didn't even have to take a step. She just lifted her arm up into the air until it landed right back into her hand like magnets colliding.

Woah. Just when I thought Skye couldn't get any more attractive, she reveals that she has a killer arm.

"That was incredible. You sure you haven't ever played baseball or softball?"

She shook her head. Skye already told me in the car that she never even touched a baseball in her life.

"Can you have a catch with this thing?" I asked, reaching for the boomerang, grazing Skye's hand.

"I guess a catch standing next to each other, but it's kind of a one person game."

"How about I'll catch your throws, and you'll catch mine."

"So I have to run all around the desert and you get to stand in one place?" Skye smiled with her hands on her hips.

"Hey, that was only my first try. I'll get the hang of it! Watch." I took the boomerang and aimed higher, trying to mimic Skye's technique. It took flight and made its expected turns, but then came back at us really high. Skye dropped her stance, like an outfielder moving back for a big hit. She tracked the throw and caught it about ten feet behind me.

I didn't expect her to toss the boomerang immediately. She sailed it right past my head. I turned around to follow its glide. I expected it would hover back to Skye, so I took a couple steps toward her.

"Stay there." She directed. The boomerang went directly to the spot I was standing in.

I looked back at her and smiled. Skye knew she was good.

Skye returned to standing at my side. "First your throw was too shallow, then too far, so now put it in the middle."

I wound up again and knew from how the release felt that it was a good one. It soared and tumbled and returned back to us, right into Skye's hand. She didn't even have to take a step.

"There you go!" Skye was excited *for me.*

"These things move fast."

"Well, it was a method of hunting for the Aboriginals."

"The what?"

Skye looked at me in disgust. "*Of course,* you don't know who the Aboriginal people are. The Americas have Native Americans and here in Australia we have the Aboriginals."

"Oh, I didn't know that."

"Your ethnocentricity is showing."

My what? I thought, but I didn't ask.

We tossed and walked as Skye led the way into a seemingly arbitrary direction. There was nothing all around us for as far as my eye could see, except the occasional boomerang cutting across the sky.

"What if we get lost?" I said, following behind her.

"Here come the questions!" Skye announced to the desert.

"You let me ask questions before."

"That's because you were *learning* something. You need questions to learn. *This* is an adventure. And you know I don't like when you try to spoil the adventure."

"I'm just being cautious."

"You? Nooo." She said sarcastically, rolling her eyes and smiling. "Don't you trust me?"

"You almost made me drown!" I exclaimed.

"Almost, but didn't. Plus there's no way you can drown out here, so don't worry."

"Yeah, because there's no water! That's also a worry. How hot is it going to get?"

"We have plenty of water." Skye assured.

"How hot is it going to get?" I asked again.

"That's a question."

"Yes, because you never give answers!" I said kind of annoyed. The desert could get really dangerous. "How hot is it going to get?"

Skye stopped in front of me and turned around, putting her face *really* close to mine. "It depends on how hot you want it to get." She said just *centimeters* from my face in the *sexiest* voice, leaving me speechless.

She turned on her toes and kept walking.

"There's a big tree I usually hike down to about two miles northwest of here. It's a good spot for a snack and spotting kangaroos." She informed, slowing her pace.

"Okay."

"Just trust me, Lucas." Skye grabbed my hand and looked up at me. Her eyes had a way of saying when she wanted to kiss me.

So I leaned down and kissed her lips.

"I'm sorry I'm so paranoid."

"Just be cool..." She said squirting the water bottle into my face.

We walked, watching the sun move higher and higher up into the sky.

"You know, I was surprised how openly I was able to talk about my parents last night."

"I think the weed helped you chill out to be honest. It was cute seeing you all giggly and loose."

"I wasn't that giggly!"

"I had to revive you with CPR multiple times, that's how hard you were laughing."

"If you always give *CPR* like you did last night, expect me to start choking on thin air…" I began grabbing my throat and coughing, pretending to fall to the ground.

Skye rolled her eyes laughing. "You can't collapse yet, we still have half a mile to go."

I stood up and in the distance I saw something move across the haze.

"What's that?!" I pointed as it hopped. "A kangaroo!?"

She squinted. "Nice eye! But no, that's actually a wallaby."

"What's the difference?"

"A wallaby is usually much smaller. Their height, their legs.. when we see kangaroos they'll be double that little guy's size. We're almost there."

Kangaroo or not, I was still interested in the wallaby, but he moved in the opposite direction any time I tried to get closer.

Then like a mirage in some movie, a tree appeared in the distance. Waving its big shady branches, a little different, but all together. I didn't ask if it was real, because that was a question and a stupid one. But we seemed to be heading straight for it, so I assumed it must've been real and hopefully our destination because I was getting tired and hungry. Just as I was in a daze staring at the tree I saw something in my periphery. Actually I saw some *things,* off in the distance. I squinted.

"Kangaroos!" I pointed like a little kid at a zoo.

Skye nodded and laughed, probably at my reaction.

I changed my direction from the tree toward the group of kangaroos.

"Don't charge at them, Lucas. You'll get whacked in the eye and people will think I did it. Let's go eat under that tree.

Aha! So the tree is real.

We sat at the roots of the big shady tree and Skye emptied her bag revealing two protein bars, two apples, a bag of almonds, and a box of Tim Tams.

"Won't these melt?" I asked, picking up the Tim Tams, hoping their chocolatey goodness was still intact.

"You're right… we should eat them *all* first."

I looked at Skye like she was crazy, because she was, and I loved it.

She peeled open the box, grabbed two cookies at one time and chomped them both in half.

"They melted a little, but it's perfect because the softness resembles a Tim Tam Slam."

I followed and took a bite too. "Mmmm." I licked my lips.

"Tea would be nice, but just not in this heat." I commented.

"We can have Tim Tam Slams tonight when it's not as hot."

"But I thought we had to eat the whole box right now."

"Yeah. *This* box. I have more back at the site. In the cooler."

Skye didn't just say: *another,* back at the site, she said: *more.*

"You're perfect." I said to Skye, getting flushed immediately. I looked down and took another bite.

"You talk to your Tim Tams?" Skye said deflecting the compliment. "Everything's better with chocolate." She winked.

We didn't eat *all* the Tim Tams, but we devoured most of the box before beginning to eat the other, far healthier selections. Some of the kangaroos in the distance moved closer as we ate. One even wandered about twenty feet from where we were sitting. Skye insisted I stay seated and told me not to appear too excited. They were after all, wild animals. I saw what looked like over a hundred kangaroos in the distances all around us.

We got back to the campsite around noon. I was sweating from the hike. Skye got into the car and started the engine. I hurried into the front seat to feel the cool AC against my face. After a few moments the car was moving. *I thought we were just enjoying the AC*, but apparently we had plans to go somewhere. I knew we weren't heading back to Byron yet because we left the tent pitched. I kept trying to think of ways to ask what we were doing without *actually* phrasing it as a question.

"Today was awesome." I said.

"We got lucky with good weather."

Lucky.

Skye realized she said it because she gripped the steering wheel a bit tighter. But I liked hearing that word.

"We're *very* lucky." I replied. And I saw her grip loosen and her shoulders relax.

"So... next stop...." I hoped Skye would fill in the blank.

"La Hermosa Mariposa." She replied.

The beautiful butterfly? In Spanish?

Although she filled in the blank, I had no idea what she meant..

"We're like an hour away."

Okay, I didn't know where we were going, but I knew a time frame.

"Are we going to see butterflies?"

Ignoring my *question,* Skye turned up the radio and began singing. Bumping to the beat, she drummed on the steering wheel and sang every word to a song I've never heard in my life. Skye had a terrible voice, but I still could listen to her all day.

After an hour of karaoke we pulled up to a wooden house in the middle of nowhere. Above the porch entryway was a sign that read, La Hermosa Mariposa. I could tell by the smell that it was a restaurant and I couldn't have been happier because I was hungry, even after all those Tim Tams.

Skye told me that was her favorite spot to eat in *all* of Australia.

"More than Burgeroo?" I said eyes wide in surprise.

"Yep."

"And HideAway?"

"Mhmm. It's a Mexican chef who married an Aboriginal woman and they opened up this place that has the best enchiladas in the world."

"You don't think Mexico would have the best enchilada?"

"Exactly. They do. And Chef Javier brought that enchilada *here,* to the middle of nowhere. It's even better here because the recipe has traveled so far and yet still has kept its authenticity."

Just then a woman came over to our table. "I thought it was you." Her smiling eyes were aimed at Skye.

"Hey Sophie." Skye said rising to give her a hug. Sophie was in her forties and stood at a generous five feet tall. She had leathery skin and a soft welcoming smile.

"And who is this handsome man?" Sophie asked winking at me.

"I'm Lucas. Nice to meet you."

"Ooo an American boy, how *exotic.*" She giggled. "Do you two know what you want, or do you need a couple of minutes?"

Before I could think of an answer to Sophie's question, Skye responded. "Two of Javi's best enchiladas."

"Coming right up."

"I thought you were vegan…"

"This place is one of my exceptions…"

It wasn't long before the restaurant had filled up and I was stuck wondering where all the people had come from. There was nothing around. We were in the middle of nowhere! Skye and I drove for an hour and all we saw was a one pump gas station that had a convenient store attached to it. *Not very convenient,* I thought when we passed, considering its location. But where there's good food, there will be people, and La Hermosa Mariposa had plenty of people.

I had high expectations by the time the enchiladas came out. As the plates sizzled in front of us, my mouth watered beyond control. I didn't listen to Sophie's warning that the plates were hot and rushed to take a massive bite of cheesy beefy goodness, only to burn the roof of my mouth. The last thing I wanted to do was embarrass myself or *worse,* insult La Hermosa Mariposa by spitting out the scorching bite I just took. My eyes watered as I felt the tenderness of the skin that was just burnt against the heat of the food. Each second that passed was a little more bearable as the enchilada cooled down. Skye was busy cutting her's up into smaller pieces, letting the steam release like I *should have* done. I finally managed to swallow. Even with all the pain of what felt like third degree burns in my mouth, the flavor erupting from the enchilada stood out above all.

Skye looked up at my teary eyes and chuckled as she blew her first bite. "Is it hot enough?"

I took a huge gulp of water. "Yeah… I think so."

I cut my next bite, blew it cool, then chomped down.

"Afraid a dingo will steal your food?" Skye joked.

"No… but this morning I overindulged on cookies and my stomach is seeking vengeance."

"Tim Tams are more than just cookies, Lucas. They're delicacies that feed your soul."

"I feel the gateway to my soul opening right now." I chomped on another bite.

The enchilada was huge, but no match for two hungry desert hikers. Part of me hoped Skye wouldn't finish it all and she'd let me have her remaining bites, like we've done at Burgeroo. But Skye was just as hungry as I was. Just as we were finishing up our meals, a guy in tribal clothing began playing an instrument that I've never seen before. It was about five feet long, wooden, with a cylindrical shape. It got more narrow as it moved closer to the top. The performer used his mouth to make a low bellowing sound I've never heard before.

"What is that?"

"A didgeridoo?"

"A didgeri-who?"

"An instrument of the Aborigines."

I focused on the performer with the instrument I've never heard nor seen before. Although he was sitting off to the side, in the corner, most of the people in the restaurant had their attention directed toward him. He was a one man show who played for five minutes before receiving a full applause from everyone.

"That was incredible!" I exclaimed to Skye. "How does he play that long without ever stopping to take a breath?"

"A special breathing technique. They don't just play on the exhaled breath, they also make sounds with their inhale."

"So all you do is breathe into it?"

"It's not as simple as that. It's a very difficult kind of breath. Especially to make a sound on the inhale."

"Is it like the trumpet?"

"No, nothing like a trumpet."

I looked at the performer in admiration as he played the next song.

"Have you ever played one before?"

"Yeah, every Aussie goes on some field trip at some point with school to learn about the aboriginals. And the trip isn't complete without a didgeridoo lesson."

"I want to try to play one. Could you teach me?"

"Teach you? I couldn't even teach myself. I couldn't ever really get it."

"Is it really that hard?"

"A lot of people have trouble."

"But this guy makes it look so effortless." I turned to watch the performer again. I was so interested, I even thought about asking the guy to let me borrow his, but after rethinking it I decided that would be almost as gross as borrowing a stranger's toothbrush.

When we left the restaurant and went back outside, the air had cooled quite a bit. We went to the car and rode with the windows down the whole ride back. We talked about surfing and work. Baseball and books. Music and travel. There wasn't a point of silence in the car, not even when we stopped to fill up with gas.

Skye made me feel so happy and it was a feeling I was so thankful for. She has shown me so much about Australia, but mostly about myself. She helped me remember what life is *supposed to feel like. What would this experience have been without Skye?* I shook that thought.

As we pulled up to the tent I held Skye's hand and memorized the way her fingers felt laced with mine. I usually didn't like holding hands because my palms would get so sweaty so fast. Probably because I was always nervous around girls and I tend to sweat when I'm nervous. Skye made me nervous and comfortable at the same time. But with Skye it was more like butterflies in my stomach, which I prefer over sweat.

We parked and sat quietly in the car for a minute. I wondered how Skye knew that location so well in the darkness when everything looked the same. Kind of like how she navigated through the dark to the cave. She had an innate sense of direction.

"Ready to build that fire?"

"Let's go, pyro."

We grabbed wood from out of the trunk and piled it high in a way that allowed air to flow. Then we stuffed paper in the middle to act as kindling. We placed large rocks in a circle around the wood. It was very dry, so when the paper went up in flames the wood caught quickly. Skye fanned the flame, causing it to crackle and grow. Starting a fire with Skye required little effort. I just lit a lighter.

"I have vegan and regular hot dogs we can roast on these sticks." Skye said as she unloaded the cooler. "You want to eat again now or wait?"

"I could always eat." Between the didgeridoo performance and the long drive to the tent, my appetite was working itself up again.

"Good because we have vegan marshmallows to roast and of course, the slam."

"You're prepared."

"Always."

"Speaking of prepared." Skye pulled a J out of her pocket.

"You've been smoking a lot more." I loaded hot dog onto a stick.

"We're on holiday." She sparked her lighter. "Do you mind?"

I shrugged. "No." I didn't like the *idea* of smoking weed, but the last time it made me feel really relaxed and loquacious. It put an introspective spin on the night.

"You can have the first hit."

Skye passed it to me. I held the hot dog on a stick over the fire in one hand, and took a hit with the other, then something compelled me…

Maybe it was the way the fire was shining against her lips or how she looked at me with anticipation in her eyes as I inhaled.

…With my cheeks full of smoke, I leaned over to Skye's lips and passed the hit to her mouth. She inhaled the smoke, then began kissing me until it exhaled through her nose.

"I wanted *you* to have the first hit." I winked.

I moved my hot dog out of the flame. Part of it was on fire.

I blew out the flaming hot dog and grabbed a bun for Skye and I.

"Boli would be proud." I joked after my second bite.

"Yeah, us and our *gourmet* hot dogs."

Skye had two hot dogs and I had three. I was going for the fourth when she brought out a bag of vegan marshmallows, which I didn't know existed. I turned from the hot dogs and went to Skye and the fluffy sugar clouds. I hadn't roasted a marshmallow over a fire since I was a kid with my parents at Lake Michigan. The sight of the mallows brought back warm memories.

I popped one in my mouth as I roasted another on the stick.

"I also have Tim Tams for later, so save room." She smiled.

"There's always room." I said patting my stomach. Food was one thing I never turned down. Probably because I've always been very active.

"Your marshmallow is on fire."

I looked down and the sugar cloud was aflame. I blew it out.

"Good thing you're not working in the kitchen. Everything would catch fire."

Skye twirled her stick as her marshmallow turned golden brown.

"I like the marshmallow burnt. It's crispier." I ate the whole marshmallow in one bite.

I grabbed another from the bag. "We should put them in our tea when we do The Slam."

Skye's eyes lit up big like she just saw a shooting star. "Brilliant!"

First, we had to boil water over the fire for the tea. Then I put a burnt marshmallow in one mug and a golden brown marshmallow in the other. Skye got the Tim Tams out of the cooler. The marshmallows began melting into the tea and I resisted the temptation of taking a sip without the Tim Tam as my straw. Both Skye and I bit the ends off of our cookie, then gulped as much marshmallow camomile tea the wafer would allow. The best part was eating the melted cookie and washing it down with more tea.

We sat beside the fire with the last few sips of our tea and looked up at the stars, which were getting brighter and brighter as the night darkened. I let our full bellies justify the empty conversation as I lethargically leaned against Skye. It was a long day that I didn't want to end. Hiking the outback, boomerangs, wallabies, kangaroos, and didgeridoos. We adventured, ate, and relaxed in perfect proportions.

"There's a meteor shower tonight." Skye said after a while of silence.

"Really?!" I exclaimed. "I've never seen one before."

"It won't start for another few hours."

"What's going to happen?" I asked, feeling foolish that I didn't actually know *what* to expect during a meteor shower.

"Shooting stars. Hundreds! *Thousands* if you looked *all* night."

Woah.

"And the outback is the best place to watch it. It's pure darkness out here."

"Yeah, and look." I pointed up to the moon. "It's a crescent, so doesn't that mean even better visibility because there's less light?"

Skye nodded, impressed. "You're catching on."

Besides the night before, I had never seen so many stars at one time in my life. Before Skye, I never gave more than a second thought about the stars. Sure, I speculated with friends about space or if we'd ever get the opportunity to travel to the moon, but I never leaned back and *enjoyed* the sky at night. With Skye though, everything was different. Stars shined brighter. Smiles grew wider. Laughs lasted longer. With her it felt like there was a universe of possibilities.

We poked the dying fire with our sticks as we waited for the meteor shower to commence. I had already seen a couple shooting stars, but Skye assured me that the *shower* would be much more intense. I thought intense would be seeing two shooting stars back to back, which caused me to jump up out of my seat. Skye still insisted I hadn't seen anything yet.

The more I looked, the more amazed I was. Stars were dancing across the universe one after another after another… I saw so many I lost count. But it never got old. Each shooting star was even more exciting than the last. My eyes scanning as much of the sky as I could, seeing stars falling from every direction.

It was so dark, I couldn't even see that her eyes were closed, but I could feel her breathing slow. That's when I knew Skye fell asleep. She was still holding my hand and even though I wanted to get the blanket we left outside, I didn't because I didn't want to let go of her. And I didn't want to wake her up.

I didn't know how late it was, but my body declared it late enough. I was battling my heavy eyes so I could keep watching shooting stars, but the steady deep breathing beside me was a lullaby I could resist no longer. The stars kept falling. My eyes kept drooping. I didn't want that perfect day to end.

I love you was the last thing I remember thinking or maybe even *saying*. I couldn't tell which were my thoughts, dreams, or reality. I just knew Skye was in my thoughts, dreams, and reality. And on that perfect day as stars fell and I drifted to sleep, all that was on my mind was how I loved her.

Chapter 32: Didgeridoo

I woke up to the sun peeking out from the horizon. Like a flower gradually opening its petals, the sun revealed shades of yellow, orange, pink, and blue. I looked over at Skye who was sound asleep. The beauty before me matched by the beauty around me, which made me wake with a smile. My final thoughts of the evening became my first thoughts of the day.

Letting Skye sleep, I unzipped the tent and went to the car to get a drink out of the cooler. It wasn't until I was gulping water that I realized we weren't alone. A group of kangaroos were congregated less than twenty feet away. They were *big*. Way bigger than *I thought* based on what I saw from the distance the day before. Some were looking over at me, which got me a little nervous as I remembered Skye's warning the previous day. I stayed quiet and tried not to make any sudden movements. I ducked behind the car and continued watching them. The kangaroos were probably making fun of me. *Look at this human, crouched behind that car, thinking we don't see him...*

"What are you doing?" The kangaroos weren't the only ones watching me. Skye was stepping out of the tent.

"Shhh." I said pointing toward the kangaroos.

"Get into the car slowly." Skye told me. I followed her directions and moved toward the front door.

"Faster!" She yelled. I sped up, got in the car, and slammed the door. Skye got into the car casually.

"Why did you tell me slowly, then yell for me to move faster?"

The kangaroos weren't paying much mind to us. They barely even got near our site.

"Because it was funny to see the look on your face."

"Are they ever aggressive?"

"Not usually, unless they feel threatened. You never know the interactions the kangaroos have had with humans, so going into the car is the safest bet."

We ate toast inside the car and took advantage of having a close up of the roos. Skye made me eat vegemite just to confirm again that I didn't like it.

When the mob of kangaroos were far enough, we packed our supplies and drove off. As usual, I didn't know where we were going until we arrived. We pulled up to a wooden house with a small sign that read, *Magic's Music Shop*. We were the only car in the small dirt lot.

"Is it open?"

Skye stepped out of the car. "Let's see."

I was skeptical as I observed the faded yellow house that looked vacant. But still, I followed Skye to the door. I thought she would have knocked, but she just turned the doorknob and walked right in. A bell above the door frame jingled. I walked into a bright big room with a display of didgeridoos of all different sizes hanging from stands on the walls and floor.

From my right, I heard a voice.

"Welcome!" The voice said with delight. We were greeted by a big smile on an even bigger man who stood behind a counter.

"Hey," Skye began. "I was hoping you were having lessons today. Sophie at *La Hermosa Mariposa* said to talk to Magic."

The big man's smile got even bigger. "I'm Magic!" The big man said, raising his hand like a young schoolboy. "Sophie is my cousin." He clapped his hands together, then walked to a big circular rug in the center of the room.

"Join me!" Magic said in an announcer voice, as if a show was about to start. We walked over to the rug and took a seat on stools. Magic grabbed two didgeridoos off the stands beside the rug and handed one to both Skye and I. He took another from a case that rested on the floor.

"A lesson must begin by introducing yourself to your instrument." Magic stated, still using his announcer voice.

"Hi Elsa, It's Magic again." His voice was back to the chipper *welcome* tone he greeted us with earlier. "Now you try!" He clapped his hands once again.

"Seriously?" Skye rolled her eyes.

I didn't mind the unusual request. "Hi, I'm Lucas." I said to the didgeridoo.

"Her name is Wanda." Magic whispered, as if the didgeridoo might get offended that I didn't know its name.

"Hi Wanda, I'm Lucas."

Magic clapped.

"And that's Hermione."

Skye looked down at her instrument. "I will only partake because of the Harry Potter reference…" Skye mumbled. "Hi Hermione, I'm Skye." She said with as little enthusiasm as possible.

Magic was pleased and of course, clapped.

I was really excited to have a private lesson, but I could tell Skye was barely tolerating it. She didn't have an interest in playing the didgeridoo, nor was she a fan of Magic's enthusiasm. She told Magic to use all his *powers* on me and not to *waste* any on her. She was there to *watch* and *support me.* Which secretly (but not so secretly) made me really happy because Skye went out of her way for me. She saw I was interested in the didgeridoo, so she organized a lesson with a true Aboriginal.

I realized we'd come a long way from her *using me* to install the cargo net. And even further from the first Bondfire when she got mad at Spigs for inviting me. Skye still had her typical sassiness as she sat there listening to Magic's superfluous descriptions about proper breathing. Even though Skye *insisted* she was only spectating, numerous times, Magic still *insisted* she participate in the breathing exercises because *her energy* affected my playing, and according to Magic, *Skye's energy was like tangled vines on a tree.* When he told her that she rolled her eyes.

"Seeeeee!" He said. "You're not breathing enough so your eyes are rolling back."

The lesson lasted about an hour. By the end I was able to play *pretty well for a first-timer* according to Skye and *amazing, incredible, outstanding, A+* according to Magic. Either way, I felt proud of myself when we walked out of that faded yellow house.

"Thanks for taking me here. I know Magic... frustrated you."

"Magic? No, I loved him!" Skye sneered sarcastically opening the car's trunk and reaching into the cooler.

"I've been thinking about these Tim Tams for an hour." She took two out of the box then passed it to me.

"How many boxes did you bring?!"

"Oh three, four... maybe five."

"Savage."

"I'm not the only one eating them." She defended as I devoured my third cookie.

"And you're missing your mouth." Skye fake-scolded as she licked some chocolate off of my cheek.

After that lick, I began missing my mouth on purpose. But Skye had already started driving, so chocolate stayed on my face making me look like a slob until I found a napkin in the glove compartment.

"I want to listen to a podcast on the way back." Skye said.

"Alright, what's it about?"

"This group who backpacked around South America finding the best surf and the best coffee beans. I went to school with one of the guys."

"That sounds like a trip designed for you."

"I know… I wish."

We drove and drove and at some point I drifted to sleep. It wasn't that the podcast was uninteresting, I just was so tired from staying up late to watch the meteor shower. I wish I stayed awake though, because my dream was not a pleasant place to be…

At first, I was surfing with a big crew. Skye, Kenny, Spigs, Budd, Zane, Coco, and Jade. The surf was perfect until the rain moved in. I was in the middle of a perfect swell as the sky went from a powder blue to a dreary grey. I turned around expecting to see Skye and everyone following on their boards behind me, but they all disappeared. When I looked forward again, LC was in front of me, surfing on the very same wave. I was so surprised, I almost slipped off the board, but I caught my footing. I made eye contact with LC and she gave me a concerned look, followed by a smile of relief. The space between our boards was getting less and less.

Then suddenly, she jumped from her board *toward me.* She cleared the ten feet of ocean between her board and mine, then tackled me into the thrashing wave. My body was submerged and only sank deeper and further into the water's depths. I could feel hands wrapping around my throat and pushing down on my shoulders. But I wasn't screaming, instead she was. *Loudly.* As if I was the one choking her. I kept trying to push her away, shut her up, make her stop… but she wouldn't. We just kept sinking down to the ocean's endless depths that morphed into a black hole.

I shook awake to the sound of Skye's voice.

"Are you alright?"

"Huh? What? Yeah. Why?" I gripped the seat to confirm I was no longer drowning into darkness.

"You looked like you were having a nightmare."

It was pouring outside.

I realized I was breathing heavy. Skye handed me a water bottle and then pulled a joint out of the center console. She lit it and passed it to me without asking if I wanted to smoke. I took a long inhale and an even longer exhale and my heavy breaths seemed to calm.

"Do you remember the dream?"

I let her question linger with the smoke that was floating around the car.

"Yeah."

I took another hit, avoiding further elaboration. But Skye was still curious.

"What were you just dreaming about?"

I just shrugged. Skye had no idea what she was asking.

"You can talk to me about it…"

I knew Skye probably thought my nightmare was about my parents, but it was LC who was haunting me now. I couldn't get the whole situation out of my mind. It's been eating me up inside and the worst part is that I haven't been able to talk to anybody about it. Who could I talk to? This was not a *normal* problem. People just don't see the deceased *alive* and chit-chatting on the beach. How was I supposed to explain that?

"I don't think I should talk about it."

"I thought you said talking things out helps."

"It does… this is just, hard. I don't want to freak you out."

"You won't freak me out. Do you trust me?"

I hated when Skye asked that. It made me feel guilty a little. I did trust her. But Skye was known to be unpredictable.

"I trust you." I *really* didn't want to scare her, but I *really* did want to vent it out.

I took one last hit and passed it back to Skye.

"Remember when I thought I saw someone running into the water on the beach? Well, she was just in my dream, trying to drown me."

"Who is it?"

I took a moment to think carefully about my response.

"That's the thing, I realized she's… not real." I finally said.

"How do you know it's not real?"

"I know *she's* not real because, well… she's not alive."

"What do you mean? Like a ghost?"

I shrugged, "I don't know, I don't really believe in ghosts, so it's freaking me out."

There was a silence that filled the car. Skye flicked the ash of the J into an empty water bottle.

"Who is it?" She finally asked me.

"I don't want to tell you because you'll think I'm crazy."

"What's wrong with crazy?"

"There's two types of crazy, Skye. *Cool* crazy and *crazy* crazy. You're cool crazy. I think I'm going *crazy* crazy."

"Don't be ridiculous, Lucas. You can talk to me."

"Maybe you should pull over." I suggested.

"No, we still have over an hour to go."

I sighed.

"Who do you see?" She persisted. "Is it your mum?"

"No."

I thought about how I would react if I saw my mom. *Would it freak me out or get me excited?*

"Your dad?"

"No."

"Who Lucas?" I could tell Skye was a little annoyed.

"It's too crazy."

"Bottling it up will make it more crazy."

She had a point.

"You won't even believe me."

"I took you all the way out to the outback to go camping. This is a no judgment zone. Tell me." She said firmly. I knew Skye would not drop the topic until she got an answer. I thought about lying, but I didn't want to get caught and more confused in a web of lies.

"Remember when I told you about Elsie… the person I saw walking into the water the night of Zane's birthday?"

Skye nodded.

"Well, I realized that she isn't real. I mean, what I saw that night wasn't real. And I saw her a bunch of other times before and after that too."

"How do you know she's not real?"

"Well…" I hesitated.

"Elsie stands for LC and LC stands for… Lessie Carter." I said holding my breath.

Skye swerved the wheel a bit.

I did tell her to pull over.

"LC? Like my mom?" Skye had a look of confusion. "That's what people around town called her. That was her surf name. You sure it's not just some other LC?"

"Who looks exactly like your mom?"

Skye paused to think. "How do you know what my mom looks like?"

"That picture from the *Legend's Board* at The Shack. I realized when I went to the Memorial and saw the pictures and well, it all hit me. That's why I felt *sick* after that."

"But how?"

"I don't know Skye. It's really freaking me out."

"How do you know it was my mom if you saw her on the beach in the dark from so far away?"

"That wasn't the only time I saw her."

"Did you see her up close?"

"We would talk, Skye."

"Are you sure it wasn't a dream or something?"

"It was too real to be a dream. We would have deep conversations. And like I said it wasn't just once... it was numerous times."

"When? Where? What did she say?" Skye looked excited, confused, and scared all at the same time. I didn't know how much I should be telling her.

"I met her before I even met you. I always saw her down by the beach. Usually by the rocks."

"Near the cliffs?" She perked up.

I nodded.

"You have to take me."

"What?"

"If you can see her, maybe I can too."

"What do you mean? You think she's real or something?"

"I don't know what to think, Lucas. But you're talking about my mom like you know her and I'd take any shot to see her again, even if it's *crazy crazy*."

I stayed quiet, collecting my own thoughts.

"What are you thinking?" She asked me.

"That I'm crazy and no matter what I do, I'm going to let you down."

Silence filled the car.

"When was the last time you saw her?" Skye asked.

"A couple days ago. On the beach."

"What did you talk about?"

"Nothing, I ran away."

"Why!?"

"Skye, I'm freaked out, okay! This may seem *cool* to you, but to me it's *crazy*. And scary."

"Maybe if you take me to her, we can figure out what's really going on."

"I don't know, Skye. I don't believe in ghosts and I don't believe in magic, so that just leads me to I'm crazy!"

"Chill out, Lucas. It's crazy, but that doesn't mean you're crazy."

"Yeah… maybe your mom just has a look alike or something." The thought of a realistic solution put me mildly at ease.

"Or maybe it's really her."

"How? What are you saying?"

"They never found my mom's body. Maybe she's not actually dead."

Chapter 33: Clues

Skye still never told me the *actual* cause of her mom's death. I only knew what Kenny told me. Skye just said, *there was an accident out in the water.*

Accident.

The word alone gave me shivers recalling the car accident on The Night My Life Fell Apart.

Part of me wondered if Skye didn't know *how* her mom actually died. Maybe when she was a kid, they just told her: *it was an accident.* That was the only solution to justify why she didn't tell me her mom died cliff jumping. Although, I bet the *real reason* she wouldn't tell me was because she thought I wouldn't go back to the cave with her. I don't know how I would have reacted if Skye told me instead of Kenny. Around Kenny, I had to keep my cool. But if that information came from Skye, I probably would have flipped on her for having me jump off the same cliffs that killed her mother…

We picked up lunch on the way home and ate it in the car. Skye said we didn't have time to stop to eat. She was driving even faster than before, and before she was driving pretty fast. It was clear she wanted to get back to Byron before it was too dark, so we could go down to the beach…

I couldn't believe I agreed to Skye's plot to try to *meet* LC, but I couldn't say no to her. It's like I would do anything Skye said because I believed her string of hope more than I believed myself. Or at least I really, really wanted to.

We dropped off the camping supplies and the car, then walked to the beach. I would have preferred to go back to Neptune's to shower, but Skye insisted we head straight to the rocks to find *her mom*. Every step in the sand felt heavier and heavier. My neck felt hot. My hands were cold. I looked around, part of me hoping to see her, but most of me wishing I never saw her ever again. Ever since the Memorial, the thought of LC made me anxious and paranoid. Being back at the rocks *looking for her* added a whole new layer of anxiety. I'm sure Skye must have noticed, but she didn't say anything.

"So, we just wait?" Skye plopped herself cross-legged in the sand.

"Yeah, I guess." I sat to join her.

Skye put her fist up to the sky and closed one eye, like she was measuring something.

"We have about an hour until sunset." She estimated. I assumed that's what she was measuring with her fist: the distance the sun was from the horizon. Kenny did that too, but at sunrise surf when he has to know the time he must leave for work.

Skye grabbed my cold hands and warmed them up in her lap. She kissed my nose, which forced my smile and for a few moments, I forgot what was so scary. I only remembered *why* we were waiting there when I noticed Skye looking around rather than at the sunset. I was trying to look away from the sand and focus on the beautiful sky.

I knew LC wouldn't appear with Skye sitting next to me.

"I've only seen her when I'm alone." I confessed.

Skye sat with the words. Her fingers loosened around my hands.

"Should I leave?"

"No!" I held her hands tighter.

"Well, not leave, but maybe hide down by The Shack?"

"That's too far." I shook my head.

"Do you want me to hide closer? Behind the trees maybe?"

I stayed quiet and looked down at the sand. I wished I could rewind to the night before. Skye and I laying below thousands of shooting stars. I let go of Skye's hands and scooped up a mound of sand.

"This is how many shooting stars we saw last night." I said as I let the sand slowly fall from my hands.

I was trying to change the topic. To make sure Skye didn't walk away from me. To make sure she didn't leave me alone because if she did, LC might appear. And even though Skye wanted to go to the beach to find her mom, that wasn't the reason why I went. I went to the beach for Skye. Because the slight look of hope in her eyes made it impossible to say *no*. And of course I wanted to spend more time with Skye, always. I wanted all the moments I could get with her because she helped to mask the fears that festered inside of me. Skye helped me feel good in times when I didn't know how to feel good by myself.

"If that sand were shooting stars, what would you wish right now?" She asked.

I thought about the obvious wish, for my parents to be alive and well, but I knew that wasn't possible anymore. I had already wished that on so many fallen stars. I knew it would never come true. I bet Skye had probably had the same wish for her mom. And now she was hoping that wish *would* finally come true. I wanted to help her, I really did. But I was scared.

"I would wish to feel happy." I finally responded.

Skye sat with the words for a moment.

"You're not happy here?" Skye's shoulders stiffened.

That's not what I meant.

"Being in Byron has made me happy. *You* have made me so happy."

"But?"

"I'm not happy with myself."

I don't know what I expected Skye to say, but I didn't expect her to say *nothing*. I guess both of us were too lost in our own complicated minds. Too distracted by the empty hope inside of us. The silence turned our gaze to the sunset upon the horizon. In Byron, I've learned to appreciate the sunset so much more. With Skye, I've learned a whole new side of the world. *There's happiness all around me, but how do I get it inside of me?*

Skye kissed me on the cheek and whispered in my ear, "I'm going to swim. I'll be right over there."

She jogged away, tossing her shirt back toward me. It landed on my shoulder, draping Skye's lavender scent past my face. I watched her run out toward the sunset into the water. I hoped I didn't hurt Skye's feelings. The way her cheeks drooped when she asked, *"you're not happy here?"* As if *Skye* took the blame for my unhappiness. But her kiss eased my worry, at least a little. I hoped she understood that there's a difference between looking happy and being happy. That sometimes no matter what happiness is happening on the outside, the inside just feels off. Voided of something. And it was up to *me* to fill it. Somehow...

I was thinking so much about not feeling happy with myself that I got lost in a daze. As the colors in the sky faded with the light that dipped below the horizon, I watched Skye drift further while wondering how life could shift so much, so fast.

"You never come around anymore. You avoiding me?" I heard from behind.

I tensed up at the sound of her voice, then turned around quickly.

"Who are you? What's your name?"

"Lucas, what's wrong?"

"Elsie or *LC?"*

"*LC.*" She laughed, "but I can see why you thought Elsie. It could be an accent thing."

I narrowed my eyes at her. "What does LC stand for?"

"Are you alright? You don't look good."

"What? No, I mean yes, I'm fine." I looked out at the ocean.

Skye! I needed her to come.

"Are you sure you're okay?" She asked again.

"Yes. I'm fine." I saw Skye in the distance and darkness creeped in more and more. Why did she wander so far?

"Skye!" I yelled. "Skye!"

Skye was already looking at me.

"Go to her, we'll talk later." LC began to walk away.

"No! Stay." I told her. "Skye!" I yelled again as I waved for her to come in.

LC walked further away.

I heard Skye swimming in.

"Wait, no. Come back!" I followed her.

She kept walking as if she didn't hear me at all.

"No. Please. Skye is *right* there."

LC turned around and looked at me. She was standing on the edge of where the beach met the line of trees.

I stared into the eyes who gained my trust. She was as real as the first time I saw her, and last time, and every time in between. I rubbed my eyes. LC looked just like the picture at The Surf Shack I saw on my first day in Byron before I went kayaking. As she stood in front of me, there was no way I could be mistaken.

"Please. Just stay right here." I begged. "Skye *needs* to see you."

"Lucas!" I heard from behind me. I looked to Skye for half a moment, but when I turned back around there was no one in front of me.

"LC!" I panicked, looking in every possible direction. Someone was screaming. I ran past the line of trees calling out her name.

"Lucas!" Skye called from behind. "Why are you running away from me?"

I stopped where I was and turned to see Skye staring at me with desperation.

"She was here. I was just talking to her." I walked back toward Skye.

"I was watching you the whole time." She paused. "I didn't see anybody."

"If you didn't see her, why were you screaming?" I asked Skye.

"I never screamed, Lucas. No one was screaming."

I dropped down onto the floor and punched the sand in frustration. I was shaking my head over and over, hunched to the ground. Skye placed her hand on my back.

With my hands over my face, I just kept shaking my head.

"Can I get you something? Water? You're sweating."

"No!" I screamed. "Don't leave."

Skye rubbed her hand on my back in circles.

"If you leave, she'll just keep coming back."

Skye kept saying that they never found her mom's body, which left the possibility of her still being alive. She was trying to sell that story as much as I was trying to buy it. Although I really wished for it to be true, there was way too many details that just didn't make sense. Where was she for the last ten years? Why wouldn't she have found Skye or Kenny instead of me? Skye came up with this elaborate story about all the possibilities, like her mom lost her memory and didn't remember anyone or anything from her life... I let Skye imagine. I stayed silent as my skepticism grew.

There was still that possibility, Skye insisted. They never found her body.

I couldn't wait to get back to Neptune's to shower away the camping grime and scrub my mind of LC, but unfortunately I was only able to do one of the two. My mind was racing everywhere, there was no way I could fall asleep. I gave up trying after an hour of *trying to relax*, which didn't work because you're not relaxed as soon as you have to *try*.

In an attempt to distract myself, I went down to the lobby and logged onto one of the computers. I hadn't been on a computer in months, or on a phone in even longer. It was nice to take a technology cleanse, but a bit stressful when I finally opened my inboxes. Messages upon messages of people who were thinking of me, asking about me, *worried* about me. Family, friends, teachers, classmates, neighbors… from all periods of my life all clueless about where I was and if I was alright. Many people sent multiple messages. As I read, I could sense the anxiety in their words, causing trepidation to rush through my whole body. I felt so selfish. Running away without looking back, like nobody would notice. I took a deep breath and began responding to the messages. All three hundred and seventy-nine.

My Uncle Will emailed me every single day and I was gone for over two months. Uncle Will was my mom's brother. He lived in Brooklyn near our first apartment. I used to see him every weekend before I had to move away.

All of his emails were really thoughtful. Sometimes it would be just a picture that he thought I'd like or a quote he wanted me to read. He'd send reports of how the Yankees were doing and videos of Puerto Rican bomba dances that were sent to him from family back on the island. But most times it was a plea for a response or a reminder of how much they all missed me. And he wasn't just talking about his wife Maria and all of my cousins, but everyone back in Brooklyn who I grew up with. I got messages from childhood friends and teammates from little league. All letting me know they would be there for me *if I wanted* and they were thinking of me. Some even included pictures of us from when we were little kids in oversized fitted hats, that we insisted on wearing even though they looked so silly swallowing our heads. The pictures made me laugh and to my surprise, most emails made me smile.

The most recent message from Uncle Will was from that very day, sent 21 minutes before. There was a green circle beside his name which meant he was online. *Where do I begin?* I thought. But before I could even comprise a message I saw that he started a direct chat with me and was typing…

I stayed up messaging my uncle for hours until darkness turned to sunrise. I barely got two hours of sleep that night, before I had to get up to go to work. On the dewy walk over to HideAway I dragged my feet along the sandy pavement and replayed the messages in my head. My uncle begged me to come back and even offered to take the trip all the way out to Byron with my Aunt Maria so I didn't have to travel back alone. The desperation in his messages was palpable and as they piled on top of the plethora of emails, I sunk deeper into the regret of abandoning my problems. The problems never went away back home… they festered and grew because when I left, some people assumed the worst. There had even begun an *investigation* for me. Search parties, flyers, and apparently I was in the local news. I didn't tell anyone where I was going and I abandoned my phone before I even stepped on the plane.

How could I be so inconsiderate? Again. How could I let everyone I love suffer even more after facing the death of my parents?! When it was my fault… How could I think it was all about me? How could I be so selfish?

"No offense, but you look like you've been trampled by an emu. Is everything alright?" Kelsey broke me out of my trance as I wiped coffee stains off the HideAway countertops.

"Yeah, I'm just tired."

"I bet you are. You and Skye went camping in the outback, right?" The last few days registered in my mind. "Oh, yeah. Exactly."

"She wore you out I see." Kelsey winked, chuckled, then headed through the kitchen door.

Work went slow. I even managed to fall asleep in the back freezer for I don't know how long. Boli woke me up by dropping a huge sack of coffee beans onto my lap. He didn't seem too happy. Thankfully there wasn't many customers that day and Kelsey took charge of the big groups to make the day more manageable for me. I kept zoning out, hearing the voices of my family and friends in New York, my parents, LC... voices that seemed to float around my head beyond my control. Voices that felt like they were taking over. Since there weren't too many customers (and because I fell asleep in the freezer a second time) Boli told me to leave work early. I gladly did, cutting myself a slice of cherry pie to-go and eating it on my walk back to Neptune's.

I stopped to throw out the licked-clean pie plate and realized I recognized the bar I was standing in front of: Coral's Pub. I had never been inside, but I heard Kenny talk about going there a lot. I peeked in the big paneled windows to see a bar half-full of people watching what looked like a rugby game. I spotted Kenny at the far end of the pub talking to the bartender as she poured him a pint. LC's voice surfaced in my head, urging me to go inside. I hated that I still felt inclined to listen to her. I hated that she was somehow able to get so deeply inside my head.

A bell jingled when I opened the pub door, but it could barely be heard over the announcers on the television and the chatter amongst the fans. Coral's Pub had a wraparound bar that led to an outdoor deck. The deck overlooked the water and had a few tables that were all full of people eating. I realized I was still hungry when I felt my stomach grumble. *I'm always hungry.* I felt a mixture of relief and panic as I walked toward Kenny. *What was I actually going to say to him?* I went the long way around the bar trying to give myself more time to think.

Thankfully all eyes were on the TV, so Kenny was looking upward and not at me approaching. He cheered loudly and then clanked his glass with another guy who was whistling through his fingers. There was a barstool next to Kenny that was free, so I took it, almost tripping over his prosthetic leg. He was so into the game, he didn't even realize that I sat down.

The bartender walked over to me. Her hair was tied up with a bright yellow bandana and she had sunglasses on, inside. She nodded her head which I assumed was her way of asking, *what can I get you? so* I ordered a burger and a beer. Kenny noticed me once I put my order in.

"Lucas! When did you get here? Good to see you, mate! How was camping?"

"Epic. That meteor shower was the most incredible thing I've ever seen."

"Yeah, I bet. The amount of stars you can see out there is unreal." He sipped his beer. "Skye said you were able to play the didgeridoo pretty well."

"She said that?" It wasn't often that Skye gave out compliments.

"Daisy!" Kenny perked up as the bartender placed a pint in front of me. "This is Lucas. Lucas, *this* is *Daisy.*"

I could tell by the way he said her name that he liked her, a lot. And I could tell by the way she suddenly perked up that she liked him too.

"Oh hi, Lucas. Nice to meet you. You're just in time for the last quarter of an intense Footy Game."

"Footy?"

"Yeah, Aussie Rules, you know."

I didn't know, and based the intensity of the game, it didn't seem like the best time to ask.

"Bloody hell! C'mon Franklin!" Screamed a guy about to punch the television.

"What the fuck was that!?" Yelled another.

"Lucas, let's take a shot. My mates are losing, so I need a pick me up." Kenny motioned to Daisy who poured three shots of tequila.

"You're taking two?" I asked, looking at the three shots.

"The third is for Daisy," Kenny chuckled, "But you're right, we should all take a double."

Daisy took out three more shot glasses, but all I really wanted was that burger I ordered.

It wasn't a surprise that those shots and the beer loosened me up quite quickly, especially with just pie in my stomach. The alcohol made it much easier for me to bring up Skye.

"Kenny, I've been thinking about what you said about the cliffs... and Skye." My liquid confidence said.

"What do mean?" His attention moved away from the TV screen.

"Well, after you told me about the cliffs, I noticed Skye headed in that direction one day and I asked her what she was doing, she said she was looking for clues." I knew it was a bit of a lie, but unraveling the truth behind my curiosity seemed way too messy.

"Clues? About what?" Kenny asked with a look of fear bubbling in his eye.

"Skye said something like..." I hesitated for a moment, "Her mom's body was never found."

Kenny broke eye contact and looked down at his lap.

I felt guilt surge through me and for that moment I wished I hadn't said anything at all.

"They didn't find a body..." Kenny swallowed hard. "But... they found *some* body parts."

He ran his fingers through his hair anxiously.

"I didn't have the heart to tell Skye *what* they found, she was only eight years old. But it was enough to know... that it was her... and she was... gone." Kenny took a deep breath, his mind lost in the horrific memory.

"I'm so sorry..." I began. I put my hand on his shoulder. "I shouldn't have brought it up."

"No, no... I'm glad you told me. You're not the first person to say she's been over by the cliffs." He took a long chug of his beer, finishing everything that remained, and without a word Daisy came over and refilled his pint and placed my burger down in front of me.

Although I thought knowing the truth about LC would be a relief, it only made me more scared. Lessie Carter died. She's been dead for ten years. Yet I see her, hear her, interact with her. So I was clearly going crazy. No... I was *already* crazy. This just confirmed it.

Chapter 34: "You have nothing to be sorry for..."

I slept the rest of the day then stayed up all night thinking about Skye. How much we've shared together. How close we've gotten. I couldn't fathom that just when things finally felt good, it all started crashing down. Maybe it was some sort of sign.

My mind raced in every direction all the way until the sun peeked through the windows. My first thought was Sunrise Surf, but then I quickly realized there was no way I was going back to that beach. I contemplated my next move down at the breakfast buffet as I ate a blueberry muffin and English Breakfast tea with honey. My mom always loved that tea in the morning. It was her favorite. I twirled the tea with a spoon as if the herbal whirlpool would give me all the answers.

In the afternoon, I went to catch Skye coming off of her shift at HideAway. I took the street route and barely even let myself glance over at the sand. The thought of being near the beach frightened me. I waited off to the side of the trees for her to come out, both excited and nervous to see her.

Skye's eyes met mine as she walked down the HideAway steps. The way she smiled at me with her deep blue eyes was something I will never forget. *Forneverget.* Then, Skye walked over to me, like she knew exactly what I wanted to tell her, but she knew *this* took priority. We both needed *this* first. Skye brought her hands to my cheek, pulled me toward her, and kissed me deeper than the depths of the cave's entryway. Her lips sent fireworks erupting through my veins as our tongues flowed like a surfboard on a wave. I held her close to me, trying to memorize the way her body fit beside mine. I felt like I could kiss her forever, but knew that forever ended too soon.

When our kissing slowed she asked me, "Do you want to go down to the beach for a little while?"

She must have seen my expression change and quickly said, "Actually, I'm hungry.."

"Burgeroo?" I suggested.

"It's like you can read my mind." She grazed her fingers down my arm, lacing her hand into mine.

Skye always took the lead and as always, I loved to follow her. Each and every step.

"I'm sorry about the other day." Skye began to apologize. "I shouldn't have asked you to go to the beach when you said it made you uncomfortable."

"I'm sorry too… for bringing this on you."

"I'm glad you told me. Really, you have nothing to be sorry for."

"Yes I do, Skye."

I stopped walking and took both of her hands, kissing them, then took a deep breath.

"Skye, I'm leaving."

My words hung in the air while she looked up at me nodding with a vacant gaze. It's the first time I looked at her and didn't see an ocean in her eyes. Just an empty pool of water. She kept nodding her head.

"I bought my flight back to New York this morning."

Her nodding stopped and she continued walking, letting go of one of my hands but still holding the other.

"I knew you'd go, so I don't know why I am even surprised." She tried to let go of my other hand, but I quickly clasped it tighter.

"I don't want to go." I told her. "I have to."

"No, you *could* stay. You even said you considered it. You could." Skye looked upset.

"Yes, but not right now. Right now I-" I exhaled a big breath. "I need to get away from the place that's causing these hallucinations."

Skye looked over at me as we continued walking. I kept my head forward. I felt embarrassed admitting my own hallucinations- even to Skye who has heard me talk about it before.

"But what if they're not hallucinations, what if somehow-"

"No, Skye. Please. There's no way!" I interrupted. "You know it's not possible. She wouldn't be sneaking around town only talking to me. *Someone... everyone* would have recognized her."

Skye fell silent, dragging her feet on the sidewalk.

"I can't ignore it anymore. I need to address these hallucinations. This isn't healthy."

"What are you going to do about it in New York?"

"I spoke to my uncle. I'm going to stay with him in Brooklyn. He says he knows of a good doctor that could help me."

Skye stopped walking.

"When do you fly out?"

"Saturday."

Skye squeezed my hand tighter.

"That leaves tonight and tomorrow." She said with heaviness in her voice.

I still had my head down. Only two more days with Skye. Only two more days in Byron. Less than two days...

Suddenly, I felt her lips on mine.

"Let's make the most of it," she said as she stepped inside Burgeroo. Skye always could make me smile, even when she wasn't even trying, but especially when she was.

After Burgeroo Skye came back to Neptune's to help me get my belongings together. There wasn't much to pack, so we spent most of the night laying together on the crammed bottom bunk talking about everything and anything around the sun and beyond. The conversation flowed as smooth and deep as when we went camping. As soon as Skye got started on a topic like the solar system and the endless possibilities of space, there was no halting her excitement. I told her more about my family, what I left behind, and how guilty I felt for it.

"Guilt is just our consciousness telling us we could have been better. And since we can't go back and change it, that's all you can be expected to do, be better."

"Be better. Like I have any clue what *better* is supposed to look like."

"Well, you must have some sort of direction if you're going back to New York."

"But it's not like I'm certain that is going to make it all better. For all I know, I'm running away from something great here in Byron. From the possibility of *better*. From you."

"It'll be hard to find peace here if there's guilt inside of you about how you left things back in New York. Sometimes being a better version of yourself means making it through all the pains that feel like they're trying to pull you down. Facing them will take that guilt away and help you go forward."

"Or come back."

"What do you mean?" She questioned.

"Come back here. After I've figured it out in New York."

Skye sighed.

"What?"

"If you came back Lucas, that would be a dream..."

"You seem skeptical though."

"It's not that I don't believe you really *want* to come back, I just..."

"Don't believe I will?"

"I don't think you should make promises like that, without knowing what the future holds."

I squeezed her tighter. "I want to hold *you* in the future."

"Very corny." She smiled up at me, but within seconds her smile faded. "I'm sorry. It's just hard for me to believe in happy endings when life for me hasn't been much of a fairy tale."

"But doesn't every fairy tale have some sort of shitty beginning for the princess?"

"Ha! I'm not a princess, Lucas, nor do I want to be. I'm not looking to be saved." She rolled her eyes.

Her attitude made me laugh. "You're right, you're like the dragon slayer who can surf on fire."

"And *you're* the princess in the tower that needs saving."

"I'll be the princess if the surfing dragon slayer is coming to my rescue."

Skye leaned in to kiss me and after a moment said, "I don't get it."

"Get what?"

"I usually hate when people are corny. But something about you... your way. I can't help but smile."

"You also said you hated Americans."

"True. I do."

I narrowed my eyes at her.

"I mean, I did. I guess... you're the exception."

Skye dosed off to sleep and I didn't want to wake her. Seeing Skye at peace is a rare occurrence. Since it's a shared dorm room, I was kind of nervous about others in the hostel room seeing Skye and I asleep. I didn't want anyone to get pissed and call the front desk... as *if* they would *even* get mad. The creepy night shift guy would probably give me a high five after I saw how he handled the situation when I found drunk Anna in my bed after karaoke. The memory of that night seemed so long ago. That was before I even met Skye.

I'm not even sure if Skye left later that night or early the next morning, I just found the note she left beside my duffel.

I work today. You should stop by.
xo Skye

P.S.
Bondfire tonight ;)

Even though the note was written on the back of a crumpled up Burgeroo receipt, I wanted to keep it. I ironed out the creases with my hand and went to put it into the pages of my notebook.

The notebook felt heavy in my hands. I flipped through the letters I wrote my parents, all left unsent. Unread.

I wished I was going back to New York to tell my mom and dad all about my trip.

I wished they were waiting for me back home, even if it's the home in Connecticut and not New York.

I wished I could run into their arms, even just one last time, one last hug, *something*.

I hugged the notebook, and because of all the emotions and contemplation that wove into my writing, the notebook held me back. I released a lot onto those pages and reading those raw emotions made me realize how far I've come. I decided to bring it along with me on my last day in Byron. I also realized I would definitely be writing in it more when I went back to New York.

Chapter 35: For You

I went to HideAway for an early lunch and got a panini, a coffee, and a slice of mixed berry pie. The pie had just come out of the oven that morning and was a perfect balance of a fruity, flaky crust.

Marcos usually stopped at the cafe on Fridays to check the inventory before the weekend rush. I got a second cup of coffee and stayed a bit longer because I needed to tell him I was leaving and wouldn't be able to work anymore.

It wasn't too far into my second cup of coffee when Marcos strolled in. His heavy steps let me know he arrived without even looking toward the door. From the same direction, I heard a loud shriek causing me to cover my ears abruptly.

"NOOOOOOO!" The piercing voice cried again.

I turned to see Marcos sweating, with a baby in his arms.

"*No* is his favorite word..." Marcos meekly announced to the handful of customers who glanced in his direction. As if the baby's favorite word was justification for the shrieks.

Skye came out from behind the counter and walked toward the now crowded doorway. Marcos had plopped the baby bag on the floor and was standing cluelessly with a group of customers behind him.

Skye reached out her arms to the baby and took him from Marcos's arms.

"Woa, woah, woah... why you crying Benny? Did you miss me that much?"

Like magic, the shrieks settled and the baby was smiling up at Skye as she wiped his tears and walked him behind the counter with her.

I got up to intercept Marcos before Skye would be forced to go back to the customers, which could cause Benny's shrieking to erupt again.

"Hey Marcos, is that your son?" I small talked.

"Lucas, hi." We shook hands. "Yes he is… if he wasn't my kid, I wouldn't volunteer to babysit, if you know what I mean. He's a handful." Marcos rubbed his baggy eyes. "Aw, but mate, I love him. Being a dad is great." He said with minimal enthusiasm.

"Yeah, it looks it... Listen Marcos, I unfortunately can't work anymore. I'm actually going to be moving back to the states tomorrow."

"Oh really, well that's perfect then."

"Perfect?"

"Yeah well, my staff who was on vacation is coming back and I was going to fire you for sleeping in the freezer-"

Boli...

"But since you're quitting, I don't have to have an awkward *you're fired* speech on this beautiful Friday. So, it's perfect."

"Yeah..." I stood there slightly embarrassed.

"I have this little guy crying all night-" And day... "But I'm not sleeping in the freezer. But you know.. that freezer keeps out a lot of sound..." Marcos walked away continuing that thought to himself.

I took the remaining sips of my coffee. Skye had put Baby Benny in a jolly jumper with a stuffed kangaroo.
"No!" He yelled at nothing in particular.

Skye disappeared to the back and returned with something in her hand.

"I'll see you tonight?" Skye asked as she cleared the table.

"Absolutely." I looked up at her from my seat.

"Here. Marcos said to give this to you." Skye handed me an envelope. "It's the money for the days you worked. Today's lunch was on the house."

"Thanks." I took a 20 out and put it on the table before putting the envelope in my pocket.

"Best food. Best coffee. Best service. Put that in the tip jar."

"Noooo!" Benny's cries began again.

"Apparently Benny doesn't agree." Skye laughed.

His cries persisted.

"Maybe Marcos should do something… where is he?" I asked.

"I think in the freezer. I better go…"

She leaned down and kissed me, but not for long enough. It never felt like long enough.

I spent the rest of the day walking through the town taking mental pictures of each shop, sign, and street corner. Promising inanimate objects that I'd be back while hoping with uncertainty that I would be able to keep that promise to myself. I stopped on a bench outside the ice cream shop and opened my notebook. I felt the urge to write to my parents, even though I knew they would never read it. The writing helps me to release.

Dear Mom and Dad,

It's hard to describe what the last few months have felt like. It's been a tidal wave of emotions, confusion, and regret. I've found happiness in Byron, but guilt won't let me enjoy that happiness, so even that feels off. It's just so hard to make decisions when I don't know where it will lead me. How am I supposed to know what's for the best?

Skye is someone really special… I don't usually talk about my love interests, especially since we moved to Connecticut, but I need to tell someone about her. She makes my heart race when we're sitting still and gives me the uncontrollable desire to smile, even when I'm feeling down. Her brilliant mind brings us on adventures through the universe without even moving our feet from the sand. She's challenged me to step out of my comfort zone and do things I would have never done on my own. She is the most talented surfer I've witnessed and I aspire to ride waves like her one day. And her eyes…

It's hard to leave someone who has grown to mean so much to me. I love her, but I'm scared that telling that to her will make leaving even harder… I've been so selfish with too much, and I didn't want to be selfish with Skye's emotions. I thought about how much easier it would be to leave Byron if I didn't care for Skye so much… But I know that I would never give back the times Skye and I spent together. The pain of leaving is worth it. Knowing her, makes it worth it. This experience has been so much more meaningful with her by my side.

But I keep circulating back to the thought: then why should I leave? I feel selfish leaving her after we've grown so close and I feel selfish for abandoning the other people in my life. But when I think of my hallucinations, the decision seems more obvious. Something is wrong and it scares me beyond words. It's not something I even feel ready to talk about…

I can't properly be there for anyone else unless I take care of my health. I need to figure out what's going on.

I wish I could talk to you about this.
Am I doing the right thing?

Love always,

Lucky

I read the letter over another few times. Absorbing my words in hopes to release my trepidation. On my fourth time reading it to myself someone sat next to me on the bench.

"I heard you're leaving back to the states."

I looked up to see Budd in his ice cream shop uniform. I remembered when Skye took me for ice cream on our first date.

"Yeah... tomorrow." My head fell back down toward my closed notebook.

"I'm going to be honest with you, Lucas. Skye really likes you." He took his hat off and twisted it in his hands. "So when she told me you were leaving, I got angry." He raised his voice. "You know, I knew this would happen when you started coming around and I saw her crushing on you. And now you're just like all the others who pass through here, just looking for a good fuck."

"Budd, that's not it at all."

"You're leaving right after you *finally* got to have sex with Skye. Get what you worked for and then go. Leave and never see her again. Probably never even talk to her again... You know, that's the very reason she hates Americans! They stomp through and disappear without looking back! I know she told you about her father, so how can you go and play her like that?"

"Budd, it's not what it seems."

"But that's what it is. You get with her and then the day after you get back from your little holiday-on-holiday, you tell her you're leaving! Are you bloody kidding me? That's just fucked up Lucas. She's an amazing person who's been through hell. How could you go and disrespect that?"

"I respect her!" I yelled standing up from the bench. "I don't want to leave her, but I need to go back to New York. I don't know how long I'll be there for and I'm sorry because I wish I knew all the answers! Maybe I am a fuck up, but I never meant to mess with Skye, or hurt her, and certainly not take advantage of her. If that's how you see it, well I'm sorry, but that's just not how it is at all." I took a deep breath and sat back down on the bench. "I love her. I haven't told her that, I didn't think it was fair to say with me leaving. But I do."

There was a short silence that felt like an eternity.

"Please don't think I'm like Skye's father. I care about her. I really do."

Budd stood up. "My break is over."

"Wait..."

But the bell above the ice cream shop's door was ringing and Budd was already inside.

Part of me wondered if I should even go to the Bondfire. It was at Budd's house and I clearly was not on his good side... but it was also Spigs house and Coco's too. *Did they think the same thing as Budd? Was the whole surf crew against me now because I was leaving?* My excitement to go to the Bondfire morphed to worry. I wish I could call Skye to ask her if people were upset at me, but I didn't have a cell phone. Being without a phone has helped me connect more with the world, but in times of need, it was really inconvenient.

Of course I had to go to the Bondfire. I couldn't just disappear on a flight the next day without saying goodbye to everyone, that would just prove Budd's stereotype correct. Running away from the problem sounded so much easier, but it also makes the whole situation worse. I needed to leave things in Byron on a good note, so that one day I could come back to the place that I love with people willing to welcome me.

Before walking over to the Bondfire, I stopped at the front desk. Bradley sat behind the desk wearing a turquoise Neptune's polo and a welcoming grin.

"Hey, mate. How you going?" He said as I approached.

"I'm good. I was just coming by to set up a taxi to the airport for tomorrow."

"Aw, yeah. I see you're checking out tomorrow. We're sorry to see you go, mate." Bradley sighed.

As we worked out the taxi reservation, we talked about the books we've read from the borrow bookshelf and my experience learning to surf. Our conversation made me realize I was in my longest gap without surfing since my very first lesson. I had been too paranoid to go to the beach… and especially too paranoid to go back to the cave.

I wrote Skye a letter and kept it securely in my pocket unsure of when I would give it to her. I didn't want her to read it in front of me and I definitely didn't want anyone else to see it either. There would be a lot of people at the Bondfire so Skye and I would hardly have time alone, unless we isolated ourselves on the beach, but I told myself I wouldn't wander there. In my hand was a bag of groceries I picked up on the way over, as my last BBQ offering. Every week these guys open their home and feed so many people, including myself. It was the least I could do.

When I opened the front door Zane was there with his usual vibrant smile and beer in hand.

"Delivery guy is here!" Zane joked as he threw his arm around my shoulder. "Whatcha got in there?" He asked looking inside the grocery bag.

"No way, mate!"

Jade and Coco were coming down the steps toward us.

"What's so unbelievable Z?" Coco asked.

"Lucas brought kangaroo burgers."

Their faces lit up in excitement.

"You didn't have to bring food to your own party." Coco said.

"My party?"

"Yeah, this Bondfire is your going-away party." Jade pointed to a hand drawn sign that read, *Safe Travels, Lucas!*

I was speechless. I attempted to formulate words, but just as I opened my mouth to speak, Skye entered the room from the kitchen making me speechless yet again.

Breathtaking wasn't enough to describe her.

Words are never enough to describe Skye.

"I think we've shocked him." Kenny said as he entered behind Skye. "Breathe, mate."

"I- I don't know what to say. Thank you. I definitely didn't expect this."

More people started crowding into the living room.

"Let's all head out back where the real party is!" Kenny announced.

"Remember though, if the neighbors ask, it's not a party!" Coco added.

Spigs was out back grilling as usual. When I greeted him with the bag of groceries he threw his arms around me in a big embrace.

"Lucas, I can't believe you're flying out tomorrow. How long has it been?

"I've been in Byron for about two months... Australia for almost three."

"It's easy to get comfortable here, huh?"

I nodded. "Thanks for teaching me to surf. Without The Surf Shack, I'd be hopeless."

"No, mate. You're a natural."

"I call one of those kangaroo burgers!" Zane yelled. "Buddy, Lucas brought kangaroo burgers!"

Budd stood behind him with a placid expression. "I'll take a hotdog." He said then walked away.

"He's so grumpy lately, uhhhh." Zane rolled his eyes. "I'll take his, if there's extra." Zane rubbed his hands together in anticipation, then walked away to chase Budd.

The crowd by the grill was getting bigger, so I gave Spigs space to focus and walked over to Skye who was sitting with Jade by the fire.

"What is hotter, this raging fire or the people sitting around it?" I joked.

"I thought you said his corny was cute?" Jade said to Skye.

"Usually."

They both laughed.

"Skye look!" Jade exclaimed pointing behind me. "She finally came!"

I turned around to see Kenny walking with a woman I recognized. "Sorry we're late. You remember Daisy?"

Daisy, still in sunglasses (at night time), smiled warmly.

"Great to meet you again, sorry to hear you're going. I've heard such great things about you."

Really? I thought. I wondered what she's *heard…*

Skye seemed *so* happy to see Daisy there. They immediately wrapped themselves up in a conversation, leaving me and Kenny to talk off to the side.

"I got to thank you Lucas for helping me out."

"Helping with what?"

"You helped me remember to seize the moment."

"Me? How?"

"After we talked at the pub I was thinking about Skye climbing up on those cliffs and how dangerous it was. But still, it was totally something her mom would do and *honestly,* something I use to do with her mom." He let out a sad smile. "I used to be so adventurous up until Lessie died... after that I felt like I had to grow up and get serious and put adventure to the side. Everything just fell into a routine and life eventually... settled." Kenny took a sip of his beer. I still had no clue what any of this had to do with me. "And in you come, adventuring by yourself reminding me when I ran away from home."

"Why did *you* run away?"

"I wanted to prove to people that missing a leg doesn't make me less capable. So I went off on my own for a while to find out that yeah, it was *much* fucking harder to do *everything* without a leg. So really, my parents and everyone was right..." Kenny laughed to himself. "It's funny having realizations decades after they happen by just reflecting on that point in time. But I'm glad I was stubborn and didn't just accept the inept fate that so many people predicted. I ran away and had to figure shit out on my own. And it was hard, but I did it. And I went back stronger and more capable than before when I had two legs."

"That's incredible."

"I hadn't broke the routine or stepped out of my comfort zone in years... too many years."

"But you shred out on the water! That's a huge thrill."

"That may be out of your routine and comfort zone, but that's been my norm since I was a young kid. When you left I thought, *what can I do right now that makes me step out of my comfort zone?* And you know what I did?"

"What?"

"I finally asked Daisy out after over five years of wanting to. Every time I thought I had enough courage, I would talk myself out of it when I got down to the bar and the vibes were good. I never wanted to ruin those good vibes. Like if she turned me down, nothing would be the same... I would have ruined the vibes..."

"But she didn't turn you down. She's here."

"Yeah, *with me*! I can't believe it." Kenny had a grin ear to ear. He wrapped his arm around my shoulders. "Thanks, mate. Now, do me a favor, Skye and Daisy are talking over there... Before Skye reveals everything embarrassing there is to know about me, bring her to the living room and look on the mantle."

"What?"

"Skye. Living room. Mantle." He walked away and took Daisy from the conversation, leaving Skye's eyes to fall onto mine. We smiled simultaneously as I walked over to her. I grabbed her by the hand, leading her toward the house.

What was in the living room on the mantle?

Skye followed along and her lack of questions made me realize she knew exactly where we were going.

"Ready for your gift?" Skye said.

"Gift? What?"

On the mantle was a long box. How could she get me a gift when I didn't buy her anything? All I had was a note in my pocket. It wasn't even in an envelope...

"Skye you shouldn't have gotten me anything..."

"You'll need this, you'll see."

Need?

It was way too slender to be a surfboard...

Skye took the box off of the mantle and placed it in my arms. I opened the box to reveal a long wooden object. I pulled it out of the box and that's when it clicked.

"You got me a didgeridoo!? Fucking awesome. This is so cool!"

I couldn't contain my excitement, I brought the mouthpiece to my face, took a deep breath, and played remembering the lesson that Skye took me to after our trip in the outback. The vibrations bellowed past the sofa and into the kitchen. It caught many people's attention as they crowded into the living room to listen to the didgeridoo.

I didn't know any songs or even what I was truly doing to be honest, but people were bouncing and vibing and coming together. It was almost as if the Bondfire suddenly became a house party. People typically stayed in the yard. I hope Spigs didn't mind.

A flash went off in my face and I saw Zane standing there with a polaroid camera and a cheesy grin.

Finally when I was completely out of ideas and breath I moved the didgeridoo away from my lips and looked up at the crowd of people. They cheered and that embarrassed me, but I savored the moment, stood up, and hugged Skye. "Thank you." I whispered into her ear. "That was so incredibly thoughtful." I remembered the note in my pocket. I wanted to give it to her, but there were far too many people around.

"How could you neglect to tell me that Lucas can blow a didgeridoo like that?" Zane whisper-yelled to Skye.

Spigs came forward and motioned his hands for people to quiet down. I got nervous that my show brought too many people inside the house at once.

"Many Fridays ago, in my kitchen, I remember telling Lucas to avoid Skye because she didn't particularly like Americans, and as we all know she's *usually* pretty rude to them." The crowd nodded their heads and laughed. "I noticed them together more and more and wondered, what *magic* does this guy know to have Skye being so nice *to an American?* Then more time passed and I was caught wondering, what magic does this guy know to have Skye looking *so happy, so often.*" Spigs looked over at us and smiled. For the first time ever, I think I saw Skye blush.

"But as Skye got to know Lucas, so did I. And all my questions were answered quite simply. Lucas is not a magician, he's an incredible person. And no matter how thick-skinned and stubborn someone may be," Spigs narrowed his eyes at Skye, "she still couldn't deny that Lucas is a quality guy with a heart of gold. So here's to Lucas," Spigs raised his bottle and everyone else followed. I even saw Budd put his cup up. "May you keep an ocean close and a surfboard closer... even if it's a rental. May you surf the waves of your life without fear of falling... even if the wave is massive! And may you never forget those you've met along your journey, and always remember that all the oceans are connected. Save travels, Lucas. You're always welcome in Byron Bay." Everyone lifted their drink into the air.

I never had a toast *about me,* in my entire life. Skye wasn't the only one who was blushing.

"Buddy got me this dope polaroid for my birthday, so I think we should take an epic group shot right now. Lucas hold the didgeridoo like you're about to play it. Skye go next to Lucas, obviously... Jade move to the front, you're too short. Buddy, get *in* the picture." Everyone listened, but Budd didn't seem too happy about it.

"Alright I'm taking it like a selfie because I need to be in the picture too, duh... okay, ready... three... two," FLASH!

"You pressed it too early!"

"It's called a candid. Or a semi-candid, since we were kind-of almost expecting it."

"You're crazy Z." Coco moved from the crowd and took the picture out of the camera and shook it until it developed.

"This actually came out really good."

"Ha! Look at Kenny in the back!"

"Are you holding your prosthetic leg in the air?"

"Ah! That's hilarious."

"Here Lucas." Zane handed me the picture. "It's for *you*."

"Really? You sure? This picture is gold."

"Of course it is, because look, my face is right there, huge!"

"And trust me, we got plenty of his face floating in this house." Coco rolled his eyes.

"He's been taking *a lot* of selfies with that camera since he got it…" Jade agreed.

"And Skye, here's the picture of Lucas playing the didgeridoo and you sitting next to him. Both of you looking gorgeous, as always."

Zane loved being the center of attention and although he was funny *most of the time*, I worried about Budd's reaction. He already didn't like me because he thought I was taking advantage of Skye. I didn't want him to hate me more because his boyfriend called me gorgeous.

My eyes noticed Budd standing off to the side looking pissed off as Spigs said something into his ear. It wasn't often I saw Spigs looking so serious. I wished Budd understood why I was leaving and how much I cared about Skye. I wished he saw me through the same lens as his brothers or Kenny. Suddenly, Budd glanced in my direction causing me to quickly look down at my didgeridoo. I hoped he didn't realize I was staring, but at the same time I wanted him to read my mind.

It was the best Bondfire I could have possibly wished for. I showed up hoping that the whole house didn't hate me and left realizing how much they actually cared. Jade even touched up my braids, so they were looking fresh and clean. It made leaving the Bondfire all the more difficult, but I was glad that Skye said she would walk me back to Neptune's one last time. We walked slowly trying to stretch extra moments out of each step. My left hand held hers and my right held the didgeridoo. I still couldn't believe she got me a didgeridoo! I would be the only didgeridoo player in New England and the Tri-State area. I hadn't even heard of the instrument before this trip.

We stopped outside my room and I rested the didgeridoo box on a bench, to free up my arm to hug her properly. I took her in my arms and I held her so close that I think her feet were levitating above the ground. Floating like my hovering heart because holding Skye took away gravity itself. I would have held her tighter if I could. I would replay that hug forever if time allowed. I already had her touch… scent… and taste etched into my heart. With her face against mine, I could taste her salty tears flowing down to our chins, but that didn't stop our embrace.

I know that I only knew Skye for a short time, but it felt like I lived a whole different life in those months. A life where I loved her, from the very moment I saw her gliding on the waves like a sea goddess. I love her like the Earth loves the sun. Although I was leaving, I hope she understands that sometimes the earth must turn away from the sun, in order to see the stars. When Skye pulled her lips from mine I realized that it was both our tears that had fallen.

"What time do you have to leave tomorrow?" She asked me.

"Noon."

Skye nodded.

"Wait, how are you getting to the airport?"

"A taxi."

Skye rolled her eyes. "No. I'll take you. Why didn't you ask me?"

"Because Kenny usually has the car and you have work tomorrow." I reminded her.

"Kenny is flexible and Kelsey will cover me. She just doesn't know that yet…" Skye poked at her phone, probably texting Kenny about the car and Kelsey about the shift. It felt good to know that I had just a little bit more time with Skye.

"We should squeeze in a sunrise surf."

Skye looked up from her phone. She looked like she was about to speak but stopped herself.

"You sure?" She finally said.

"Yeah. I want to surf before I go. I haven't been on the beach since…" I stopped myself from bringing up LC. *If I stay with a group of people,* I rationalized in my head, *I won't see LC.*

"If you feel up for it… sunrise surf *has* missed you."

I wanted to surf. I didn't want the hallucinations to take even more away from me.

Chapter 36: LC

My body and mind were restless on that final night. I woke up with a heavy feeling in my chest and familiar screams ringing in my ears. Screams that always brought me back to the night of the crash.

I took a shower with hopes of steaming away the tension in my head, then wandered down to the lobby to grab a muffin before sunrise surf. On my way out, I stopped at the front desk. Creep was still working from his overnight shift and stared at me begrudgingly when I told him to cancel my taxi for the airport.

"You want me to call the taxi company before 6am," he looked at his watch, "to tell them you *don't* want a taxi. Do you know how stupid that sounds?"

It was clear he hated his job.

But that encounter was only 45 seconds out of my final 6 hours in Byron Bay, and I wasn't going to let Creep's bad vibes bring down my last morning in any way. Even if I got a bad night's sleep and woke up in the middle of a nightmare, I still had the rest of the day. *I'm going to surf again*, I repeated in my head, letting my excitement overpower the fear that still lived inside of me. *One last sunrise surf.*

Skye was waiting for me at the entryway of the beach with her surfboard in one hand and coffee in the other.

"You're up extra early." I said walking over to kiss her good morning. Kissing her hello and goodbye had started to become a regular thing. I hated how that would end too soon.

As my feet moved from pavement to sand, Skye grabbed my hand and we walked the beach together in the morning darkness one last time. I kept counting *Lasts* then tried to remind myself they were the Lasts of *this trip*, but not the Lasts of *forever*. At least I hoped.

The whole squad was putting on their wetsuits as the sun began to peek over the horizon, winking good morning. I focused on what was right in front of me and getting out to the water. It's not like LC would appear swimming at me. *Although I did hallucinate her running into the water...* I put that thought out of my mind and focused on paddling out as fast as I could. For once, I made it out to the break first.

"Eager to get out there, mate? Hell yeah!" Kenny paddled up beside me. "I'm missing a leg and move faster than you!" He teased Coco who arrived next.

"That's because getting out is all arms!"

"And riding it..." Kenny began to paddle. "Is all about balance..." Kenny caught the wave but didn't stand up on his prosthetics. Instead, he put his head to the board in a praying position and the next thing I saw was Kenny on his head riding the wave like nothing I've ever seen before.

Skye paddled up alongside me. "He's been practicing that headstand for months. To be honest, I didn't fully believe him the other day when he said he was going to do it while surfing. He told me he wanted to see if he could take surfing out of his comfort zone."

Kenny was still upside-down as the wave began to die out.

"Ever since he asked Daisy out, he keeps talking about seizing the moment. She has really had an affect on him." Skye continued. I nodded and with a smile thought about the conversation I had with Kenny the night before.

"Your uncle is the man." Jade said to Skye as she arrived to the group with Spigs, Budd, and Zane.

"Challenge accepted!" Spigs yelled to Kenny as he paddled back toward us.

"Oh yeah? Well, I have more yoga poses in the works if you want to make this a competition." Kenny boasted.

Spigs began paddling hard to catch the next wave, eager to show off some moves. Skye, Budd, and Zane followed in his trail complimenting his motions as their surfboards cut through the ocean. I hung back enjoying the pristine view of the crystal blue water and the sand that hugged the shoreline. I missed that view... and knew I would miss it even more after I left. Coco and Jade caught the next wave, while I sat stuck, my eyes transfixed at the sand in the distance.

I saw her all the way at the end of the beach wearing a white sundress. Staring at me. Like she was frozen on the hot sand. I tried to ignore her, but every time I looked away I felt her eyes burning into me. Skye surfed up next to me and yet I could not look away from LC standing at the end of the beach.

"You alright?" She asked.

I shook my head out of the daze. I looked at Skye and then back at LC. "Do you see someone down by the rocks?"

Skye looked over to that direction. She stared longer than she had to in order to answer the question. Each second that passed was another scoop of certainty that I was hallucinating again.

"Yeah, wearing white?" Skye finally said.

I stared at LC in her white sundress that flowed with the wind. I squinted to try to focus better. *It certainly looked like LC.*

"Who is that?" I asked hastily.

"You know I can't see that far away. I just see a person wearing white."

"But you *see* a person?"

Skye nodded. "Do you think it's...?"

I paddled closer.

"Big one coming your way, Lucas!" Spigs yelled.

I looked back and a perfect wave was building behind me. I looked back over at LC, staring.

"Paddle, mate!" Coco called from further back.

Jade was ahead of me already paddling full speed.

I tried to keep up with her and put my arms to work.

I could ride the wave in to see if it's really her, I thought.

I paddled faster and harder until I had enough speed as the wave was curling right behind me. I popped up to see Jade who was gliding just ahead of me. Kenny was further ahead of her. The wave curled like it was in slow motion.

I looked to see if LC was still down by the rocks, but instead my eyes met Skye's who was surfing behind me. It was the first time I felt like I had total control of the board. Before, I could never ride alongside so many other surfers without the fear of getting in their way and then bailing as a result. I saw the white figure down by the rocks. It was LC and she was still staring at me.

Ride the wave in. I thought.

Stay with the surf crew. My conscience battled.

I cut the wave, like I always see Skye doing, and landed it. Coco whistled from behind Skye. I didn't even see him.

The perfect wave kept us on its pathway and I resisted the temptation to cut out and head into the shore to see if it was really LC.

Why? I asked myself.

Why go through the anxiety of chasing the very thing I've been avoiding?

Why ruin the moment?

Why focus on what's tearing me down when I could be raising myself up?

I got lower on the wave as it was beginning to die out. I picked up some speed to join Kenny and Jade who were up ahead together. We had surfed even closer to the rocks. Even closer toward LC. She was still staring at me. I was sure it was her.

All I had to do was ask Kenny if he saw her. If he saw LC in the distance. If he could see his sister who died ten years ago…

LC smiled and waved casually as if daring me to point her out to someone. I turned my back to the rocks and watched Skye surf over, followed by Coco. Spigs and Budd were on a wave behind us headed in our direction .

"We could paddle in and check." Skye said from behind me. "If you want."

I looked over at LC. Paddling in to *check* would only cause me more trouble and certainly raise questions within the crew. We hadn't been surfing for too long. It was far too soon to leave. I didn't want to let the hallucination of LC ruin more than it already had. I couldn't drag anybody else down that messy pathway. I couldn't let it ruin my last sunrise surf. It was my last few hours with the people who taught me how to glide on the waves in ways I thought I'd only witness from a distance.

"No, let's catch up to the crew and surf some more." I replied, already moving away.

Skye half-smiled and nodded her head. I could sense her curiosity wanted to ride the next wave in. I paddled forward, unsure if Skye was following behind me or heading in toward the white figure standing at the end of the beach. *What would I say to the guys if Skye went back to shore?*

There was another wave about to curl just beyond us. A choppy one. I could either ride that wave in, or dive under it to rejoin the crew further back. Behind me was Skye, except I couldn't tell which direction she was headed. From the shore, I could see LC's white dress shining as bright as the sun.

The wave was coming.

I needed to make a decision.

Ride the wave in

or

dive under

or

wait too long and get trampled.

I paddled as hard as I could.

Swimming hard.

Pushing my hands quickly through the water.

Then took a huge breath before diving under the surface of the water as the wave passed above me.

I came up for air and Skye was paddling right beside me.

"Let's get back over with the crew." I said and Skye followed.

We surfed for over two hours weaving the waves like they wrote out the story of my stay. I wished we could surf forever, but forever ended when Budd made his way back to The Shack to open up for the day. Zane went with him, Coco and Jade followed soon after, then the rest of us. No one seemed to be in a rush to go anywhere. Everyone sat on the sand around The Shack joking and discussing the morning's surf. That's when Zane brought out the Tim Tams.

"Oh sweet goodness. I love you." Budd kissed Zane and grabbed the box of Tim Tams.

"Well, they're for everybody, so you need to share."

"Alright, alright." Budd passed the box back to Zane. "I'll get the tea ready."

"Lucas, take *this* box to bring back to the states."

"That is if he doesn't eat them all on the plane." Skye said.

"True."

"Lucas, they're the caramel kind. They're my favorite." Zane salivated.

"Always thinking of yourself, huh Z?" Coco criticized. I was thankful for any type of cookie.

"Treat others the way you want to be treated… and I would want caramel Tim Tams." Zane defended.

"Treat others the way *they* want to be treated." Coco corrected. "I believe *these* are Lucas's favorite Tim Tams." Coco revealed another box of Tim Tams. Double chocolate.

"You guys are crazy!" I said accepting another box.

"Looks like we all had the same idea when we heard Lucas was coming to sunrise surf…" Kenny pulled out another box of cookies.

Everyone started laughing.

"Great minds think alike." Zane added.

"Everyone knows you can't leave Australia without a box of Tim Tams for your mates back home." Skye said passing the box from Kenny to me.

"Or three." Jade reminded.

From over my shoulder I heard Budd's voice.

"Here."

He handed me a cup of tea, nodded his head, and gave me an almost smile. It was surprising that Budd gave the first cup to me. Maybe he doesn't hate me after all…

My paranoia had me glancing down toward the rocks every minute. I think Skye noticed when she slipped her arms around me and whispered, "Let's go over to my place and I'll make you breakfast. Kenny is going over Daisy's house." My attention was immediately on Skye…

and food. I thanked the guys, said my goodbyes, and felt lucky to have people who showed such care for me. One thing my Puerto Rican and Italian backgrounds had in common was that they both show appreciation for others through food. When I'd do well on a test or win a big game, it showed by what was for dinner. Sometimes the way to the heart is through the stomach.

The morning went by too quickly and soon it was time to return my Neptune's key and load all my stuff into the trunk of the car.

"You sure you don't want to drive to the outback instead? We can make this another camping trip!" Skye suggested, less than ten minutes into the ride.

"That sounds amazing." My jaw dropped just thinking about the temptation. "I wish." "We'll go again one day." I almost said I *promise*, but remembered what she said the other day about promises. But still I was silently making that promise to her.

The airport was a distance away so we had time to spend together in the car. I don't know if I should have brought it up or not, but I wanted to talk to someone about how I woke up that morning.

"I heard that screaming again. But this time it was in my dream."

Skye lowered the music. "What was your dream about?"

"It must have been a nightmare, but I don't really remember what it was about... I just remember feeling really scared then hearing the screams. As they got louder, I saw someone moving closer to me and then I woke up."

"Who was moving closer to you?"

"I'm pretty sure it was my mom." I paused a moment, caught in a daze out of the window. "When I woke up it was like the screams were still echoing. I've been thinking about it, and I realize it was my mom screaming all along. They were the same screams I heard the night of the crash."

"You mean you heard your mom screaming the other day on the beach?"

"I think so… yeah. And some other times too." I thought about how crazy it sounded to say out loud.

I avoiding looking over at Skye and wished I didn't mention it at all.

After a few minutes she broke the silence.

"I brought you something." Skye said reaching to the back seat. *She already got me a didgeridoo, what else could it be?*

I hoped she didn't see me wiping my tears. Suddenly a slice of blueberry pie in a takeout container appeared on my lap. My eyes grew wide.

"I figured you might be hungry."

"I'm always hungry."

We laughed together then Skye put her hand on my thigh.

"I'm glad you landed in Byron, Lucas."

I thought back to when Skye *hated me.* or at least how she hated her own stereotype of an American. She didn't want anything to do with me when I met her at my first Bondfire.

"I'm glad you gave me a chance." I said, beginning to dig into the flaky crust, coated in blueberries.

"I'm glad you came in for blueberry pie."

"Delicious pie, good vibes, the beautiful Skye… couldn't ask for much more." I said taking a bite.

"Coffee."

"Yes, coffee." I began with my mouth half full. "But without extra espresso shots. And with sunshine and rainbows."

"How did I know?" Skye pointed to two iced-coffees from the cupholders in the back seat. "Grab those."

I did and we both took refreshing gulps. I noticed that Skye only had one straw.

Skye always had a way of making me feel like I was levitating above the clouds. Like I was somehow removed from the rest of the world.

It was too hard to formulate words when Skye dropped me off at the airport. I knew I wasn't going to be able to say what I was actually feeling in that moment. All I could do was hug Skye long and tight until the security guard at the airport whistled for her to move the car out of the *No Standing Zone.* But I didn't want to let go of her. Ignoring all the honking and whistles and airport traffic, I kept my arms around Skye and slipped the note into her pocket. Writing to her was the best way I knew to tell her how much she means to me. I grabbed my duffel with the didgeridoo popping out of one side.

"Have a safe flight." Skye said as she backed toward her car. "Text me when you get a phone again." She added as she opened the driver's side door.

"Hey, Skye." I said before she climbed into the car. The whole entire ocean stared back at me.

"Do you think you'd take a trip across the world? To New York."

"Me?" Skye replied with wide eyes. "In America? With all the Americans asking me to repeat what I just said because they *loved* my Aussie accent and *need to* hear it again?"

I stared at her without reply. Half smiling at Skye being her usual self, and half frowning that she was halfway in the car, moments from zooming away from me without any assurance that I'd get to see her again.

"Maybe… for you." She winked then jumped in the car.

"I love you." I whispered underneath my breath.

Skye turned up the radio and it poured out of the windows. It was one of the songs I never heard before, but now because of Skye, I heard it over a dozen times. I turned to begin walking toward the terminal's entryway, humming the song's melody.

Then, I heard the car door open again, the music turned down.

"Wait." I heard Skye's voice. "You forgot something."

I turned while checking my pocket for my wallet. It was there.

What did I forget?

By the time I fully turned around Skye's lips were pressed against mine, as her hands held my cheek pulling me in tighter.

"I love you too." She whispered as she hovered beside my lips.

Floating.

Frozen.

She made a single kiss feel like an entire evening together.

She made the whole universe pause. For us.

She left me standing there with only her scent lingering. She slammed the door, blew me a kiss, and drove away with the music blasting. I watched the car pull away, hoping something else was forgotten so that Skye would turn back, but the car kept going and going until it disappeared out of sight. I was left replaying Skye's words and her kiss over and over in my mind, until I boarded the plane and dreamed of sunrise surf, underwater caves, and the unforgettable Skye of Byron Bay.

Jillian Linares

Epilogue: Final Letters From Lucky

Dear Skye,

You brought shooting stars into my life before you ever even took me stargazing. You immediately caught my attention, sparked excitement on my soul, and made me hopeful. You changed the perspective in which I saw the world. You changed the perspective in which I saw myself. You tested my limits and forced my comfort zone to widen. You helped me to discover who I was in a time when I felt lost.

I didn't want to leave, but I feel like I have to. My hallucinations got too overwhelming. I needed to get help before it got worse. I feared that all of my problems would eventually scare you away, so I need to fix them, before I lose my mind... and you.

I also left many people very worried in New York and Connecticut and I realize I need to start taking more accountability for my decisions. Thinking my parents' death only hurts me is selfish. Running away without looking back has started to pile up on me. I need to untangle that part of my life to fully heal the wounds that I've tried to continuously push to the side.

Thank you for letting me love someone as brilliant, adventurous, and breathtaking as Skye Carter. It has been an honor to surf and hike beside you, to lay in your thoughts in a secret underwater cave, and to kiss the lips that hold the most beautiful smile I've ever laid my eyes on. Skye, you changed my life for the better and I truly hope we have a future together. Because of you I will forever be a:

thalassophile- a lover of the sea

astrophile- a lover of the stars

Also, there's something about an astrophile that you didn't mention to me: It's not just a lover of the stars, but a lover of the sky, which makes me a triple astrophile.

Love,

Lucas "Trip" Catano

P.S.: please message, text (when I finally get a phone again), email, send smoke signals (you pyromaniac), or even write snail mail. I know we are in completely different time zones and you're basically in the future, but I hope somehow we can work it out that my future ends up with you in it...

P.P.S.: was that super corny? Are you smiling?

Good, I adore your smile...

Dear Mom and Dad,

I moved in with Uncle Will and Aunt Maria, I'm sure that eases your worries at least a little. I saw many doctors to understand why I was hallucinating, including my current psychiatrist.

I know what I saw out there, which is the scariest part. I didn't just speak to LC once. Those conversations felt as real as when I sat down to talk to my psychiatrist. I can't accept the conclusion that she was a mere hallucination. But she was... She had to be...

Schizophrenia is what my psychiatrist diagnosed me with. Seeing LC, smelling burning that doesn't exist, hearing screams that aren't there... these are all symptoms of schizophrenia. My doctor said that awareness and acceptance are the first steps to recovery. That's why she had me write down my whole story. So that she can help to pinpoint certain times where I showed the symptoms and discuss how to manage them for the future. She says LC was my conscience and the conversations we had were extensions of my own internal conflict. In other words, I was talking to myself. I guess it could make sense... but it's so hard to accept with interactions so vivid.

The screaming I would often imagine was you Mom, from the night of the crash... it's a sound that is etched into my eardrum when I'm in a state of panic or feeling stressed. The burning smell I also remember from the crash... They were all hallucinations...

I'm learning to appreciate the little moments more. The moments I use to coast through before realizing how meaningful and impactful they truly were. Moments when I wasn't 100% there. Maybe I was on my phone, computer, or

watching TV, whatever the excuse, I wasn't fully there. I can't change the past, but I'm learning to grow through it with the lessons I've learned.

Mom... Dad.... you continue to enlighten me, even in your absence. So long as I look close enough, with careful scrutiny, you're still here with me. You live through me, in the lessons I've learned and will continue to learn. I don't know if I would have ever realized my oblivion without this tragedy.

As I look around, I see how many people are trapped in a false reality; going through the motions without appreciating the moments. I want to tell them to wake up because the ground can crumble at any moment, when you very least expect it. But some things people need to realize on their own, hopefully before it's too late.

Love always,

Lucky

schiz-o-phre-ni-a - (noun) a mental disorder concerning the breakdown of the relation between emotions, thoughts, and behaviors, leading to incoherent perception, inappropriate actions and feelings, withdrawal from reality into fantasy and delusion, and a sense of mental fragmentation.

Dear Reader,

  My psychiatrist said to write my story to help myself. To help me understand. But as I was writing I realized it's not just about me. So I began writing for you... to help people understand... to help you understand.

  It's painful to look back on your life and wish you acted differently. I did for so long... I'm not just referring to The Night My Life Fell Apart, but all the moments I treated my parents unfairly. And all the moments I focused on the world inside a screen rather than the world all around me. When I acted like I was the only person with problems. When I'd have an attitude toward someone just because things weren't going smoothly in my life.

  It took the death of both my parents for me to realize all the moments I lost with them. And not just future events like graduating from college... getting married... telling them they're going to be grandparents... but also the moments of the past. Their death made me realize that I should have been a better son and for a while that thought alone wrenched my heart and ached my bones. But not anymore. No. I will not let my life be squandered away by dwelling on something that cannot be changed. This experience, as painful as it was, has made me into a better person and I hope that I can help others becomes better versions of themselves as well, with a lot less pain.

  That's why I'm writing this. To help people realize there's happiness and pain all around, it's just whether you choose to pay attention to the storm clouds or the rainbows. Because happiness does not depend on sunshine, or pay checks, or weekends, or people. Happiness depends on you. Your perspective. Your ability to find sunshine when it's raining, have wealth in your soul even when your pockets are empty, everyday of the week. No matter who is with you, or who is not.

Maintain a good perspective and not just a positive perspective, but one that allows for a good vantage point. To be fully present in those moments that deserve your attention. So they don't slip away like a cloudy memory. So you can reminisce and smile at the vivid mental memories you've compiled. So moments can be cherished, not regretted.

Life throws a lot of unexpected twists and turns, but I've learned that life is 10% what happens and 90% how you react to it. You can't change the past, but your actions dictate the future. So I'm focusing on bettering myself, for whatever the future entails. To make my parents proud and to live a life worth living. I don't know what the future holds, but I hope it somehow involves a bright blue sky with an ocean in her eyes gazing back at me and a smile rooted deep in my soul.

Everyone deserves their slice of happiness, but often it's up to you to cut your own piece.

Your friend,
Lucas Catano

Author's Note & Acknowledgements

I started writing *I Ran Away to Find Myself* during my senior year at UCONN in 2013 for a class with one of the most inspirational teachers I've ever had, Dr. Wendy Glenn. What started as a 15-page sample became my personal project over the next four and a half years. It was a teacher who pushed me to keep going, that has brought this book to fruition! Thank you Wendy, and all the teachers who enable others to be the best versions of themselves.

I wasn't always actively writing *I Ran Away to Find Myself*, however. It was tough to balance student teaching, graduate school, and my first years of teaching in Puerto Rico while attempting to write a book for the very first time. I mostly utilized summers off and my travels, in which I was without a cell-phone and cut off from communication for large chunks of time. *I Ran Away to Find Myself* was written in 13 different cities, as well as under candlelight in the aftermath of Hurricane Maria. This book has been with me through my most memorable and challenging moments. The journey has been truly remarkable.

None of this would have been possible without my parents' support of my dreams and ambitions. Thank you for having confidence in my ability to navigate 21 countries (often alone) in the last 8 years and supporting my decisions to live in London, Puerto Rico, and Denver. The inspiration for this book would not have been as vast and vivid without those experiences.

I would also like to thank all the people who have helped to sculpt *I Ran Away to Find Myself* throughout this journey, especially those who had a hand in the editing process. From advising me to delete the first 100 pages, to essential punctuation additions, and comments in the margins, I would not have been able to do this without my trusted editors who read the book and gave me helpful feedback. Cesar Linares, Jon Schisselman, Emma Cohen, Gabriela Deambrosio, Tara Higgins, and Gabriel Castro. Thank you!

Made in the USA
Middletown, DE
30 December 2018